THE CROSSBOW MURDER

THE CROSSBOW MURDER

by
Wayne Minnick

CREATIVE ARTS BOOK COMPANY
Berkeley · California

The Crossbow Murder is published by Donald S. Ellis
and distributed by Creative Arts Book Company

For information contact:
Creative Arts Book Company
833 Bancroft Way
Berkeley, California 94710

For ordering information call:
1-800-848-7789
Fax: 510-848-4844

ISBN 0-88739-301-2
Library of Congress Catalog Number 99-64933

Printed in the United States of America

For my wife, Lenore, whose help with
this book was invaluable

The Crossbow Murder

Chapter One

Wade Davis, homicide detective, Atlanta Police, went to the hearing as a favor to his colleague, Cyrus Orovac. Orovac, an enthusiastic crossbow hunter, gave Davis choice cuts of venison every deer season and, when invited to join Davis in a bachelor dinner, skillfully grilled steaks and regaled his host with implausible tales of how he had stalked his prey and killed it with a bolt fired from an improbable distance. Because of Orovac's largess, and because he liked the man, Davis felt obliged to humor him occasionally. So, against his inclination, he consented to attend the hearing.

"Hunters have to have as many people there as the animal rights people," Orovac told him. "The Bambi crowd will be there in force, ready to damn hunters to hell and bow hunters to its hottest corner. We need numbers and strong, persuasive voices to counter the bastards."

Davis, aware of the battle between hunters and members of animal rights groups, felt some ambivalence about attending a hearing of a senate subcommittee that was considering a bill to ban bow hunting of deer in the state of Georgia. He had, without any sense of guilt or notion of ethical impropriety, hunted deer often when he was a boy. Born and raised on a farm, he was used to the rearing of animals for slaughter. He had helped his dad kill and butcher sheep and hogs when the animals were too few to be sent to the big markets in Chicago and Kansas City. His father never questioned the killing of animals for food and never suggested to his son that such killing was wrong. The Bible, he told his son, gave man dominion over the birds of the air, the beasts of the field, and the fish of the sea. For him that was justification enough for eating the flesh of God's creatures. Davis, now a well-known homicide detective, who daily witnessed human beings maiming and killing one another had, until quite recently, never given a thought to the possibility that the deer he hunted in his youth could have rights human beings were morally obliged to respect. It was a disquieting notion, one that challenged traditional thought. He felt bound to grapple with it. The debate over the abolition bill would offer, he hoped, a reasoned contrast of views about the way people ought to treat animals. In that assumption he could not have been more wrong.

Cyrus Orovac, a colleague with whom he had worked on a couple of homicide cases, was a man whose judgment he respected and friendship he valued. Cy had been a hunter for years and saw nothing wrong with killing deer by bullet or by arrow. Now, finding his right to hunt seriously threatened, he had recruited Davis to help influence a senate committee that was being pressured to report an anti-bow hunting bill to the state legislature.

"You needn't take part in the debate," he told Davis, "unless you want to. Anyway, I think the chairman, Senator Griscom, has got the proceedings tightly structured. Nobody gets more than two minutes of formal presentation, and no more that ten speakers are allowed for each side. Of course, there'll be an open forum afterward when people can ask questions or make thirty-second statements."

Davis acknowledged his companion's remarks with a diffident smile.

"I doubt I have the eloquence to influence the committee, nor do I know that I'd want to," he said. "You'll have to rely on your own matchless rhetoric, Cy."

Cyrus was the division's media officer, (he had graduated from the School of Speech at Northwestern University before becoming a policeman) and was respected by his fellow officers for his terse, on-the-scene, TV accounts of who had allegedly killed whom and why. He bowed toward Davis in acknowledgment of the compliment.

"My lone voice won't be enough to influence the committee," he said. "We need others to speak up. You can say a word or two, can't you, Wade?"

Davis smiled but made no commitment. He was watching the people milling about the room—an odd assemblage of fervid advocates. The supporters of the abolition bill bore placards printed with inflammatory slogans: "Bow hunters are sadistic killers." "Bow hunting is cruel and unusual punishment." "Bow hunters cripple more deer than they kill." "Bambi killers ought to be ashamed."

Opponents of the bill carried more logic-based, less emotion-arousing signs. Davis liked the implied argument in a large green sign hoisted by a man dressed as Robin Hood, who strode about the room with a quiver of arrows over his shoulder and a longbow firmly clutched in his hand. "It's better for a deer to die from a swift, merciful arrow than starve to death or be pulled down and eaten alive by a pack of coyotes." Another, held aloft by a woman of muscular build and fierce expression, asked, "Why don't opponents of bow hunting quit eating steak?"

There were more signs, but Davis's preoccupation with them was brought to an end by the voice of Chairman Griscom speaking over the public address system. He was visibly irritated.

"I want all those signs put down on the floor, out of sight. This is a serious congressional inquiry, not a carnival! Proper behavior and decorum in speech will be observed at all times."

He paused, glaring about belligerently. His eye fastened on the costumed archer, who stood with his bow raised as if rallying an outlaw band in Sherwood Forest.

"You, Robin Hood," he said sternly, "if you don't get rid of that archery get-up right now, I'll have you ejected."

Robin Hood complied reluctantly, surrendering his bow and arrows to one of the Capitol Police officers. He then sat down next to Davis with a great show of being unfairly put upon. Davis was amused at his pouting.

Griscom, round of face and abundantly bearded, had a thatch of white, wavy hair and pink, dimpled cheeks. He was almost a caricature of a pompous politician, but he left no doubt in anyone's mind who was in charge of the meeting. He pounded a gavel on the rostrum, and quickly hushed the babble of voices rumbling throughout the room. A man about whom no one held moderate views, Griscom was to his supporters the spirit of benevolent government personified, a good man wrestling with rogues. To his detractors, he was the symbol of government gone amok, the embodiment of a corrupt politician. Whatever their estimate of his character, every one in the room knew he would conduct the hearing with dispatch. After serving four straight terms in the senate, he had recently announced his intention not to run for a fifth, and being thus freed of the obligation of answering to the voters in the next election, he was now enjoying the pleasure of acting exactly as he pleased.

"The proponents of this bill," he announced, "have agreed to allow one speaker to use the twenty minutes allotted to them instead of having ten speakers talk for two minutes each. The decision strikes me as a sensible one. I hope those opposing the bill can agree upon a similar course. Assuming their cooperation, I am postponing the opening of the hearing for ten minutes to allow them to consult with one another."

Agitated conversation erupted from the ranks of the bill's opponents. A group of them clustered in a corner of the room, where they argued vehemently for a few minutes, then, with a show of hands, elected a spokesman.

Davis, observing this activity, had some misgiving about the chairman's decision to change the format of the meeting at the request of the bill's sponsors. It had the appearance of favorable bias, and many bow hunters clearly interpreted it that way. Angry scowls shown on their faces and they grumbled loudly.

Robin Hood expressed his disapproval to Davis bluntly.

"Damn him," he said. "He's tilting things in favor of the bleeding hearts. They don't need help. Animal rights people have been brainwashing the public for years. Now they've started a legislative offensive. This move against bow hunting is only a first step. Next they'll sponsor legislation to ban deer hunting altogether."

Davis wondered if all bow hunters felt as threatened as this hot-headed man. Fierce emotions seemed to be felt by everyone in the room.

Griscom, wielding the gavel vigorously in the manner of a medieval executioner lopping off heads, pounded the assemblage into silence and announced that formal statements were about to begin. There would be, he said, in view of the fact that time was of the essence, no formal introductions. He would simply announce the speaker's name, said speaker would take the floor, identify her or himself, and hold forth for the allotted time.

The room was laid out with the stodgy utilitarianism of overworked and apathetic staff members. There was a raised platform at the rear where, behind a long table, committee members sat, peering at the audience from behind microphones that sat like toadstools before a litter of briefcases and file folders. A small table with two chairs faced the phalanx of senators, an arrangement which compelled speakers who sat there to direct their remarks to the committee rather than to the audience behind them.

"Our first speaker," Griscom intoned, "is Madelin Gelbart."

Gelbart had the intense, high strung, messianic bearing of the true believer. A handsome middle-aged woman, she projected an aura of steely competence and icy determination.

As she approached the witness table and sat down, Robin Hood, or Stephen Gault, the name Davis had finally wormed out of him, sighed loudly. "Madam DeFarge, no less," he whispered. "Ready to send every hunter in Christendom to the guillotine."

After hearing Gelbart's inflammatory rhetoric, Davis decided that Robin Hood's opinion of her was a not unfair judgment.

Gelbart repeated her name and identified herself as spokesperson for an organization called the Society of Animal Conservators, Inc. She launched a vicious attack upon hunters. They were, she said, sadistic perverts, who enjoyed inflicting pain upon helpless animals. Bow hunters were the worst of the lot because they used a weapon that, being notoriously inaccurate, often resulted in a deer being wounded and escaping to die hours or days later in agony from infection or loss of blood. Some authorities, she said, estimate that sixty to sixty five percent of deer targeted by bow hunters are merely wounded and die two to five days later of infection.

Hunters were sadists because they killed not out of necessity, but for fun. They covered their true reason for hunting by arguing that deer needed to be "harvested" because natural predators no longer were abundant enough to do the job. If deer were not "harvested" or "culled," (coward words used by murderers to hide the true nature of their crimes) large numbers of deer would allegedly starve to death. Hunters neglected to mention that in this kind of culling, unlike in the processes of natural selection, the strongest and best animals are killed, as hunters compete for trophy deer, rather than for the weak and ill. The result is weakening of the gene pool. They also fail to mention that state game and fish commissions deliberately manipulate herds to increase the numbers so there will be more animals for hunting.

Gelbart carried on in this fashion for about twenty minutes, and, after characterizing hunters as incredibly cruel and insensitive slaughterers of innocent animals, implored members of the committee to stop the carnage by passing the bill.

She rose from the table to hisses and applause.

Davis grinned at Cyrus Orovac.

"A pretty tough customer," he observed. "I hope your spokesman can measure up to her."

"He will," Orovac replied. "He's Harry Paulson, CEO of Edgeware Pharmaceuticals and a long time enthusiast of bow hunting. Uses a crossbow. He's not only dedicated to the cause, he knows how to talk to politicians. Watch him."

Davis watched as Paulson, with that indefinable air of authority that men acquire who have fought and won their share of laurels in the marketplace, strode from the audience to the witness table, sat down, buttoned his beautifully tailored jacket, and adjusted his shirt cuffs meticulously. Davis was amused at the man's pretentiousness. "Regal" was the term that came to his mind. A bearing a little too grand for present company, he thought. But, he appeared to be mistaken, for members of the committee came to attention smartly, and beamed upon the witness with respect that was almost fawning.

Paulson sat calmly for a few seconds, nodded familiarly at selected members of the committee, and began to speak.

"I have never had much sympathy with animal rights extremists. Madelin Gelbart," he bowed slightly and condescendingly toward her, "is, fortunately, less emotional than some. I'm sure she would not agree with the statement made by a member of Last Chance for Animals, 'Even if animal testing resulted in a cure for AIDS I would be against it.' Or the group that calls itself, 'Killing People to Save Animals,' who argue that there are many non-human animals the lives of which are more valuable than the lives of many humans. Yet, about the hunting of deer she can become quite passionate. Unfortunately, her opposition is based on errors of fact and unreliable opinion."

Paulson went on to dispute the charge that bow hunters are poor marksmen and injure large numbers of deer who die painfully of infection. Bow hunters were humane people who recognized the limitations of their weapon and all but a small minority would not target an animal that was more than forty or fifty yards distant. At that range, bow accuracy was equivalent to that of a rifle. "I do not know," he said, "where Ms. Gelbart got the figure that sixty five percent of deer targeted by bow hunters are merely wounded and left to die in agony. The figure is nonsense. I honestly think animal rights people are often guilty of making up statistics to support their arguments. There is, to my knowledge, no reliable source for the figures she cited."

Amid a chorus of "Boos" from the animal rights supporters, Gelbart sprang to her feet.

"Are you calling me a liar?" she demanded.

Paulson, looking a bit rattled at this direct challenge, opened his mouth to speak, but whatever he was about to say was never heard.

In the front row of seats, a thin intense youth, who sat directly behind Paulson, opened a knapsack on his lap and took from it a round sealed bag. Carefully lifting the ball-shaped bag in both hands, he stood up and, in the manner of a basketball player going for a shot, he lofted the bag squarely at the back of Paulson's head. On impact it broke, showering Paulson with blood and propelling his head forward onto the desk. The young man turned to the audience and cried out.

"Blood to the bloody butcher!"

He raised both hands, fingers spread in a V for victory sign, and bowed to right and left like an actor expecting applause. His look of satisfaction astonished Davis, who found it incredible anyone could be congratulating himself for such an assault upon an unsuspecting victim.

Paulson appeared, momentarily, to be stunned. As senators leaped to their feet, and audience members rose and started toward him, Paulson pulled himself to his feet and staggered a few disoriented steps toward one of the doors. With blood running down his face, with his shirt and jacket slowly turning crimson, he looked as if he had been the victim of an assassin's bullet.

A long-protracted "Ah" of astonishment swept over the audience.

Senator Griscom, leaped to his feet and roared, "Arrest that man. Don't let him get away."

Although the room was in pandemonium, people milling about, pushing and shoving, climbing over chairs, and creating confusion that could have made flight possible, the young man made no attempt to escape. Orovac and Davis, who had instinctively begun pushing their way toward the assailant, found their intervention unnecessary as two Capitol Police officers closed in on the man, wrestled him to the ground, cuffed him, pulled him to his feet, and pushed him in rough fashion toward a rear door.

Senator Griscom, clearly outraged at the turn of events, brought his gavel down in a series of resounding blows that settled the milling of the crowd. He spoke with asperity.

"Those who think they can influence the judgment of this committee by such uncivil behavior are seriously mistaken. I will hold no more hearings on this bill! It will not be reported out of committee."

He cast belligerent glances at the now vocally complaining supporters of the bill as if daring any of them to contest his decision.

He gave one final rap of his gavel and declared, "This meeting is adjourned."

A group of supporters hovered around Paulson, dabbing at his bloody face and clothing with handkerchiefs and paper tissues. He endured their concern graciously but with evident impatience. Doffing his sodden jacket, he pulled off his necktie, unbuttoned his shirt collar, and accompanied by devoted partisans, made it out the door.

As they left the hearing room, Cy Orovac apologized to Davis, for the fiasco that ended the meeting. Orovac admired Davis and had for a long time hoped, in spite of Davis's reclusiveness, to forge a closer friendship with him. He was worried, now, that Davis, put off by the disruption of the hearing, might identify him with such tactics. The viciousness of the attack on Paulson had sickened and disgusted him. His companion, he was sure, had been similarly affected.

"I'm afraid I dragged you into an ugly mess," he said. "I don't see, though, how I could have known what Gearhart would do."

"You know him, then, this crazy guy?"

"Not personally, but by reputation. He's Basil Gearhart. Well known among animal righters. Belongs to the Society of Animal Conservators, Inc., the group Madelin Gelbart runs. It's a militant outfit that resorts to direct action at the drop of a hat. To my knowledge, however, this is the first time one of its members has attacked anyone."

"I hope the Capitol Police throw the book at him."

"I'm sure they will. They want to discourage what the animal rights people call civil disobedience."

"Humph," said Davis, "more like uncivil disobedience, if you ask me."

CHAPTER TWO

Henry Paulson's seventeen year-old daughter Kimberly often walked the trails that wound through the four acre tract adjoining the family home on the northern outskirts of Atlanta. Near Buckhead, close to a private golf course, the parcel was like a miniature game preserve or arboretum, into which Kimberly retreated when the stresses of growing into womanhood, complicated by the discord that existed between her father and mother, seemed about to overwhelm her. Rarely, but often enough to arouse pleasurable expectations, she had seen deer flitting through the wax myrtle that grew like green curtains beside the trail. Other animals—raccoon, possum, fox—were so common, she could almost be assured of running across at least one such wild creature every time she went for a late afternoon walk.

On this day, dusk was approaching, and shadows grew long and heavy. Stately pines reared high into the darkening sky. Massive live oaks spread their wide limbs in all directions, each limb clothed with resurrection ferns and Spanish moss. Shafts of late sunbeams cut through the gloom, forming a pale, gold lattice work that deceived the eye, creating shapes that had no substance and movements where nothing moved. Kimberly felt a momentary chill and fought an impulse to run toward home, an impulse that grew stronger as she saw, or thought she saw, a human figure slipping furtively through the underbrush.

"Greta," she called out. "Is that you, Greta?"

Gretchen was her sixteen year-old sister. Mature for her age, and favored by a pristine loveliness, Gretchen had never been close to Kimberly in spite of Kimberly's repeated attempts to build an affectionate relationship between them. Greta consistently rebuffed Kimberly's overtures with a sullenness that approached hostility. Perhaps, Kimberly thought, it was because of rivalry for the attention and affection of their father. Gretchen's emotional attachment to Harry Paulson had become, during the last two years, more clinging, more possessive, more infused with jealousy. She seemed to resent any attention her father paid to his wife or to Kimberly. In her own mind, though reluctantly, Kimberly admitted her father favored Gretchen over herself, perhaps because Gretchen had an adolescent ripeness that grew out of early and enticing sexual development, while Kimberly, flat-chested and scrawny-limbed, still lacked those endowments that make women appealing.

Rousing herself from such thoughts, she called out again.

"Greta, if that's you, please come here."

Silence. She had been mistaken, Kimberly told herself. It was not a person she had seen but an animal, possibly one of the deer that visited the area occasionally. She had only a short distance to go until the trail turned and headed back toward the house and she resolved to continue on despite the fading light. Ahead of her, lighted by a shaft of sun that pierced the limbs of a giant oak, she could see a man's jacket lying in the underbrush as if flung there by a careless hiker.

As she walked toward it, she saw hands protruding from the sleeves of the jacket and, almost concealed by weeds, the lower part of a body projecting from beneath it. She halted in terror. There was something dreadfully familiar about the inert figure lying face down before her. To learn who it was she would have to turn the body over, a task she felt incapable of doing from fear of what she would discover. Hands trembling and heart beating wildly, she grasped the form by the shoulder and pulled till the face became visible. What she saw wrung a plaintive cry from her throat.

"Daddy. Daddy. What's happened to you?"

She released her grip as if she had received an electrical shock and as she lurched backward her arm brushed against the thing sticking from her father's back.

Chapter Three

Davis and his colleague, Leda Fulford, stood silently looking down at the body of Harry Paulson as it lay, crumpled like a discarded scarecrow, in the weeds beside the trail. They had not been the first to arrive on the scene, but nothing had been disturbed. Two patrol officers riding in a red and white near the Paulson residence had answered the call, had taped off the site, and were standing guard over the body. Two officers from another red and white, were talking with family members who had been asked to remain in the house until Detectives Davis and Fulford could interview them.

"I heard him speak just a few days ago," Davis said to his companion, nodding toward the victim's body. "Before a senate committee. He was opposing a bill that would have banned hunting deer with bow and arrow. Ironic, isn't it?"

"It's a kind of stubby looking arrow," Fulford said as she got down on her knees to inspect the feathered shaft buried in the man's back.

"It must have hit him with great force." she observed. "There's just a few inches of it showing front and back. It almost went through him entirely."

"He was probably shot at close range," Davis said, "and with a powerful bow. I don't know much about them but I do know that compound bows made of magnesium and epoxy shoot arrows at high speed, high enough, at close range, to punch a hole like this in a person's body."

Fulford looked at the arrow's tip, a three bladed affair with blades that appeared to be razor sharp. "Looks like the head was made specifically to penetrate flesh," she said.

"Yeah." Davis replied. "But the flesh of a deer, not a human being."

Forensic people were now on the scene, and Davis and Fulford watched as they took photographs and began searching the area.

A few minutes later, Christopher McCalmon, the medical examiner, came up quietly behind them and offered a flippant remark, something he did often when faced with a murdered body.

"What kind of carrion have you enterprising ghouls found tonight?" he asked. "Given the wilderness we're in and the full moon that's showing, I'd guess a werewolf."

"Wrong," said Fulford, replying in the same vein. "Here's a straight-laced business man killed with an ancient weapon, a bow and arrow."

Her casual remark concealed the sadness she felt. The man had been a beloved husband and father, she reflected. A man still youthful, still pursuing cherished dreams, still harboring great expectations, suddenly brought down by a brutal attack. His death was, in her mind, the essence of tragedy—the destruction of a life before its time. She felt like crying, but forced back the tears. She was, she reminded herself, a police officer inured to violence.

She had joined the Homicide Division less than a year ago and had seen her share of murdered bodies, but she had not succeeded in viewing a dead person without an upwelling of emotion. She looked up and smiled at McCalmon, a light-skinned man of African heritage, like hers. The ME knelt down, and peered closely at the shaft sticking out of the man's body.

"You're right, Leda, it's from an ancient weapon, but it's not from an ordinary bow. What went through this man's back is a bolt from a crossbow. A bolt is much shorter than an arrow, only fourteen to eighteen inches long. That's why so little of it is still showing on either side."

Davis, hearing the ME's comment, recalled that Cy Orovac was an expert in crossbow hunting, and resolved to contact him as soon as circumstances permitted.

"I suppose," McCalmon said, as he knelt, taking the corpse's temperature and moving its limbs to test for rigor, "you want to know how long ago he died?" He turned the man on his side, opened his shirt and inspected the stomach for lividity.

"A good off-the-wall guess will do us," Fulford said. "It can't have been very long. His daughter called the police the minute she found the body and a cruiser answered right away."

"You're assuming," McCalmon said, "he was killed shortly before she found him?"

"Wasn't he? We need your expert opinion, Chris."

McCalmon's attempt at a neutral expression failed to conceal the liking he had for Leda Fulford. She was a woman who, in addition to physical beauty, which he found breathtaking, had an engaging personality marked by simplicity and directness. He did not deceive himself about his emotional involvement. He was, to use an expression he had heard on a BBC historical drama, besotted with her. He knew she had dated her partner, Wade Davis, and he suspected they had been intimate. But while that knowledge was painful, and while the one date he had with her was pretty much of a dud, his infatuation remained undiminished.

"You're right, Leda." he said. "He's been dead about two hours. I'd say six o'clock almost exactly."

"Which means," said Davis, "he was, in fact, killed just a few minutes before his daughter found him."

The Crime Scene people combed the area for clues. Their search uncovered nothing in the way of footprints, cigarette butts, fibers, hair, or other leavings that might be used to identify an assailant. The area immediately behind the victim failed to show any trampled spot that might indicate where the assailant stood when he fired the bolt.

Davis shook his head, shrugged his shoulders, and said to McCalmon, "I think we're wasting time here, Chris. Looks like any help we get in tracing the assailant will have to come from your autopsy. Maybe a fingerprint on the bolt. Do they have batch numbers or anything like that?"

Chris smiled. "I doubt it. But the type of bolt and its manufacturer should certainly be traceable."

"OK. We'll check with you in the morning." He turned to his companion. "Let's go up to the house, Leda, and talk to the family. Maybe we'll get a lead there."

The three women, soon to be described in obituaries as survivors of Harry Paulson, were in a study that had floor to ceiling book shelves, an antique roll top desk of polished walnut, and French doors opening upon a formal, well-tended garden. Lucinda, the wife, sat at the desk in a tilt back chair; the two girls occupied either end of a richly upholstered sofa.

Lucinda Paulson had nothing of the matriarch about her. Although a bit on the fleshy side, she had a smooth, unwrinkled face, pert breasts, and, Davis thought, sensuous buttocks. She dressed in a youthful style that accentuated her physical beauty, wearing a peach blouse with maroon lace at the wrists and neck and a pair of russet brown slacks. She almost seemed, not their mother, but a slightly older sister of her daughters. Gretchen, her eyes red from crying, looked at the detectives with a kind of adolescent insolence. Kimberly, gently dabbing at her nose, stared blankly into space.

Gretchen, barely sixteen years old, had the figure of a designer's model. Her skin was of unblemished translucence, her hair, of a color between blond and auburn, was as fine as silk. The contrast between her physical ripeness and the immature body of her sister, Kimberly, was remarkable. Both girls sat stiffly with tears clinging in the corners of their eyes. Fulford, who despised the necessity of questioning them at such a time, thought they were both probably in shock. It was especially important, however, that a deposition be taken from Kimberly, who had discovered the body.

Because they had agreed before entering the house that Davis would question the mother while Fulford would talk to Kimberly and Gretchen, Davis asked Lucinda if they might move into the kitchen where he would appreciate a glass of Coke. She seemed to understand the purpose of his request.

"I could make some coffee, if you'd like," she said as they left.

Alone with the girls, Fulford said, "I'm sorry about your father. I know his death is a terrible blow to you. I don't like having to ask questions at a time like this, but it goes with my job."

She smiled reassuringly at the girls. "Would either of you like something to drink? Your Mom is making coffee for detective Davis."

Gretchen shook her head silently, her expression resentful and oddly apprehensive.

"No, ma'am," Kimberly replied, "I'm not thirsty. I just want to get this over with. Will they take my father to a morgue?"

"For the time being, yes."

She wondered if either of the girls understood the necessity of performing an autopsy on a murdered body. They were both tight-lipped, holding their emotions under control with great effort. I must try to do this swiftly, she told herself, for their sake.

"What was your father doing out there where you found him?" She addressed the question to Kimberly.

"He walked there lots of times in the evening, especially if he'd had a hard day at the office. He did it to relax."

She spoke those words with a peculiar inconclusiveness, as if her father might have had other reasons for venturing into the woods. Fulford decided to explore.

"Do you suppose he might have gone there to meet someone?"

Kimberly rejected that possibility emphatically.

"No, ma'am, I'm sure he didn't. The golf course lies at the end of our property. No one is allowed on the course except members. If someone wanted to meet my dad in the woods, they would have to have gone past our house. We would have seen or heard a stranger going by, or even a friend, for that matter."

"Isn't it possible some one could have slipped by the house without anyone noticing? Didn't you tell one of the officers who responded to your 911, that you heard the sound of movement in the underbrush just before you found your father's body, movement made by someone you couldn't identify?"

"Well, yes. I did. I thought perhaps it was Greta. She likes to walk in the woods, too. Don't you Greta?"

Gretchen was clearly annoyed with her sister. She seemed to take Kimberly's remark as an accusation. "Why did you say that, Kim? I wasn't anywhere near the woods. I was watching TV."

"Well, you sometimes go there. Anyway, I knew it wasn't you, or you would have answered me when I called your name."

"Then why did you say it? It was mean of you."

Gretchen's anger with her sister seemed unwarranted to Fulford. She could not understand the reason for it—unless it was jealousy.

"When you saw the body," Fulford asked Kimberly, "and discovered it was your father, did you think to yourself, 'I wonder if so and so could have done this?'"

Kimberly seemed to find the question profoundly disturbing. She covered her face with her hands and shook her head in vigorous negative.

"No! No! No!," she cried. "I didn't think that at all. I couldn't imagine anyone wanting to kill my father. It's impossible."

To Fulford, her reaction suggested that, despite her denial, she had thought of a possible assailant but that the idea of that person having killed her father was too painful to face. She posed another question.

"Was there any trouble between your parents? Did they ever quarrel?"

Gretchen and Kimberly looked at one another before answering, expressions guarded. Their glance told Fulford more than their words. Kimberly spoke first. "Everybody has little arguments, don't they? Our parents never had any real fights."

Gretchen said, "Mom and Dad were very much in love. They never really got mad at each other."

"I'm glad to hear that," Fulford said. "You girls are lucky to have such a loving family."

She looked squarely at both girls, neither of whom returned her gaze. She said nothing, hoping a prolonged silence might be awkward enough to provoke one of them to say something. It was Kimberly who finally responded.

"He was killed with a bolt from a crossbow. I think someone did that because Daddy was in favor of bow hunting. He spoke at a senate hearing on bow hunting and a man threw blood all over him. He could have killed Daddy."

"We're investigating that man. He's a prime suspect. But we have to consider other possible suspects."

"Well," Gretchen said, with apparent pleasure at the discomfort she was causing her sister, "lots of people know how to use a crossbow. Kimberly's good with one. Daddy taught her."

Kimberly flushed with resentment. "He taught you, too, Greta."

She looked at Fulford, her expression that of a person trying to neutralize incriminating information. "Everybody in this house knows how to use a crossbow."

"Are you suggesting someone in this house might have killed your father?"

Kimberly flushed in anger. "Of course not. I only meant that a crossbow is easy to use. Anybody could shoot one. Even if they hadn't had much practice."

In the kitchen Lucinda Paulson made instant coffee for detective Davis and herself. Davis found the kitchen unbelievably opulent—a built in refrigerator had doors of oiled walnut; the stove, of black enamel-ware with decorative chrome bands, had a panel of dials set within a mosaic of colored lights. It had a grill with downdraft exhaust, and ceramic covered burners. Cabinets were of some exotic wood. Teak, Davis supposed, from its rich tan hue. As he sat down at the table, his feet felt uncomfortable on the Italian marble floor tiles. Henry Paulson, he concluded, if nothing else, had been a first-rate bread winner.

"Cream or sugar?" she asked.

"Just black."

"The best way," she said. "The way I like it."

In spite of her effort to be congenial, Davis felt little rapport with her. The carefully applied make up and the resolutely youthful demeanor she projected seemed false, undermining the impression of the mournful wife she was trying to convey. Nor did the appearances of grief she exhibited, the red rimmed lids, the furrowed brows, the tremulous voice, ring true. Lucinda Paulson, he concluded, was less bereft than she pretended to be.

"Did your husband often walk through the wilderness area where he was found?" he asked. "Often enough, I mean, so that someone intending to attack him, would know he might be found there?"

"His job was tough. Decisions he had to make were critical to the prosperity of the business. At the end of the day he needed to unwind, but, unlike many executives, he did not relax by drinking cocktails. He loved nature. The birds and animals in our modest zoological park, as he liked to call it, provided him with a way of unwinding after work." She paused briefly. "I guess that answers your question, though I don't see how anyone outside our immediate family would be aware of his habits."

"He could have talked about it at work, or mentioned it to friends."

"I suppose so. Most likely to his hunting pals."

"And who are they?"

"A partner of Harry's, a chemist, and an enthusiastic bow hunter, Roger Godwin, and two of our best friends, whom we entertain often, Adam Wharton and his wife, Pamela. But none of those people could possibly have wished to harm Harry. We were like family, especially with the Whartons."

"I sense you were less close to Roger Godwin. Am I right?"

"Roger is single and when we entertained it was sometimes simpler to leave him out, especially if he didn't have a date. But that didn't happen often. After all, he was Harry's partner."

"But you were on cordial terms with him, were you not?"

"He's a charming man. I like him a lot. We included him in our social events most of the time. I don't want to give the impression we didn't enjoy his company." She inspected her fingernails for a second or two, then said, "I am particularly fond of him."

Davis made a mental note to talk with Roger Godwin and the Whartons as soon as possible. He was curious about the nature of Godwin's role in the Paulson menage. He turned his attention once more to Lucinda Paulson.

"Is it possible," he asked, watching her reaction closely, "your husband could have gone into your zoological park this afternoon to meet someone? I understand the rear of the park joins the golf course. It would have been easy for him to have met a person there."

"He would never have done that. Why should he? He has on occasion met people after hours, but always in our home, in his study."

She seemed to be thinking of the implications of Davis's question.

"To me, it makes more sense to suppose that someone who wanted to attack Harry would sneak up on him from the golf course."

"Yes," Davis agreed. "Do you know of anyone, Mrs. Paulson, who might have wished to harm your husband?"

"Basil Gearhart," she said without hesitation. "The man who threw blood all over Harry. He's an extremist. I'm sure he would think, like some anti-abortionists do, that it's perfectly all right to kill a man to prevent him from killing a fetus, or, in Harry's case, to stop him killing deer."

"Other than throw that bag of pig's blood at your husband, did he ever threaten to do him bodily harm?"

She nodded her head. "Yes. Harry received a hate letter a day or two after the episode at the hearing on bow hunting. Although it wasn't signed, both of us were convinced it came from Gearhart."

"Mrs. Paulson, did you saved that note?"

"Of course I saved it. You don't think I'd be foolish enough to destroy it, do you? It's in the desk in the study. Shall we go get it?"

"OK," said Davis. "Let's do." He felt sure Fulford had finished questioning the girls and was relieved when, as they entered the study, he found Kimberly and Greta gone. He indicated to Fulford she should remain while he continued questioning Mrs. Paulson.

Lucinda went directly to the desk, opened one of the file drawers, searched quickly, and withdrew a single sheet of paper. She handed it to Davis.

The letter had no address, no salutation, and no signature. It consisted of just two sentences.

"You had best watch your back, you bloody butcher. One day
you may know how a deer feels when it's shot with an arrow."

Beneath the text was the image of a deer. In the middle of the deer's chest a protruding arrow had been drawn in black ink.

"Was there an envelope, a postmark?" Davis inquired.

"No. The sheet was folded in half and put in our mail box, presumably by the sender."

Davis passed the note to Fulford.

"See anything distinctive about this?"

Fulford inspected the note and nodded her head. "I'm sure it was written on a computer and then printed."

"Exactly. The big question is: Can it be traced to a particular computer?"

"I doubt it. Albert Saffron would know."

Mrs. Paulson interrupted with irritation.

"Why waste time trying to trace it. We know it came from Gearhart," she said, emphasizing her words strongly. "I don't think there can be any doubt about it. The expression 'You bloody butcher' shows he wrote it. He used those same words the day he hit Harry with that bag of blood."

"Yes, he did," acknowledged Davis, remembering the incident at the hearing. "However, I don't think he would use a phrase that would tie him to the threat so convincingly. Someone else probably used it to implicate Gearhart."

Lucinda frowned. "Maybe. I think Gearhart used it because he knew that's exactly what you'd think. I hope you won't be fooled by such a trick."

"We'll investigate him, you can be sure," Davis told her. "Before I go, however, there is one question I must ask. Please regard it as a routine inquiry.

Did you and your husband have any marital problems, any conflicts that caused tension between you?"

She looked at him with disdain, as if he had violated a basic canon of good taste.

"How impertinent! Harry and I were the happiest of couples. We never quarreled."

Davis pretended contriteness.

"We have to ask such questions in a murder investigation," he said. "No offense intended."

In an atmosphere strained by Lucinda's resentment, they expressed condolences with the usual ineptness they showed when trying to voice difficult emotions. They left Lucinda sitting in the study, assuring her they could find their way out.

As they neared the door, they saw Gretchen sitting on the stairway, crying silently. When she saw the detectives, she hastily wiped her eyes and sprang to her feet.

"I know I look a mess," she said, "but I can't help it. Mascara tends to run dreadfully, don't you think?"

She addressed this question to Fulford, who assured her mascara was difficult to manage, then added, "We're sorry about your father. The loss of a parent is a terrible blow. Especially when you're so young."

"You can't know how hurtful his death is to me," Gretchen said. There was something incredibly sad and moving about the way she spoke the words.

Her tears started again.

"I loved my Dad. I loved him better than anyone else. More than my mother or Kimberly did. We meant the world to each other." She buried her face in her handkerchief, sobbing.

Davis found her behavior odd, something he could not put a finger on. She seemed genuinely grieved at her father's death, but she seemed also to be... he could not think of a proper word to describe it. Finally, "unburdened" came to mind, though why that word seemed right he could not have said.

Fulford, harking back to a remark Kimberly had made, said. "When we were talking a few minutes ago, your sister thought you might have been in the woods near where your father was found. You said you were in the house watching TV. Is it possible you didn't remember the exact time and were actually in the woods?"

Gretchen bridled, did not allow Fulford to continue. She spoke in shrill, angry tones.

"No! I was never near the woods! Kimberly's a bitch, she really is. Jealous. Always has been. She hates me because I'm pretty and she's a dog. Daddy

19

always favored me, and Kim couldn't stand that. She was always trying to cause trouble between us."

She stopped abruptly, conscious of the surprise the detectives showed.

"You think I'm terrible, don't you?" she said. Tears welled in her eyes again. She gave them a resentful glance, turned, and ran up the stairs.

As they went out, Davis looked at Fulford, and smiled. "A bad case of sibling rivalry, wouldn't you say?"

"About the worst I've seen."

Kimberly heard her sister run up the stairway and into her room. She got up from the sofa and went slowly up the stairs. Greta's heart must ache as bad as hers, she thought. Perhaps even more because of how close she was to their father. She felt a tug of regret, a twinge of resentment because she had never been able to share with her father the affection Greta had found. Now, however, there was no room for envy, she told herself. It was a time for healing, a time for her and her sister to share the pain of bitter, irretrievable loss. She resolved after some hesitation, to try to make things right with Greta.

She opened Greta's door quietly, just a crack, so she might withdraw immediately if met with hostility. Greta was stretched out on her bed asleep, but a sleep disturbed by inner turmoil. She rolled from one side to the other, flinging her arms about as if warding off some terror. She spoke words Kimberly could not make out. She drew closer, bent over the bed, and listened carefully. The words became clearer.

Kimberly bit her lip in dismay at what she heard. Not that it was a surprise to her. Upon finding her father dead, she had the same thoughts as were now tormented Greta's sleep. But to hear them tumbling out of her sister's mouth with such anguish was appalling. With hands trembling, her thoughts in turmoil, she shook her sister violently.

"Wake up, Gretchen! Wake up! We have to talk."

Lucinda Paulson waited a tediously long time after the detectives were gone and longer still until she was sure her daughters were both in their rooms. Then she picked up the phone and dialed a familiar number. When a voice responded she said, "Can you talk?" After a pause she said, "OK, I thought as much. Just make out I'm someone inquiring about business and listen carefully. You've heard about Harry's murder. It's all over TV and radio. We're in a difficult spot. The police were here—two homicide detectives. They wanted to know who all our friends and acquaintances were. They intend to contact everyone. They mustn't find out about us. If they do, we become prime suspects. When they talk to you, just say the same thing over and over again—we're friends of long standing, nothing more. There's no way in the world they can uncover our relationship unless we give ourselves away. Do you understand?"

She paused, listened briefly, then said, "Don't worry. The police have enough suspects to keep them busy."

She hung up.

In an upstairs hallway an extension phone was gently replaced in its cradle. Kimberly crept silently back to her room and quietly closed the door. What in the world had her mother meant? What was it that must be so carefully concealed from the police? And who was she talking to?

Breakfast the next morning was a glum affair. Both girls were red-eyed from weeping, from lack of sleep, and from the acrimonious discussion they had had late into the night. Gretchen seemed especially depressed. Neither girl spoke to their mother. They sat down silently and toyed with bowls of cereal. A few listless bites and both were done.

Lucinda's appetite seemed unaffected. Impeccably made up, wearing a silk, flowered dressing gown that revealed the curves of her figure to good advantage, she ate toast and raspberry yogurt with relish. Her daughters watched her with frowns of disapproval.

"Mom," Kimberly said at last, "how can you eat like that? Aren't you sorry Daddy's dead?" Her question carried a strong tone of accusation.

"Of course, I'm sorry. I'm just as sorry as I can be. No one deserves to die the way your father did."

Her face assumed an expression of grief, but there were no tears in her eyes. "If I don't seem as broken up as you girls think I should be, I've reason for it."

She leaned closer to her daughters.

"Let me tell you how things were between your father and me," she said with an air of resignation. "They were not good. Although we tried to hide our troubles from you, you couldn't have missed our quarreling entirely. What you don't know is the reason for it." She paused, biting her lip. Her voice was strained with emotion and her expression was an entreaty for understanding. "Your father was unfaithful to me during all of our years together. That may be hard for you to believe, but it's true. He began cheating on me less than a year after we were married. He took up with a woman who worked for a company he had dealings with, thinking I would never know. But I found out. A friend told me about her and I confronted him. He begged me to forgive him, promised never again to get involved with another woman. But he didn't keep his word. I knew he had other women because he lost all interest in me. He repeated acts of infidelity over and over again."

She paused as if she were reluctant to disclose what she was about to say. "He was carrying on with someone when he was killed. For me, that someone was the last straw."

She paused, looking at her daughters intently. She seemed to stare especially hard at Gretchen, who was deeply affected by her mother's revelation. Her face flushed a bright crimson and she blew her nose softly into a tissue. She was unable to suppress a sob. Some private misery of her own, seemed to gnaw at her heart.

Kimberly had known of the friction between her parents, but her mother's disclosure of her father's repeated offenses stunned her. She found herself rebelling, unwilling to believe her father, whom she adored, could have been guilty of such conduct. She, too, began to cry softly into a handkerchief.

The three sat in silence for a long time. Kimberly absently stirred the cereal in her bowl. Gretchen glanced now and then, furtively, at her mother, a strange expression on her face.

Suddenly she rose to her feet, said, "What a horrid mess," and ran swiftly from the room.

Kimberly and her mother continued to sit and stare at one another in silence.

Finally Lucinda said, "You find it hard to believe your father was unfaithful, don't you?"

"How can you be sure of something like that?" Kimberly asked. "Maybe it was just your imagination. How do you know there were other women?"

Like Greta, she sprang to her feet and fled from the room.

Lucinda stared into space her face twisted with pain. The old adage about the pot calling the kettle black rang in her mind. She was certain that one of her daughters knew that she had been unfaithful to their father. And one of them, knew, without question, the name of the woman Henry Paulson was playing around with when he was killed.

What a mess, she thought.

Chapter Four

In the ME's lab Harry Paulson's body had been laid out on a steel table. He had been positioned on his left side. His clothing had been cut away and Chris McCalmon explained to his companions the reason for his odd position.

"I've laid him out this way because the bolt went all the way through him and I can't put him on his back or his stomach without disturbing it. As you see, about three inches of the tip sticks out just below the sternum, and there's seven or eight inches protruding from the back. Figuring seven or eight inches as the depth of his torso, we have a bolt approximately eighteen inches long. Cy, does that make sense? I'll take the thing out in a minute and measure it, but I like to do a little guess work in advance. Adds to the fun."

He directed the question to Cyrus Orovac, who was the nearest thing the Division had to an expert on crossbows. Davis and Fulford had brought him along hoping he could provide much needed information about a weapon they had never dealt with before. Cy nodded to McCalmon.

"Your guess is about right, Chris. The length of the bolt depends on the make of the crossbow. The one I own, a Camelot Lance, has a bolt exactly eighteen inches long but a slightly more powerful Camelot model has a twenty inch bolt."

"Can you tell from looking at the bolt what brand of crossbow was used?" asked Davis.

"Not really. Nothing like the way you can link a bullet to a particular gun. A crossbow archer might buy his bolts from the same firm that made his bow, but again, he might not. There's no way to show what crossbow fired a particular bolt. The bolt doesn't have any marks on it like those left on a bullet by the lands in a pistol's barrel."

"But a store-bought bolt would have the manufacturer's name or some other identification on it, wouldn't it?" asked Fulford. She was intrigued by this weapon, one she knew practically nothing about. She listened to Orovac's comments intently.

"Oh, yes. When Chris gets this thing out, we should be able to tell who sold it, unless, of course, the archer made it himself. In that case, you'd have no idea where it came from."

"Do people actually make their own bolts?" Davis asked.

"Sure," Cy assured him. "Just the way some riflemen cast their own lead bullets."

Chris was impatient to extract the bolt. He looked around at the group as if trying to anticipate their reaction.

"I don't want to cut this thing out." he said. "That would be messy as hell and would make examination of his viscera difficult. I think I can pull it out. If so, I won't have to butcher him to remove it."

Fulford found the prospect unpleasant. She wrinkled her nose in distaste. Cy made a suggestion.

"You can unscrew the head, Chris, and take it off. Then you can pull the shaft out backward.

"I didn't know you could do that," said McCalmon, "I thought it was permanently attached. You want to do the honors?"

Cy unscrewed the head which flared at the base in a way designed to prevent extraction. As he did so, the three razor-sharp blades fell away from their metal frame into his hand.

"Hey, that's neat," Chris said involuntarily. "A really ingenious device." He glanced swiftly at his colleagues in slight embarrassment. "In a gruesome kind of way," he added.

He suddenly became very businesslike, walked around the body, wrapped a piece of heavy cloth around the shaft, and pulled. The bolt did not move. He gave another hard tug but the bolt remained firmly embedded in Paulson's body.

"Jesus," Chris swore. "Whoever said the flesh is weak."

He handed a mallet he used to chisel bone to Cyrus. "Here, Cy, take this and hit the end of the bolt while I pull."

Cy complied, tapping the bolt as Chris pulled. The thing barely moved.

Exasperated, Chris said, "You're going to have to really wallop it, Cy, or it'll never come out."

He looked at Fulford apologetically. This distasteful task was causing her revulsion, something he was feeling, too.

"Okay," Cy said. "I'll give it a real belt."

As Chris tugged, Cy struck the end of the bolt with great force. The shaft, with a strange sucking sound, slipped out abruptly, causing Chris to lose his balance. He almost went over backward. He looked at his companions sheepishly. "Not what you'd call an elegant procedure, is it?"

"It sure ain't," said Cy. "Paulson would have died if he knew what we were doing to him."

Chris handed the blood smeared bolt and the disassembled head to Cy without comment.

Cy looked at the bolt and said, "I think it's made by Camelot for their Lance crossbow, the kind of crossbow I use, but I'm not sure. The manufacturer's mark seems to have been removed. It could have been made by Renaissance or Pro Form. We have to determine its exact length and weight to get a fix on its probable origin."

Davis nodded. "Look into it as soon as possible, will you? It might give us a lead to who ever shot Paulson."

Fulford disagreed. "I don't see how it could help us much. There must be dozens of people in this area who own Camelot crossbows or Renaissance ones, or whatever. That bolt could be shot from any weapon, couldn't it, Cy?"

"Well, any crossbow that was made for that size bolt. If you tried to fire an eighteen inch bolt from a bow designed for twenty inch bolts, you'd have a problem."

"OK," Davis said. "But suppose we find that an enemy of Paulson's, Basil Gearhart for example, owned a bow that could shoot this kind of bolt. We'd have reason to suspect him."

Davis disagreed with Leda Fulford reluctantly. He had fallen in love with her, or believed he had, a few days after she started working with him on the Oaks Hospice case. On their first date, several weeks after Gerry Fillmore, the Division head, had designated them a working duo, he had invited her, after they had seen a play at the Alliance theater, to have a drink in his apartment. Mutual attraction led to their spending the night together and several nights after that. He had assumed their physical intimacy was a sign of lasting commitment, but when he asked her to move in with him, she refused, saying, that, although she admired him a lot, she was not ready to give up her independence. They had dated a few times since, and she had come to his apartment for drinks, but refused to have sex. She expressed regret that she had ever allowed herself to sleep with him.

Davis found working with her a bittersweet experience. The pleasure of her company was diminished by her aloofness.

He drove thoughts of her from his mind and turned to Cy. "For the bolt to have penetrated Paulson's body the way it did, how close would the assailant have to stand?"

"The velocity of a bolt shot from a good crossbow is only about 250 feet per second. I'd say for the bolt to have gone through his body, clothing and all, the killer had to be no more than twenty or thirty yards away."

"That's awfully close." said Fulford. "You'd think Paulson would have heard something."

"Paulson was used to the sound of animals moving about in the brush," Cy said. "And the wind blowing through the trees would mask a lot of noise. He probably wouldn't pay any attention to the slight sounds a careful pursuer might make."

"Still it bothers me," Fulford said. "If he were expecting someone, someone he knew and had no reason to fear, he wouldn't have been alarmed by a sound behind him."

"He would have turned around, wouldn't he?" asked Davis. "But he didn't turn. He took the bolt squarely in the middle of his back."

"Yeah," said Cy. "His assailant crept up on him without making a sound. A regular deer stalker."

Chris McCalmon interrupted their speculations. "I'm about ready to open this guy up. You all want to stay for the show?"

Davis spoke for them all. "Thanks a million, Chris, but we've got other things to do."

They left quickly.

CHAPTER FIVE

Albert Saffron looked at the note, that curious sheet, blank except for two short lines of type and the drawing of a deer with an arrow in its side. He ran his fingers over the surface of the paper in exploratory fashion.

"It's printer paper, all right, and the font is Times New Roman #14. The image of the deer is from a clip-art program, probably Corel Draw, or something similar. The arrow was drawn in with a pen as you people have no doubt observed. There's not much point in trying to pin the thing down to a particular computer. Any PC with a word processing program would have that font and most computers have some kind of clip-art program installed when they're sold, but it might be possible, with microscopic examination, to tell what type of printer it came from."

"How?" Davis asked.

"By counting the number of DPI, or, for you dummies, the dots per inch in the text and picture."

Albert Saffron was a man of astonishing bulk, nearly three hundred pounds, with an agility of mind that had earned him the respect of his colleagues. Some years ago, his weight had been a matter of contention within the Division because it exceeded, by a substantial margin, the restriction imposed by regulations. The brass had, accordingly, sent him a notice of dismissal.

Albert, supported by Davis and other friends, protested the dismissal before a Division Grievance Committee. The pro-Saffron arguments, honed to perfection in strategy sessions with his lawyer were ingenious. He had been within the designated weight requirements when hired and the excess poundage, coming as it did in small increments over a period of many months should have been noted by his superiors. Since no one cautioned him against his growing weight, it should not be held against him. The Division should not have waited until he bore a multitude of surplus pounds, but should have expressed concern the minute the first excessive ounce attached itself to his frame. Moreover,

Saffron had a desk job (with a chair quite capable of bearing his weight) and little physical exertion was required of him beyond an occasional trip to the bathroom or to the coffee and Coke machine. These activities he could handle with no difficulty.

The committee, some of whom had a sense of humor, listened to the arguments in Saffron's behalf with grave faces, as if they believed them legitimate. Later, they confessed they were unconvinced until Albert's lawyer, in a flash of legalistic incandescence, contended that Saffron was a man with a disability as defined in the American's With Disabilities Act recently passed by Congress. He could not, because of disabling avoirdupois, be legally fired. So Albert was restored to his job and had been, ever after, Davis's loyal friend, eager to lend him his expertise and intelligence whenever it was required.

"So how long does it take to count these DPI?" Davis inquired.

"We don't actually count them," Saffron replied. "We project an image on a comparison microscope of a particular font next to a font whose DPI has already been established. I can do it now, if you want to wait. We can test the deer image by looking at a few clip art programs."

"We'd appreciate your doing it, Albert."

When Albert had gone, Davis spoke to Fulford. He was reacting to the coolness she exhibited when he had asked her for a date.

"I get the impression you're up-tight working with me, Leda. If you want, I'll ask Gerry to pair you with someone else."

"Wade, don't start imagining things. Just because I won't go to a concert with you this weekend, you think I'm turning you off. I'm not. There are other people I like to see occasionally."

"So you're seeing someone else this weekend?" Wade asked, jealousy in his voice unconcealed.

"Look, Wade, I like you. I never would have slept with you, if I didn't." She sighed. "I'm seeing my brother, who's home on break from law school. I'm going to spend some time with him."

"Oh!" said Davis, somewhat mollified. "I thought maybe Chris had beaten me out."

"Chris is a nice guy. If you keep crowding me," she said in a mock serious way, "I'll throw you over for him."

Albert returned, holding a note pad on which he had scribbled a few notes.

"I was right about the font," he said. "Times New Roman #14. Every word processing program ever devised has it. The resolution of the letters, however, is lousy. A high number of DPI makes for characters with good sharp resolution and most printers are designed with high DPI. Canon, Lexmark, Apple all run six or seven hundred DPI. Some have two levels of resolution the operator can choose from. I know of only one printer, although there may be others, that has four levels of DPI, 1200, 720, 360, and 180. That's the Epson. This note was written at 180 DPI. I'd guess, therefore, it came from a computer that has an Epson printer attached.

"As far as the deer image is concerned, it matches, as I thought, a picture from a Corel Draw 4 program."

"So," said Fulford, who had been listening in fascination, "if we find a computer with an Epson printer and a Corel Draw 4 program, "we might have found the computer the note was written on."

"Might, is the operational word, Leda," Saffron said. "There must be hundreds of computers that have that combination."

"True," said Davis. "But if one of Paulson's enemies turns out to have access to a computer like that, well, we'd have a right to be suspicious, wouldn't we?"

Basil Gearhart, zealous member of the Society of Animal Conservators, sat in the precinct jail, charged with assualt, unable to make bail and unwilling to accept the plea bargain offered by the prosecutor. It would require him to admit to being emotionally disturbed, to attend twelve sessions with a psychiatrist who specialized in hate reduction, and to write a letter of apology to Harry Paulson. In return, he would receive a suspended sentence of ninety days in the county jail.

The denigration of his self-esteem required by the plea bargain was more than he could bear. He was, he avowed to himself, no more emotionally disturbed than the judge who denied him bail nor the prosecutor who was persecuting him. What was emotionally wrong about hating people who killed innocent, defenseless animals? Indeed, a loving concern for the welfare of animals was a sign of enlightenment, of moral superiority. He resolved to tough it out. He would rot before calling himself disturbed, either emotionally or intellectually. He was a crusader in one of the worthiest causes of contemporary times.

As the days and hours in his narrow cell began to accumulate, he was tempted to reconsider his refusal and gain his freedom. The cause for which he had dedicated himself required a high degree of selflessness. What right did he have to retire from the field of battle because of some pejorative label? He would sacrifice his self-esteem on the altar of moral obligation. On the point of calling a turnkey to announce his capitulation, he was confronted by a jailer who informed him an anonymous sympathizer had put up his bail and he was free to go.

He walked out of prison at eleven thirty a.m., July 30th, the morning of the day Harry Paulson was felled by a bolt from a cross bow.

Alone in his apartment at eight o'clock that evening, Gearhart was about to settle down to watch a favorite TV program, when a sharp knock sounded on his apartment door. He opened, alarmed at seeing the two uniformed police officers who stood before him.

"I'm detective Wade Davis," the tall, lean man announced. "And," gesturing to his companion, "This is my colleague, detective Leda Fulford. We're investigating a homicide and need to ask you a few questions. May we come in?"

Gearhart hesitated, but considering his precarious position with the law, he thought it wise to cooperate.

"I suppose so, but I have nothing to do with any homicide. I don't see how I can help you."

He stood aside and the detectives entered, glancing about the room, in hope of seeing a computer. No such device was visible. The only electronic gadgets Gearhart seemed to possess were a nineteen-inch TV set mounted on a black plastic pedestal and a compact disc player. He had tuned his TV set to a popular show based on the activities of a police department and its idealized personnel.

The room, which from some odd quirk of construction, was almost triangular in shape, had one wall just five feet in width. Against this, the TV was situated and a sofa and two upholstered chairs had been arranged opposite for optimal viewing. An end table at one side of the sofa held a lamp and the larger of the upholstered chairs was flanked by a floor lamp. The sofa appeared to be the kind that made up into a bed. To Davis the room was one of austerity and tasteless dreariness.

"Harry Paulson, whom you assaulted last week," Davis began, "was murdered a few hours ago at his home near Buckhead. You're a suspect."

Gearhart's portrayal of surprise was either genuine or superb acting. But he seemed frightened. His hands trembled and there was a nervous tic in his cheek. Davis could not tell, however, if it was fear of being found out for having committed a crime, or was just the alarm a person shows at being suddenly confronted by two police officers who name him a murder suspect.

"My God!" he said. "You can't think I had anything to do with that. I just got out of jail. I don't want to go back there again." He paused looking beseechingly at the officers. When they continued to stare accusingly at him, he declared, "I'm not a violent man. I would never hurt anyone."

"You don't call hitting a man over the head with a bag full of blood a violent act?" Fulford asked.

"No. I don't. It was an act of symbolic violence, not actual violence. I had no intention of doing Mr. Paulson any real physical harm. The bag was flimsy, designed to break on contact so as not to have enough force to injure him. It didn't do him any harm, did it? More startled him than anything else."

"I find it hard to see the difference," Fulford said, "between what you did and hitting someone in the head with a club."

"Believe me," Gearhart was almost pleading, "I would never think of hitting a man with a club or harming him in any other way. I believe passionately that to maim or kill non-human animals is evil. It is just as evil to maim or kill a human being."

There was conviction in his voice, but Davis was skeptical. How many times had he heard a brutal killer proclaim his innocence with all the sincerity and candor of a minister of the gospel. Basil Gearhart remained in his mind a solid suspect as Harry Paulson's killer.

"Where were you between six and seven tonight?" he asked.

"Here. Right here in my apartment. I was released from jail at eleven-thirty this morning. I had lunch at a McDonalds. Then I went to the grocery store and bought food for my dinner and tomorrow's breakfast. I brought the stuff home, took a nap— I had trouble sleeping in jail—and fixed my dinner. After I had eaten and washed up, I watched TV. I was still doing that when the two of you arrived. I assume that Mr. Paulson was murdered somewhere around six or seven."

Davis did not comment on Gearhart's assumption.

"Do you own a computer?"

Gearhart appeared puzzled by the question. His face expressed curiosity when he answered. "No I don't. Why?"

"Just curious," Davis replied. "You belong to an organization known as the Society of Animal Conservators, don't you?"

"Yes I do. It's a respectable organization," he said defensively. "It's devoted to the welfare of animals, especially those species that have been traditionally abused by human beings. A lot of famous people belong to it. The actors, Ned Featherstone, Julia Carton, and Michael Johns, for instance. Also a member of the President's cabinet."

"Didn't your group break into the research lab at Calumet University a few months ago, set free the monkeys and rats that were being used for cancer research, and generally trash the premises?"

"I did not approve of that project, nor did the majority of our members. A group of extremists within the organization conceived it and carried it out. Regrettably, things like that happen in any large organization."

"But you and your like-minded friends didn't publicly condemn the action, did you?"

"No. That would not have been good for the organization."

"I suppose not. Dissent within the ranks, is that it?" Fulford said sarcastically.

Gearhart gave her a resentful look and replied to Davis's next question with a put-upon attitude.

"No, I am not just a mere member. I serve, to the best of my ability, on the Recruiting Committee and the Legislative Lobby Committee. I am devoted to the advancement of the society's aims."

There was a smugness about the reply that prompted Davis to remark. "Even if it requires smashing an unsuspecting man with a sack full of blood?"

"I told you, I think of that act as a form of symbolic protest."

"In your work as a lobbyist for the Society of Animal Conservators are you responsible for sending out letters and brochures?"

"Yes. I handle a lot of correspondence. Is there anything important about that?"

"Possibly. Do you use a computer in your work?"

"Yes, I write and revise letters and bulletins on the organization's computer. Why do you ask?"

"Just curious," Davis replied. "I assume you're out on bond."

"Yes."

"A substantial figure?"

"Five thousand dollars. I don't have that kind of money. A supporter of the movement put it up."

"Then you won't be running off somewhere, will you? We'll want to talk to you later on."

"Where would I run to?" Gearhart said.

Chapter Six

As Davis expected, Leda Fulford, whom he had asked to be in his office at 9:15, was waiting when he arrived. His cool greeting belied the emotion he felt when he saw her. He thought it wise to hide the intensity of his attraction to her.

"Morning, Leda. Cy Orovac is joining us in a minute. I want him to tell us more about crossbows and about the war between deer hunters and animal rights people."

She nodded, then spoke as if thinking out loud.

"It's easy to believe Paulson was murdered because of his prominence as a defender of bow hunting, but our investigation is just getting started, and we are bound to turn up other possible motives for his murder."

"Such as?"

"Well, family discord, for one. I felt Kimberly and Greta were lying when they said there was no friction between their parents. Their answers were too pat, too positive. If I'm right, and their parents were having trouble, we could have a potential motive for murder."

"I got the same feeling from Lucinda's answers to my questions. To hear her talk everything was sweetness and light between her and her husband. We'll have to look deeper into that relationship. I suspect there was conflict between that pair."

Cy Orovac entered the room holding a crossbow in his hand.

"I thought you might like to see one of these up close. If I show you the way it works, you'll know what a murderer had to do in order to kill Paulson with it."

He handed the weapon to Davis, who looked it over and gave it to Fulford.

Fulford examined it, raised the stock to her shoulder, sighted along the groove, and returned it to Cy.

"It's seems nothing but a small longbow mounted on a gun stock," she said. "Very much like a rifle. Why has it got that D shaped thing fastened to the front end of the stock?"

"That D shaped thing," Cy responded, "is called the stirrup. When you want to cock the bow you put your foot in the stirrup to hold the bow down as you draw the string back. Otherwise you'd have to pull in two directions at once to cock the thing."

Davis frowned. "Isn't it pretty hard to cock a crossbow, especially, a powerful one." He was wondering if a woman had the strength to do the job.

"It takes muscle, all right. This bow has a draw weight, as it's called, of 165 pounds. That's a little stronger than average. It will shoot a bolt at a speed of 270 feet per second. The strongest crossbow I know of has a draw weight of 185 pounds and will drive a bolt at 290 feet per second."

Fulford voiced Davis's thought.

"Wouldn't it be almost impossible for a woman, particularly a small woman, to cock one of these, say the one with a draw weight of 185 pounds?"

"Not really. Some crossbows have a detachable windlass called a cranequin. By winding the lever, you get an advantage of 145:1. Even a child could cock a bow with it. Most crossbows, however, have a cocking lever called a goat's foot. It's a two piece hinged lever that hooks on to the string and pulls it back as the lever is pulled upward and toward the rear. It gives a 5:1 advantage, enough to enable even a frail woman to cock the bow."

"OK," Davis said. "So a woman could cock it. Wouldn't you have to have a lot of practice before you could use one with any degree of accuracy?"

"Actually, a novice can learn to shoot one pretty accurately in a short time. With a longbow, the kind we associate with Robin Hood and his merry men, the archer must learn to aim instinctively, that is, he must aim without a sight to guide his eye. He must also learn how to release the string without spoiling his aim. And that's hard to do if the bow has a high draw weight. It's easier for the crossbow hunter. He sights along the shaft of the arrow, which makes for greater accuracy than sighting instinctively, and he can release the string with a trigger mechanism that won't pull his aim off-target. In some cases, crossbows are equipped with carefully engineered sights."

Davis listened critically to Cy's statements. It seemed to him a crossbow was an odd weapon for a murderer to choose, a weapon with a much bigger margin of error than a pistol or a rifle. Even if the murderer chose it for its symbolic value, he would risk failure, and possible exposure with such a device. Why not use a gun?

"Cy, when you say, a novice could learn to use a crossbow in a very short time, how short is short?"

"Ten or twelve half-hour practice session are all an adult would need in order to take a deer at fifty yards with only a rare miss. Shorten the range to thirty or thirty-five yards, and a novice could reach a high degree of accuracy with as few as three or four lessons."

"How far away did Paulson's assailant stand when he shot the fatal bolt?"

"When you asked me that earlier, I estimated thirty yards. I now think he, or she, was closer. Given the poor light and the presence of heavy underbrush, the killer would have found it hard to estimate distance. Not wanting to run the risk of a total miss or a hit in a non-vital spot, he'd try to get really close. I'd say fifteen yards."

"Forty-five feet! At that distance, he'd risk being heard."

"Exactly," Fulford said. "I believe the assailant was someone Paulson knew, someone he wouldn't suspect was planning to harm him. If discovered, the killer could just abort the mission, pretend he was out for a walk, and wait for another time."

"You're suggesting a close friend or a member of the family," Davis said. "But so far, we have no evidence that would cause us to suspect anybody like that. Right now the most likely candidate is Basil Gearhart who had a grudge against Paulson."

He turned to Cy and said, "At that congressional hearing on the proposed longbow ban, I saw how hostile hunters and animal rightists were toward each other. Do you think someone like Gearhart is fanatical enough to commit murder?"

"A division psychologist once told me there's no one more dangerous than a single-issue zealot. And a lot of animal rights people are single-issue zealots. I don't know about Gearhart, in particular, but there's plenty of fanaticism in the rhetoric used by some animal rights people. The stuff you heard at the congressional hearing, Wade, was relatively tame. I've collected some dillies from pamphlets, books, and speeches just for your benefit."

He drew a sheet of paper from his jacket pocket and, with the eagerness of a scholar bent on sharing the fruits of his research with the uninitiated, he spoke:

"Listen to some of these: 'Hunters are sadistic rednecks.' 'Hunters are dangerous, unethical, selfish, destructive creatures.' 'Hunters don't kill for food, they kill to inflict pain and suffering.' Sounds pretty harsh, doesn't it?"

Fulford, who had reservations about hunting in general, and even greater reservations about bow hunting, offered an opinion.

"I admit those statement are exaggerated, but there may be a kernel of truth in them."

Cy frowned.

"You think I'm a sadistic redneck, Leda?"

"If you're a hunter, Cy, expect to be tarred with the same brush used against hunters," she said half in jest, half seriously.

"Well, thanks for your good opinion," Cy said sarcastically. He pretended to be more hurt than he actually was. Years of fighting the animal rights people had given him a tough hide and a high tolerance for gratuitous insult.

"All right, you two," Davis said. "Let's not take sides in this war. We're just trying to find out if the combatants get fired up enough to kill one another. Go on, Cy."

"I don't think there's much doubt that truly rabid animal lovers would murder," Cy said. "I'm not quoting exactly but one guy said something like this. 'If I had the money I'd buy an island, round up a bunch of hunters, tie antlers on their heads, turn them loose in the wilderness, and hunt them down the way they hunt deer.'"

Davis grunted. "Charming idea. But not very original. Must've read 'The Most Dangerous Game.'"

"Okay. Tell me what you think this fellow's been reading. He says, 'The lives of some deer are, by any standard, more valuable than the lives of some people.' I suppose he had in mind murderers, drug addicts, and other unsavory types."

"Probably. But still an unsettling thought," Fulford said.

"The group calling themselves People for the Moral Treatment of Animals have some pretty extreme members," Cy continued. "One of their officers said that animals have the same rights as retarded children because they are dependent on others the way retarded children are. He went on to say that arson, property destruction, burglary and theft are acceptable when used for the protection of animals."

Davis thought further speculation on the subject was unnecessary.

"You've answered my question," he said. "In your judgment an animal lover, perhaps not one of the rank and file, but a deeply committed and emotionally disturbed person, could be outraged enough about the hunting and killing of animals to commit murder. Right?"

Cy nodded. "Yes. But let's remember that most animal rights people are decent, sincere, law abiding folk. There are a few loose cannons in any society, people who can be tipped over the edge."

"Agreed," Davis said. "In fairness, let's take a look at the other camp. At the devoted hunter. Is it possible that a hunter, out of anger or sheer cussedness, might kill an animal rightist?"

Cy shrugged, "It's possible. But defenders of the status quo don't usually get so riled up. Hunters use rhetoric that is not generally inflammatory. They're on the defensive and tend to be forced into logical arguments. Still, some of them must sometimes feel severely threatened. There are initiatives on the ballot in ten different states this November that would restrict or limit deer and bear hunting. I suppose some hunter might feel his back was to the wall and that he had to retaliate by killing one of the enemy."

Fulford, who had grown impatient with all this talk about who would or would not resort to violence, voiced a cynical opinion. "Listen, guys. Let's remember one simple fact. Anybody can commit murder. Vicious psychopaths and sweet little old ladies do it all the time. As detectives, we've learned that over and over again. All a person needs to commit murder is a compelling reason. Unfortunately, any damn thing, to a murderer, can be a compelling reason."

Chapter Seven

"**W**e need to talk to Gretchen and Kimberly again," Davis said, looking at his partner with an expression that told her he doubted his ability to carry off such an interview with much success. "I'm certain they're concealing a rift between their parents. Something we need to know about. But I'm not very good at interrogating young girls. I think I intimidate them."

"You're intimidating, all right," Fulford said with a laugh. "You even intimidate me. I suppose you want me to question the girls. Is that what all this self-denigration is leading up to?"

"Yes." Davis admitted. "I'll tag along, if it's all right with you, and sit and listen. You do the talking. Okay?"

Leda agreed, and an hour later, she and Davis sat in the study of the Paulson home confronting the two girls, who were seated together on a sofa. Davis had taken a chair in a corner and tried to be as inconspicuous as possible.

Kimberly was dressed, almost starkly, in a black sack-like shift gathered at the waist with a narrow belt. Gretchen had on a tangerine-colored skirt that clung tightly to her buttocks. An off-white pullover sweater accentuated the outline of her breasts. Fulford guessed the contrast in clothing was a reflection of each girl's self image.

She smiled at the them and asked if they wanted to get something from the kitchen to drink. They declined politely and did not suggest the officers seek refreshment for themselves. There was a palpable sense of strain in the air. Fulford tried to diminish the tension by speaking in a casual, non-threatening manner.

"I know you're anxious to help us to find the person who killed your father," she began.

Both girls nodded without speaking. Kimberly looked squarely at Fulford, but Gretchen cast her eyes down. While Kimberly seemed assured, Gretchen was evasive, distant.

"For us to find out who killed your father, we have to know all about your Dad's life. Especially, we need to know about his relationship with family and friends. You both loved him and suffer greatly from his loss. I get the feeling, however, your Mom is not as hard hit as you are. Does it seem that way to you?"

Both girls squirmed uncomfortably. Neither seemed willing to respond to Fulford's inquiry. An awkward silence ensued. Fulford, thinking continued silence might pressure the girls to speak, said nothing. She sat quietly, staring at the girls. A long empty, interval went by.

Kimberly broke down first. "I don't know what you're trying to do. I know you're not being very nice insulting my mother with your questions. Are you insinuating she didn't love my father?"

Gretchen, red faced and insolent, said, "I think you're terrible. Any minute you'll be saying she killed him." Fulford sensed a lot of turmoil beneath her controlled demeanor.

"We don't think that at all," Fulford said. "But if your mother and father quarreled, if they had serious disagreements, that fact might point us to whoever had a reason to kill your father."

Even to herself, Fulford admitted the statement she had just made didn't make much sense. Suspicion, in the event of bad blood between the couple, would fall squarely on Lucinda Paulson. Both girls were bright enough to see that.

"Look," she said with what she hoped was disarming frankness, "In the investigation of a crime, police officers are trained to suspect everyone. The murder victim's spouse is always a prime suspect. We just wonder if your mother had a possible motive."

She stopped, looked hopefully at the girls.

"If you want us to help you put a noose around our mother's neck," Kimberly said, venomously, "you're badly mistaken."

Gretchen was a bit more ambivalent. "Even if our parents quarreled every day of the year, we wouldn't tell you. If you think they did, you'll have to find out somewhere else."

Fulford had the distinct impression her statement was intended to confirm that discord between her parents had in fact existed. She wondered why Gretchen would imply such a thing.

She looked inquiringly at Davis who nodded his head almost imperceptibly. As Fulford terminated the interview her words were a reproach. "I'm sorry you decided not to cooperate. Given your attitude, there's no point in prolonging this interview. You may go."

As they rose and left the room, neither girl gave a backward glance. And neither showed any sign of contrition.

When they were gone, Fulford said, "I'm afraid your theory about my being able to get more out of them than you could was woefully wrong."

"Not entirely. I'm sure the girls didn't intend to do so, but by word and action, they let us know the Paulsons were an unhappy couple. Gretchen's response was a sly tip off. She didn't deny the marriage was a troubled one. I think she really wanted us to know there was trouble in paradise but didn't want to say it outright."

"I suppose we were stupid to think they would rat on their Mom and Dad. Well, we'll look elsewhere for the information we want. As Gretchen, snippy little creature, told us to."

They were on their way to talk with Adam and Pamela Wharton. Investigation had revealed that Adam Wharton was a gynecologist. He had an office near the city's largest hospital, and, according to discrete inquiries, had been sued for malpractice only two times in fifteen years of practice, a better than average record, according to the source. In both cases the insurance company had settled for an undisclosed sum. No admission of wrongdoing had been made.

"I don't know what to make of that fact," Davis told Fulford. "How many malpractice suits do you suppose the average doctor has?"

"I'd guess quite a few," said Fulford. "People sue their doctors nowadays for the craziest reasons. I read that one woman sued her gynecologist for failure to warm a speculum before inserting it. Said it caused her emotional and physical trauma."

"What happened?"

"The insurance company paid the woman a nuisance sum, rather than spend a small fortune on legal fees contesting her claim."

"Makes sense. Or does it?"

Adam Wharton's wife Pamela was a nurse. After her marriage, she gave up nursing and devoted herself to supporting humanitarian causes. Her present enthusiasm was a campaign to provide housing for Atlanta's homeless.

The couple received the detectives in the living room of their thirty five hundred square foot home. Davis had never been in a house that big and found himself awed at the size of the room they were in. Pamela Wharton, he thought somewhat spitefully, could accommodate in that room alone at least a dozen of the destitute creatures about whose condition she was so concerned.

"We won't spoil your entire evening," Davis said. "We'll be as brief as we can."

"Don't worry about our time," Adam Wharton said. "Harry Paulson was one of our best friends. We want to do everything we can to help catch his murderer."

Adam Wharton was smooth, urbane, congenial. Of medium height, he seemed remarkably self assured and carried himself with authority. His bearing made him appear to be of greater stature than he actually was.

"We appreciate your attitude, Mr. Wharton. First off, you and Harry were prominent supporters of legislation that permits bow hunting of deer, weren't you?"

"We are...uh, were. You know what happened to Harry at the recent hearing on a bill to end the practice of bow hunting." It was more a statement than a question.

"Yes. The man is in custody and will be punished for what he did. Aside from that incident, did Mr. Paulson ever, to your knowledge, receive threats of bodily harm because of his support for bow hunting?"

"Yes he did. He was flamed several times on his computer."

"I'm sorry," said Fulford. "I'm not sure I know what 'flamed' means."

"Flaming means receiving, via e-mail, a scurrilous, obscene, or threatening message. Since an e-mail sender is remote from the recipient and unknown to him by name and may be using an alias, he can be as hateful as he wants to be with little possibility of being held accountable. The receiver of an inflammatory message doesn't know the sender."

"Did any of these hate messages threatened bodily harm to Mr. Paulson?"

"Yes. Many of them promised death by about every means you can imagine. Hanging, shooting, poisoning, you name it. Less drastic ones threatened arson, knee-capping, and castration."

"And he never told the police?"

"Flamers are cowards. They merely bluster. They don't have the guts to carry out their threats. Harry never felt truly threatened."

"You and Mr. Paulson hunted with crossbows, didn't you?"

"Yes. You may not know it but that made us unpopular with some longbow hunters. Crossbows are very accurate weapons and the longbow people accused us of getting more than our fair share of game."

"So, in addition to enemies among the animal rights people, Mr. Paulson might have had enemies among longbow hunters?" asked Davis.

"It's possible. I don't think longbow hunters are as fanatical as some of the animal rights people. I wouldn't think a longbow hunter killed Harry.

Animal rightists are something else. Most of them are good citizens, but among them there's a sizable fringe of impulsive, potentially violent zealots. Like that Basil Gearhart."

"Do you think Mr. Paulson was killed by an overzealous animal rights person?"

"I think it likely. And I think Gearhart is a good candidate."

"Can you think of any other reason why someone might want to kill Mr. Paulson?"

"About a year ago, there was a flap about contaminants in a vaccine Harry's firm sold. Several people had serious physical impairments from using the drug. Roger Godwin could tell you more about that incident than I can."

"Is Mr. Godwin a friend of yours? We know he and Harry Paulson were partners, and I had the impression the three of you hunted deer together."

"That's true. Roger was a partner and a research chemist of great ability. We not only hunted together, but we socialized at parties and receptions. I can't say Roger is a close friend, not as close a friend as Harry. Maybe close acquaintance would be a better description."

"Was there ever any friction between the two of them?"

"None that I know of. Of course, if there had been any trouble stemming from problems at the plant, I wouldn't have heard about it."

"You never heard any rumors of trouble?"

"No. Not between Roger and Harry. I did read in the paper, as I said earlier, about a flap concerning a monkey virus contaminating some vaccine. I think it led to threats of a class action law suit."

"But it wouldn't have resulted in threats against Mr. Paulson personally, would it?"

"I don't think so. I suspect Roger would know."

Davis paused momentarily as if uncertain how to proceed.

His hesitation gave Fulford an opportunity to question Mrs. Wharton. Though in her early forties, as near as Fulford could judge, Mrs. Wharton had an enviable figure, the product of disciplined exercise. Her face, unwrinkled, and attractive in a wholesome sort of way, seemed to reflect a compassionate spirit.

"Mrs. Wharton, I've seen your name in the papers in connection with a drive to increase the number of Atlanta's shelters for the homeless."

"Yes. I'm pleased you noticed. Homelessness is a difficult problem, one requiring money that, unfortunately, the city is unprepared or unable to provide. We—our organization that is—are obliged to solicit private funds. I'm head of our money raising efforts."

"Did Edgeware Pharmaceuticals contribute to your fund?"

"Only nominally. Harry Paulson, God rest his soul, had a negative attitude toward the homeless. He thought the majority of them were drug users, alcoholics, mentally impaired, or just plain lazy. He felt they should be forced to shift for themselves."

"But he contributed, nevertheless."

"Out of friendship for me and Adam."

"Was his attitude well known?"

"I don't think it was ever reported in the papers or on TV, but he talked about it at social gatherings. A lot of influential people learned about it in that way. I remember one or two spirited debates we had during parties."

"Do you think he could have offended anyone to the degree they might have wished to harm him?"

"I doubt that very much. Only a person with a strong emotional investment in the program might have wished him harm. But harming Harry wouldn't have made much sense. What would have been gained?"

"If you were a person who was homeless," said Fulford, "because of a corporate downsizing, or because of some other legitimate reason, you might be upset enough to want a little revenge against a man who thought you were lazy trash."

"I doubt if any of Atlanta's homeless ever knew of Harry's attitude toward them."

Davis said, "I suspect you're right, Mrs. Wharton." He paused looking at her as if he regretted what he was about to say. "I'm forced to ask you and your husband a question you may find difficult to answer. But when investigating a murder, we have no choice. Did either of you ever observe any indication of trouble in the Paulson marriage?"

The Whartons glanced fleetingly at one another as if conveying a signal. Adam assumed the role of spokesman. "They had disagreements. Don't we all? As near as Pam and I could tell, their differences were minor. I think we were close enough friends to have detected any serious friction had it existed."

"Is that your opinion, Mrs. Wharton?" asked Davis.

"It is. I don't think I saw even minor disagreements more than a few times. They seemed to be very much in love."

Davis and Fulford thanked the Whartons and left.

"Yes," Roger Godwin replied to Davis's remark. "We had a problem with SV 40, a simian virus that contaminated polio vaccines from 1959 to 1964."

In response to their telephone call, Godwin had agreed to meet them for lunch in the Crown Room of the downtown Holiday Inn. He had arrived promptly and had made clear immediately that the cost of the lunch would be born by Edgeware Pharmaceuticals.

"The company has a vital interest in apprehending Harry's killer. As interim CEO, I assure you we will do whatever is necessary to assist the police. My own personal feelings are involved as well. Harry was a dear friend, and I wish to bring his assailant to justice."

He was young, probably no more than thirty five or thirty six. His features were clean-cut, though his chin, jutting out a little protuberantly, gave him a severe, judgmental look. A small bald spot on the back of his head, was a sign of greater bareness to come. His muscular, well toned body, indicated regular visits to a fitness club.

Davis told him of Adam Wharton's comment about the company having dispensed a vaccine contaminated with monkey virus. Godwin acknowledged the problem and elaborated.

"Polio vaccine that was used in the fifties and sixties was grown in kidney cells of Rhesus monkeys. As a result, scientists found simian viruses in the vaccines before they were released. At least twenty-six viruses were identified and eliminated but other viruses, SV 40 among them, could not be detected by methods then in use. By the time SV 40 was identified and eradicated from the vaccine some ninety eight million people had been inoculated."

"I read in some cases the vaccine caused people to come down with polio," said Fulford. "Was that caused by SV 40?"

Godwin shook his head. "No. Why the vaccine did that to a few people was never fully explained. SV 40 was never demonstrated to cause problems in human subjects, although it did cause cancer in hamsters."

"All of this happened years ago. What relevance does it have today?" Davis asked.

"Scientists are not certain there is any relevance, but recently researchers have found genetic pieces of SV 40 in certain cancers of the bone, lung, and brain. This raises the question of whether SV 40 may have contributed to those cancers. A hell of a lot of people who were inoculated with the polio vaccine that contained SV 40 are alarmed. Some of them have become paranoid and are branding the pharmaceutical business as being run by a gang of ruthless, profit-crazy killers. Which leads me to the importance of this whole matter for your investigation."

"I don't see how all this could relate to Harry Paulson's murder," Davis said.

"Let me explain. At a recent board meeting a man named Victor Percy said, as a small stockholder, he had important information to share with the company. We have a policy of allowing stockholders the right to air concerns at our annual meetings, so he was allowed to speak. The result was a tirade, emotional to the nth degree. He was suffering, he said, from a rare bone cancer, that was cause by SV 40, which he contracted when he was give a polio vaccine from Edgeware Pharmaceuticals in the sixties.

"He alleged the company was responsible for his cancer and demanded compensation. He wanted all his medical expenses reimbursed and compensatory damages for his pain and suffering and diminished life span. Also unspecified punitive damages."

"I suppose he disrupted the meeting with his charges," said Davis, still unsure of the relevance of Godwin's story, but beginning to see a possible connection.

"He did. For a short time. Then Harry took control and responded to Percy's allegations. He pointed out that Edgeware Pharmaceuticals did not make the polio vaccine that Percy had received as a child. It was merely a distributor, and if any culpability existed, it would lie with the people who manufactured the product."

"Did Percy dispute this?" asked Fulford.

"He did, indeed. He became abusive and charged Harry with veniality, placing profits above human suffering. Harry managed to calm him a bit. He pointed out that the cancers of bone, lung, and brain, where genetic traces of the virus had been found, had never been scientifically proved to have been caused by the virus. This brought another outburst from Percy, who threatened to take action against the CEO of the corporation if he did not yield to his demands for compensation."

"Do you recall exactly what he said?" asked Davis. "It's important to know how he worded his threat."

Godwin scowled in concentration. "I think he said, 'I will take appropriate action against the CEO of the corporation if he does not agree to compensate me fairly.'"

"Did you interpret that to mean he might do physical harm to Mr. Paulson?"

"'Appropriate action' is ambiguous. It could mean no more than legal action. But in the emotional context of the meeting, and given the near hysterical tenor of Percy's language, I felt it could have meant physical harm."

"After the stockholder's meeting, did you hear from Percy again?" asked Fulford. "It seems to me his remark could hardly be construed as a physical threat without some other indication he meant it that way."

Godwin nodded. "I don't want to cast unwarranted suspicion on the guy, and I can't say for certain he was responsible for an e-mail threat Harry received shortly after the meeting. That message, which was anonymous, was a death threat."

"Did you make a copy of it?" Davis asked.

"No, but it's still in the computer file. If you want, I can pull it up."

He went to the computer, clicked a few icons, and from a file of e-mail messages selected one, which he enlarged on the screen. It read:

> *Maybe you think you can get away with what you have done to me. You have invaded my body and corrupted it for your own ends. If you do not atone for my injury, you will pay with your life. This is no idle threat. You know it is not.*

Davis and Fulford read the letter carefully. Davis asked, "Is there any way to tell who wrote this note?"

"No, sir. The message is completely anonymous."

"I thought the sender of e-mail had to give an address before the e-mail provider would accept it."

"That's true. But the sender of this note used what's known as a re-mailer. A re-mailer is a person who receives e-mail from a sender, re-addresses it and sends it on to its destination. The receiver does not see the address of the true sender. He sees only that the message came from an address like this: *re-mailer@ such and such.com*. If he tries to contact the re-mailer to find out who the true sender is, he gets nowhere."

"Surely a responsible re-mailer wouldn't allow people to send a death threat message." said Fulford.

"Most re-mailers wouldn't. But I suppose there are some unscrupulous ones who might. You'll note that the letter Harry received didn't actually use the word death but 'pay with your life.' If the re-mailer's computer is only configured to red-flag anything with the word death in it, this wordage would slip through."

"Does the re-mailer sit in front of his computer screen and read all the e-mail letters his computer receives?" Fulford asked.

Godwin smiled. "Hardly. He might receive as many as two hundred or more messages a day to be re-mailed. He would set his computer to handle them automatically. Of course, every message received is stored in his cache, so if he needed to review a particular one, he could do so."

"You said if the receiver of an anonymous e-mail message contacted the re-mailer to find out who sent the message, he'd get nowhere. What if the message were a death threat."

"I'm sure the re-mailer would reveal the source to the police."

"I see the re-mailer's address on this message is *blimpie@simpleton.com*. If we contacted him, or her, or it, would they reveal the sender of this note to us?"

"It depends. If it's the kind of re-mailer who assigns the sender a number like XXXXX, you could reply to the re-mailer asking him to direct the letter to the person holding the assigned number. If challenged by the police he would probably reveal the name of the person holding that number. However if the re-mailer is the cypherpunk kind, his computer would destroy the sender's name and address. Sometimes cypherpunk re-mailers substitute a nonsense address for the real one, something like *somebody@somewhere.org*."

"You never contacted the re-mailer to try to find out who sent it?"

"No. We just assumed it was sent by Percy. I'm still convinced he was the sender."

"Do you think Percy might have been the man who killed Mr. Paulson?"

"It's possible. He was livid with anger at the company. He could project that anger on to Harry and get satisfaction by killing him. He's a sick man. Probably doesn't have long to live. He could think, 'What the hell. If I'm caught I won't be around long enough to be executed. What have I got to lose?'"

"Aside from the computer threat, did Percy show any other sign he might be thinking of violence?"

"No. He seemed to be inclined toward litigation. He filed suit for damages against the company. That action is still pending."

"I suppose he'll be after millions," Davis said.

"His attorneys approached our people with an offer to settle for two million, a sum we could readily afford, given the cost of fighting the action. I wanted to take it, but Harry wouldn't hear of it. Called it blackmail. I reminded him that before we were through defending ourselves, we'd spend at least two million in legal fees. And, given the way juries behave these days, we might have a multimillion dollar award to contend with."

He shook his head in disbelief at his partner's obtuseness. "It's the only matter over which Harry and I ever had a serious disagreement."

Davis nodded in understanding. "Ironic, isn't it. His death gives you the authority to settle the matter the way you think best."

"Hardly the way to settle a disagreement," Godwin said.

Chapter Eight

Davis awoke Sunday morning pleased at the prospect of a day off. The weather forecast was for showers and temperatures in the low nineties, but he resolved he wouldn't let that deter him from the outing he had planned. As he prepared his breakfast, four strips of bacon, two fried eggs, basted with bacon fat until the bright orange of their yolks was covered by a thin film of white, two slices of whole wheat toast, well buttered, he thought of the dismay Fulford had expressed when he had told her what his customary morning meal consisted of.

"My God, Wade," she had said, "Think what you're doing to your arteries. Filling them with sludge. You'll probably have a heart attack before you're fifty."

He had dismissed her warning light-heartedly, but now, as he settled down to enjoy his meal, he felt a trace of guilt, a nagging sense of irritation. The mere fact that eating his favorite food could plague his conscience was, he thought, a tribute to the persuasive power of the health zealots. Nevertheless, as he dipped his toast into the runny yolk of an egg and filled his mouth, he forgot all considerations of dietary propriety and gave himself over to sheer gustatory pleasure.

As he ate, he thought about his plan for the day—a visit to the Atlanta Zoo to see and photograph the giant Panda on loan from the Chinese government. He had just bought an SLR camera with a array of settings that governed aperture, shutter speed, focus, and zoom lens settings. Designed for the mechanically inept, the camera could, with the press of a button, make all critical decisions automatically if the user chose. This "point and shoot" capability Davis refused to use. He would override it with a manual switch which he intended to lock permanently in place. He vowed he would never give up control of the camera to some internal wizardry.

He played with the controls, disabling one function after the other to see what happened. He had almost blinded himself by looking into the lens of the camera as the flash went off, when the phone rang.

"Damn," he said at the intrusion. He briefly considered not answering. He could always claim he had not been at home.

"Wade?" The voice was that of Gerry Fillmore, Division Head. "Something has happened at the Paulson household. Lucinda Paulson is upset as hell. Claims she's received a threat. Won't say what kind. Wants you on the scene right away. You, and no one else. Go hold her hand."

"Come on, Gerry! I'm not on duty. Give her some excuse."

"You give her some excuse, Wade. Go tell her to her face you're too selfish to help a damsel in distress."

It was no use arguing. He put his new camera back in its case and slammed the door as he left the apartment.

Lucinda met him at her front door holding a Teddy bear in her hands, arms stiffly extended so it made no contact with her body. The bear was a tiny, cuddly thing and its sweet, friendly little face had been transformed with a black magic-marker into a grimace of acute suffering. Its body, pierced through the midriff by an arrow, had red blotches of imitation blood, drawn with a red marker around the entry wound. The arrow was from a child's archery set and had a point crudely sharpened. The bear's body had apparently been pierced with a screwdriver, or similar instrument, and the arrow inserted through the hole. It fitted loosely.

"Take it," she said, thrusting the animal into Davis's hands.

He fumbled the thing ineptly, almost dropping it. "Where did it come from?" he asked, puzzled. "Did you find it in the house?"

"Of course not." She gave him a disdainful look. "How would anyone get it into the house?" Her face showed the strain she was under. Her jaw was clamped tight. A muscle in her cheek twitched. "It was sitting on the front porch when I went out to get the paper. I could have left it where it was, but I didn't want the girls to see it. I brought it in and put it in the closet. Then I called you."

"Are the girls still in bed?"

"They sleep in on Sunday."

"You didn't touch the arrow, did you? There may be fingerprints on it."

"No. I only held it by the body."

"Show me exactly where you found it," Davis said. "Here." He extended the bear toward her.

Lucinda Paulson took the animal and, with a distasteful look, put it down on the porch.

"Are you sure that's exactly where it was? On the edge of the step that way?" Davis asked.

"Yes, its legs were dangling down the top step. Just the way I've put it."

"So someone could have reached in through the railing and put it there without stepping on the porch?"

"I suppose so."

"Mrs. Paulson, I know you're upset about this. And I don't blame you. But I wouldn't make too much of it."

She bridled. "Do you think it's a silly prank? A practical joke? It's an omen. Just like that bag of blood thrown at my husband by Basil Gearhart. That was a warning of his approaching death. This bear is another warning. A threat of some kind."

"What kind of threat, Mrs. Paulson? Is it a threat against you? One of your daughters? Why should anyone want to harm you or your girls?"

"I don't know. But for what other reason would someone leave this thing on our porch? Don't you think it's supposed to convey a message of some sort?"

"Possibly. But my guess is it's a publicity stunt thought up by animal rights people. Someone will tip off the papers and they'll have a field day with it. 'Why did the Paulson's get a Teddy Bear impaled with an arrow? Is this just another imaginative protest against bow hunting?' That sort of thing. You haven't been contacted by any reporters, have you?

"No."

"You will be, I suspect. Whoever devised this prank will probably make an anonymous telephone call to the *Constitution*. Then you'll have reporters after you wanting you to describe the bear and how you found it. Then they'll want to know your reaction. Don't give them any satisfaction. Deny you ever got a bear. Tell them you don't know what they're talking about."

Lucinda shook her head doubtfully.

"Okay, but I still feel uneasy," she said in a tense voice. "Someone's threatening us. I don't know why." She paused, shaking her head uncertainly.

"Trust me," Davis said. "I don't think this is intended as a threat."

He took the bear from where it sat, a gloomy little icon, and put it carefully on the front seat of his car. It would go to forensics tomorrow for careful examination. He left Lucinda standing on the porch. As he prepared to drive off, he called out, "Don't tell the girls about this. No point in that."

He used his cell phone to call Fulford. It was only nine-thirty. When she answered he said, "What are you doing at this ungodly hour?

"Not so ungodly for me, Wade. I'm an early riser. Even on Sunday. What got you up so early?"

He described the arrow-pierced bear Lucinda found sitting on her front porch. "She's convinced the bear constitutes some kind of threat. She was absolutely fixed on that."

"Maybe she's right, Wade. You don't agree with her interpretation, so you tend to dismiss it."

"Okay. I plead guilty. I tend to see the world through my own glasses. Can you do better? Can you tell me why she believes it's a threat?"

"Very simple. Because she knows who sent it and why."

"How could she know that?"

"Everyone has things in their past they want to keep hidden. If we knew all of Lucinda Paulson's past transgressions, we might know why the bear could be a threat to her."

Davis thought about Fulford's statement. They knew practically nothing of Lucinda's past. "Tell you what," he said. "Let's talk about it, today. If you're up for it, we can mix business with pleasure. I'm heading for the zoo, very shortly, to see Ling Ling, the Chinese Panda. I've got a new camera and I'm dying to use it. Why don't you come along?"

"I don't have a camera."

"I'll let you use mine. Or I'll buy you one of those throw away jobs."

She laughed. "How could I refuse such a generous offer. You don't need to pick me up, though. At two o'clock, I have to meet my brother David at Rich's. He's buying a new suit and needs my advice."

"Then I'll meet you in the Safari Cafe at eleven-thirty. Okay?"

As he drove toward the zoo, he tried to guess the kind of person who could have sent the arrow-pierced bear to Lucinda Paulson. Did the sender use the bear as a symbolic threat to expose an unsavory act in Lucinda's past, something Lucinda thought lay securely buried? Perhaps a youthful sexual indiscretion? To him, that interpretation made little sense. Why would that someone choose this moment to threaten her with exposure? In spite of the publicity stunt explanation he had given Lucinda, he was starting to think the appearance of the murdered bear was somehow related to the killing of her husband. Just how, at the moment, he couldn't say.

He found Fulford standing in the door of the Safari Cafe. She was dressed casually in blue jeans and a white cotton T-shirt printed with the Atlanta Olympics logo. Her hair was wind blown, her cheeks glowing from the hot sun and humid air. She dazzled him. He hugged her, pressing her body tightly to his and didn't release her as quickly as social convention dictated. She didn't exactly melt in his arms but she didn't abruptly pull free either.

"Do you want a snack?" he asked. "Or shall we head for the Panda cage right away?"

"I'm ready for the panda, how about you?"

"Lets go. They've made a special enclosure for her in one of the gorilla habitats. Full of bamboo, the favorite food of pandas. Only a few steps from here."

In spite of the warm weather and the early hour, a crowd of curious people stood in front of Ling Ling's enclosure, staring across the moat at the exotic bear. A habitat, faithful reproduction of the panda's natural environment, had been constructed, and Ling Ling sat contentedly on her haunches munching bamboo shoots and casting an occasional disinterested glance at the crowd of onlookers.

"What a beautiful animal," Fulford said. "She looks like an oversized child's toy."

"Yeah," said Davis, his imagination sparked by the remark, "like a Teddy bear. I wonder..."

Fulford glanced sidewise at him. "You don't suppose," she said, following his unspoken thought, "that the bear sent to Lucinda Paulson was intended to implicate a child in Paulson's murder? Maybe that was why she was so unnerved by it."

Davis shook his head. "You have to strain too hard to arrive at that conclusion. What child? Certainly not one of her own. No. I'm beginning to lean toward Lucinda's interpretation. The obvious one. That it's a threat directed at a member of the household."

"But why? Why aim a threat at Lucinda and her children? Is it a threat related to animal rights. If so, what do her children have to do with that? Or Lucinda herself, for that matter?"

"Suppose it's not related to animal rights. Suppose, as you suggested earlier, it's aimed at Lucinda herself, for an indiscretion that would cause her trouble if it were revealed."

Davis was playing with his camera, focusing it on Ling Ling and turning the zoom lens to different settings. His face reflected the fascination he found with the results.

He handed the camera to her. "Point it at Ling Ling. I've turned the lens to 200mm."

She took the camera and looked through the viewfinder. The image of Ling Ling appeared so close it seemed she could reach out and touch her.

"That's really something. What kind of lens is this?"

"It's a 28 to 200mm zoom. At 200mm you seem to be right on top of the subject. If you go in the opposite direction the subject gets farther away. Turn the barrel of the lens slowly to the left and you'll see what I mean."

As she turned the lens, the panda receded further into the distance while parts of the habitat grew visible around her. When she turned the ring to the left as far as it would go she could see the head and shoulders of members of the crowd.

"Go back to 200 and take a shot of Ling Ling," Davis suggested.

"I'm right in her face," she said as she pressed the shutter release. "Ought to be a good shot."

She surrendered the camera to Davis who took several more shots at various distances.

Ling Ling provided little action to excite her spectators. She munched contentedly on bamboo, occasionally brushed a fly away from her face, and remained seated on her haunches. Children grew restless, tugged at their parents, and pulled them toward the Simba Lion Overlook, or toward the Monkeys of Makokou enclosure.

Davis felt the tug of boredom, too. "Can't spend the whole day on Ling Ling," he said. "There are other fish in the sea, or should I say other beasts in the field?"

"I'll opt for beasts," Fulford said. "And right now I'm looking at a beast I don't believe. A red elephant!"

Davis looked where Fulford pointed and saw three African elephants in a moated enclosure. One, a large female, had just arisen from a mud bath in which two others lay on their sides wallowing contentedly. Coated with red Georgia clay, this great creature was an astonishing sight, a crimson monstrosity. As Davis and Fulford approached, the other two elephants rose up out of the mud and joined their companion forming a trio of scarlet pachyderms.

Davis raised the camera and, adjusting the range and focus, took several shots of the three. A plaque on the wall of the enclosure informed them that the three elephants were Starlet O'Hara, Victoria, and Zambezi. According to the text, Zambezi was the largest and Starlet O'Hara the youngest.

Fulford laughed. "Starlet O'Hara is a cute name, but right at this moment, just Scarlet would be more descriptive, wouldn't you say?"

"Definitely." He glanced at his watch. "You know, before time runs out, we ought to see the zoo's prize animal, the gorilla, Willie B."

"Okay, I'm game. Lead on."

They moved slowly with the crowd toward the gorilla habitat, called the African Rain Forest, where Willie B. and his friends, several females, resided. People began bunching up, six or eight abreast, against the moat making it difficult for those in the rear to see inside the enclosure.

"Let's drop back," Davis suggested. "The path slopes up here so we can see over people's heads. With the zoom lens we can bring Willie B. up as close as we like. Here, you take a look."

She found Willie B. in the zoom lens and watched his antics with amusement. His favorite trick seemed to be making absurd faces at the spectators. This he varied occasionally by hurling feces over the mote with surprising accuracy. Before giving the camera back to Davis, Fulford scanned the crowd, fascinated by the rapt attention people paid the gorillas. Mostly she saw people's backs or saw profiles of faces turned in excitement toward their companions. But at the edge of the enclosure as the moat wound in a great circle, she could see people's faces, obliquely for the most part, but directly when heads were turned in her direction. Her eye was suddenly arrested by a familiar face.

"Jesus, Wade, There's Lucinda Paulson talking to some man. I can't make him out. He has his back turned to me. But she's unmistakable."

"Take their picture, Leda," he commanded. "Come on! Come on! Do it. Hurry."

"Well, hold your horses, Wade. I've got to get focused." She snapped the shutter, but as she did the man disappeared amid the shifting crowd.

"Here. Let me look," Davis demanded. He took the camera and found Lucinda at once, but she was now alone, making her way through the crowd toward the zoo entrance.

"I suppose we could cut her off," Davis said, "and confront her before she gets to the exit, but that might not be smart. She'd probably deny having talked to anyone."

"Or maintain she accidentally ran into a friend." Fulford paused thoughtfully. "And that might be true. Are we justified in putting a sinister meaning to this?"

"Want my fix on this episode? Lucinda Paulson has got a lover and she's scared to death we'll find out about him."

"Come on, Wade. Your imagination is getting the best of you."

He smiled at her. "Could be." He glanced at his watch. "And your time is running out, lady. If you're going to meet your brother at two o'clock, we'd better get cracking."

As they walked back to the car park, Davis said, "Tell me about your brother."

"He's twenty two, just three years younger than I am. A big guy. Got abs of steel and buns of iron. That's why Mom named him David. Even when he was an infant he looked like an ad for a body building spa."

"Didn't you tell me he's in school?"

"Last year at law school in Athens. Expects to graduate next semester. We're all very proud of him."

"You should be. In spite of popular prejudice," he said, somewhat pretentiously, "the law's a noble profession." He paused. "I sense you and he are quite close."

She nodded. "There's a reason for that. We used to spend a couple of weeks every summer on Martha's Vineyard. Mom and Dad had friends there. The first summer we vacationed there I learned to swim, not very well, but well enough to make me foolhardy. One afternoon, I swam out a hundred yards or so from shore, but when I turned back I couldn't make any headway because of the undertow. I began to tire, but I was too proud to call for help. I struggled till I was almost exhausted. Then I let out a yell. David, who was sun bathing on the shore heard me, ran into the water and swam toward me."

She paused, her eyes dreamy with recollection. "I sank under the water as he came near. I remember how misty green everything was. I could no longer struggle, just lay there on the bottom in a semi-conscious state, sure I was going to drown. David dove down and pulled me up to the surface just as I was about to inhale, filling my lungs with water. He was powerful enough to pull me back to shore. On the beach, I clung to him, wouldn't let go. He held me in his arms till my panic eased." She looked at Davis for understanding. "He saved my life. How could I not be close to him?"

They were at her car ready to say good-bye. Davis wanted to hug her, give her a kiss, but thought better of it.

"Be good. I'll see you tomorrow."

CHAPTER NINE

Monday morning, when he arrived at work, Davis found the crime lab report concerning Lucinda Paulson's teddy bear already lying on his desk. He and Fulford scanned it together. The bear was a gift to women who spent twenty-five dollars or more on a popular brand of cosmetics. Every department store in the city carried this promotion, and stores had no way of telling who got a bear and who didn't. The arrow came from a child's archery set sold by a national toy store chain. The arrow originally had a suction cup on its end so it would stick to a target when fired. The suction cup had been removed and a point crudely whittled with a knife. The body of the bear had been pierced with an awl or screwdriver and the arrow inserted. There were no fingerprints on the arrow nor anywhere on the bear. The grimace on the bear's face and the red around the arrow "wound" had been done with a Magic Marker, a brand sold practically everywhere.

"Not very helpful," Davis observed. "I don't see any way we could trace this bear."

"Nor the arrow or the marker," Fulford agreed. "But one thing it does show us. Whoever bought and prepared this little icon was probably a woman."

"Or a girl. My guess is, Lucinda made the thing herself. Raised a stink about it for some reason we don't know, but which served a purpose for her."

Fulford nodded. "Or," she said. "It could have been Kimberly or Gretchen."

"What would they gain from leaving a wounded bear on their mother's door step?"

"Your guess is as good as mine."

Just then a messenger from the photo lab delivered the prints from the film taken at the zoo on Sunday. The image of Lucinda taken by Fulford was sharp, well-defined. Davis was pleased with the result.

"It's a good thing the shutter speed was fast," he said, "You were shaking like a leaf."

She replied defensively. "Damn it, Wade, I was nervous as hell. You were a pain in the ass, yelling 'Shoot, Shoot' at me like a demented drill sergeant."

"So I was a little overeager. I wish you had gotten a picture of the man." He sounded disappointed, almost accusatory. "You might have got it, too, if you'd been quick enough."

"Rub it in, Wade," she said resentfully. "I don't think you could have done better. He was there an instant, then melted into the crowd. And anyway, what good would a picture of his back have done us?"

"Maybe we could have identified him."

"From the back? Not unless he had his name stenciled on his shirt."

"What kind of shirt was he wearing?"

"Nothing unusual. White cotton broadcloth. The kind you can buy in any department store. Shirts that are clones of each other."

She scanned the other three pictures Davis had taken of Lucinda making her way toward the zoo exit. "She doesn't look like a woman overcome with grief at her husband's death," she said. "She looks content, maybe even happy."

"And that supports my theory that she went to the zoo to meet a lover. Nothing like that to put a big smile on your face."

He grinned at her in a suggestive way. She ignored him.

"Don't you think the zoo is an odd place for a lover's rendezvous?" she asked.

"If you want to be invisible, there's no better place than in the middle of a crowd."

"So, what do we do now? Waltz up to Lucinda and say, 'We caught you at the zoo making nice with your boyfriend?' Want to tell us his name?"

"You can try that approach if you want to. I'm not eager to incur that lady's wrath. We could have someone follow her for a few days. If she has a boyfriend, she'll lead us to him."

"I wouldn't be too sure of that. She's not stupid."

"No. And she really has no motive for killing her husband that I know of, unless he discovered her with someone and confronted her. Or threatened a divorce and a battle for custody of the children. Even that's a pretty iffy motive. Infidelity doesn't often provoke murder these days."

"A better motive would be if Lucinda discovered infidelity on his part. A woman scorned might commit murder in the heat of anger."

He nodded agreement and walked over to a small chalkboard fastened to one wall of his office.

"Let's list the suspects who had a possible motive, as far as we know, to kill

Harry Paulson. Basil Gearhart is my first choice. You agree?"

She nodded and he wrote Gearhart's name on the board.

"We know he assaulted Paulson, and we're assuming he sent Paulson a threat accompanied by a clip-art deer with an arrow in its side. However, we have to establish his movements between eleven-thirty, when he was released from jail, and six P.M.,. the approximate time of Paulson's murder."

Fulford sat staring at the photographs of Lucinda at the zoo.

"Lucinda Paulson strikes me as worthy of suspicion. She was at home when Paulson was killed. She could have easily followed him into the brush. She knew how to use a crossbow. She had a clear opportunity. If her husband was cheating on her she had motive. I'd rate her above Basil Gearhart."

"Okay, she goes on our list beside Gearhart."

He stood at the board idly drawing small thunder clouds with lightning bolts issuing from them. Fulford viewed his art work with some amusement.

"Is that supposed to represent your state of mind?"

"Nope. It's a forecast. If you listen carefully you'll hear distant thunder. It'll rain within the hour. Speaking of forecasts, I'm predicting we'll uncover another suspect if we e-mail blimpie@simpleton.com."

"Isn't that the address of the re-mailer who forwarded the death threat to Paulson?"

"Yeah. And Roger Godwin thought it was sent by a guy named Victor Percy. Percy believed he was a victim of a polio vaccine contaminated by monkey virus. Blamed Paulson for it because his firm sold the vaccine. That makes him our third suspect. Maybe he sent the threat and maybe he didn't. We have to contact 'blimpie' to find out."

"You want to try contacting 'blimpie' now?"

"I'm going to ask Albert to do it. We have no assurance 'blimpie' will reply, even if he reads his e-mail regularly. In the meantime, let's find out what we can about Lucinda."

The search for Lucinda Paulson's supposed hidden life took, for the better part of a day, a back seat to the quest for the identity of 'blimpie.' When Davis asked Albert Saffron to make a stab at contacting the re-mailer, Saffron was discouraging. He shook his head.

"Trying to contact a source who has used a re-mailer, Wade, is like looking for a tadpole after it has turned into a frog. You don't know which of a hundred tadpoles it was before it became a frog. If I send a message to *blimpie* (what was the rest of it?) *@simpleton.com*, I have no assurance he'll ever read it, or that he'll answer it if he does."

"Give it a try," Davis urged.

Saffron complied. "Don't expect an immediate answer," he said. "Unless he reads his e-mail regularly and answers routine inquires gladly, we won't hear from him for a long time."

However, within an hour Saffron received a reply.

To: <asaffron@atlpol.gov>
From: <blimpie@simpleton.com>
Subject: Identity of re-mailer.
Sorry. Subject used chain re-mailing. Difficult to trace. Message came to my computer from Jacobol@chapel.com.

Saffron tried to contact *Jacobol* but got no response. After a thirty minute wait, he was ready to throw in the towel.

"It may be days before he responds. He may never respond at all."

Davis was disappointed. "Isn't there any way we can get a response from him?"

Saffron's tone was ingenuous, but his expression held a flicker of conspiracy. "You willing to bend your code of ethics a little, Wade?"

"How much is a little?"

"Not much, in my view. But you be the judge. There's a lad on our staff, a mere youngster, who if he turned his talents in that direction, could qualify as one of the world's most successful hackers. If we turn him loose on this assignment, I guarantee he'll get results within an hour or two."

Davis had no trouble making a decision. Sending death threats over the net gave them the right to uncover an anonymous threatener's identity in any way they could.

"Okay," he said. "Ask him to come in. I'd like to meet him."

The lad, as Saffron had described him, was not the pimple-faced computer nerd Davis had supposed, but a strapping, muscular man, deeply tanned and handsome in a rugged way. One leg was wasted, however, and he dragged it, imperceptibly, as he walked.

"Jeffrey Sailor," Saffron said. "This is Wade Davis." He motioned him to sit down. "Wade is after an anonymous re-mailer, Jeff. One who has sent a chain re-mailed message. We want you to find out who he is. We haven't had much success."

"Have you gotten anywhere at all."

"We contacted the last re-mailer who gave us the address of the re-mailer who sent him the message. We bogged down there. Do you think you might be able to be able to identify the original re-mailer?"

"Probably. All the common browsers—Netscape, Internet Explorer—use the same high tech protocol to access the web. I should be able to get into the files of any computer configured to use such systems. If so, I can follow a complex trail of re-mailed messages. If a message was encrypted at any point along the way, however, it may take me a while to discover the key to the encryption."

Davis listened with something resembling awe. What he knew about computers, were the knowledge liquid, could be poured into a shot glass. He spoke deferentially to Sailor. "Can you start right away?"

"If Albert tells me to."

Davis smiled at his bulky friend. "Tell him, Albert."

It was two o'clock that afternoon. Davis and Fulford were arguing about the best way to uncover facts hidden in Lucinda Paulson's past life. Davis wanted to revisit Adam Wharton and his wife Pam.

"If we're straightforward with them, if we stress the necessity of full disclosure of all they know, and how important that information might be to the discovery of Paulson's murderer, I think they might open up."

"I think there's a high degree of loyalty between those two families," Fulford said. "The bond between them involves more than a mutual interest in hunting and casual partying. I think the Whartons will continue to be highly protective of Lucinda's interests."

"There's only one way to find out," Davis said. "Let's have another talk with them."

Just then, the phone rang. He answered.

"It's Albert," the voice said. "Jeff Sailor has caught up with our elusive chain re-mailer."

"Great. Who is it?"

"You'd better come over here and hear what he's got to say. I don't think you'll be too happy with the result."

"Damn it, Albert, I'm in no mood for games! Who in hell is it?"

Saffron gave a sigh of surrender. He thought Jeff Sailor deserved an appreciative audience to hear how he had navigated complex and devious computer paths to reach his goal. But Davis's insistence was going to rob him of that pleasure.

"There is no *who*, Wade," he said, feeling some satisfaction at how the news would upset his colleague. "The message came from a computer at *Edgepharm@compuserve.com,* and it was sent to *gimlet@hollywood.com.*

Davis was astonished. "Jesus, Albert. Correct me if I'm wrong. That's the e-mail address of Edgeware Pharmaceuticals—Harry Paulson's own company."

"You got it buddy. Jeff tells me the office has a network of twenty computers. The message could have been sent from any one of them."

Roger Godwin greeted them without enthusiasm. He seemed harried. He sat, glancing down at the floor, a tight smile on his face, and a rigidity to his shoulders that seemed almost painful. The appearance of physical well being that had impressed them at their first meeting, now seemed to have been replaced with an unhealthy tension.

Davis assumed his demeanor was due to concern about the e-mail message. He had told Godwin what the message said and had impressed upon him the need to track down the sender. "I leave it up to you how to go about this. I don't want a police officer plodding methodically from one of your computers to another looking into e-mail files. At least not when people are working."

"I don't like that approach either," Godwin replied. "But we'll have to do it that way. Our computers are not joined in a local area network so we can't explore the contents of all of them from the one in my office. Someone is going to have to open the e-mail out-box of every one of them till we find the right one."

"Okay," Davis said. "Let's start with your secretary's computer."

"Okay."

They moved into Godwin's reception room and he made introductions. "Detectives Davis, Fulford," he said. "This is Cheryl Hargert. Cheryl, I'd like you to show them how you can pull up our old e-mail file."

"First, you have to contact the e-mail server," she said. "We use Eudora. She clicked the Eudora button and an array of buttons bearing various labels appeared at the top of the screen. She clicked *mailbox*, and from a drop down menu chose *outbox*. The screen was filled with a list of addresses to which e-mail messages had been sent, the date of each transaction, and the subject of the message.

"If you're looking for a particular message, I need to know the date."

"Look for one sent somewhere around the first of the month," Fulford said.

Cheryl scrolled through the list of addresses. "It would help if I knew what we're looking for," she said.

"We're looking for an address called *gimlet@hollywood.com*," Davis said.

"I don't find it," Cheryl said. "Are you sure it was sent around the first of the month?"

"Try the middle of the month," Davis directed.

Cheryl scrolled swiftly through a batch of addresses. "Nope. Wait a minute." She scrolled downward a few more addresses. "Ah, here it is. Sent on the eighteenth at twelve-twenty."

"Pull up the message," Godwin said.

Cheryl clicked the find button and the message appeared on the screen just as it had when Davis and Fulford saw it earlier at their interview with Roger Godwin.

Maybe you think you can get away with what you have done
to me. You have invaded my body and corrupted it for your
own ends. If you do not atone for my injury, you will pay with
your life. This is no idle threat. You know it is not.

"This is ridiculous," Fulford said. "Someone sent hate mail to Harry Paulson from a computer right in his own office."

"Not exactly," said Roger Godwin. "This is my office, not Harry's."

His face showed puzzlement. "Given that I didn't send this message, and that Cheryl didn't either, I can't figure out who could have done it. We guard access to our computers carefully."

"This message was sent at twelve-twenty," Davis said. "That's your lunch hour, isn't it? Cheryl could have been away from her desk, leaving her computer unattended. Someone slipped in, typed the message quickly, and sent it without ever being seen."

Godwin shook his head. "It's not that easy. One of us, Cheryl or I, is in the office at all times. Cheryl takes her lunch hour between twelve and one. I stay in the office till she comes back. Then I go out."

"But you can't see the computer from your desk, can you?" Fulford asked.

"No, but I think I would hear the noise of the keyboard if it were being used."

"But if you were concentrating on something, the slight noise from the keyboard probably wouldn't attract your attention."

"Probably not. It's possible someone slipped in and sent the message without my knowing it."

"Can you think of anyone in your organization who might have had a beef against Mr. Paulson?" Davis asked. "Someone upset at a reprimand or at an unwanted assignment?"

"I don't know of anyone offhand. I could have Cheryl make some discreet inquiries. But I wonder why such a person would sneak into this office to send the message. There are dozens of other computers in the building, all of them a lot more accessible than this one."

"True. But have her snoop around, will you?"

"All right. But don't expect much."

Fulford, a thoughtful expression on her face, said, "An idea just occurred to me. When you have a board meeting, isn't it held in a room in this suite?"

"It is." Godwin replied. "Board meetings are held in Room 212 just down the hall."

"Isn't it possible someone from a board meeting could have casually moved into this office at lunch time and written the note?"

"I suppose so. We're vigilant as possible, but we can't be perfect."

"So, stretching possibilities a bit, Victor Percy might have done it the day he came to the meeting to denounce Paulson."

"I'd say that would take a lot of stretching," Godwin said.

"Nevertheless, it's a possibility," Fulford said.

Davis asked Cheryl to print out the address of the first re-mailer and also a copy of the message. He folded the papers and stuffed them into his pocket as he and Fulford left the office.

Chapter Ten

Fulford was to remember this as a day of surprising events. It had begun inauspiciously, as she made routine inquiries in an effort to trace Basil Gearhart's movements after his release from prison. She contacted, first, the manager of his apartment building, a man identified by the label on his mail box, as Milford Sutter. Sutter opened the door to her in a truculent mood. A thin, arthritic man, he conveyed a sense of harried exasperation. He seemed on the thin edge of outright rudeness. He looked at her with ill-concealed impatience.

"What is it, now?" he demanded. "The air conditioning's been fixed. Haven't you tried it? Don't tell me something else has gone wrong?"

"I guess you've had a hard day," Fulford said, smiling. "I'm not here to complain. In fact, I don't even live here."

"You don't live here?" His hostility seemed to abate a little. "Then, what is it? You have to see the rental agent if you're wanting an apartment."

He seemed visibly relieved that his visitor had not come to lodge a new complaint.

She shook her head.

"All I want is a little information about one of your renters." She told him who she was and said she was trying to trace the movements of Basil Gearhart, the tenant in apartment twelve.

"The animal rights guy, the one who bashed Harry Paulson over the head with a pig's bladder full of blood?" The question was aimed more at establishing Gearhart's identity than it was an expression of disapproval.

"That's the guy. I suppose you heard on the news he was released from jail yesterday morning?"

"I did. Been up to some other kind of mischief? Wouldn't surprise me. A self-righteous rascal, if I ever saw one." He nodded his head judicially to affirm his judgment.

"He got out of jail at eleven-thirty," Fulford said. "Told the police he had lunch at a McDonalds, bought a few groceries, came back to his apartment and stayed there the rest of the day. Do you know anything of his movements yesterday?"

"Do I?" Sutter glanced at her with the air of a man who knows he has vital information to share. "I can tell you exactly what he did, and it ain't like he said. Not at all. He left his apartment at three-thirty and didn't come back till after six."

"How can you be sure of the times, Mr. Sutter?"

"I was on the roof of section C watching the air conditioning crew at work. I had a good view of Gearhart's apartment. I was just about to leave the roof to meet a mechanic who had come to repair the pump in the swimming pool when I saw him come out of his door and get in his car."

"And when did he come back?"

"Can't say exactly. But it was after six. At six, I knocked on several doors, his included, to see if the air conditioning was working all right. He wasn't home. After six, I went into my own apartment and listened to the news."

Fulford glanced at her watch. "Is he home now?"

"He works in a men's store in Underground Atlanta, Eddie Bauer, I think. He's probably there now. In his free time, he does volunteer work for an animal rights group. If you don't find him at Underground Atlanta, you can probably find him at the headquarters of 'Animal Lovers', or something like that. I don't know the actual name."

Fulford thanked him and returned to her car. She sat there for some time thinking. Gearhart, according to Sutter's testimony, had been away from his apartment at the time Paulson was murdered. So he could have done the job.

But there were problems. The Paulson estate was located in Atlanta's north side. Fulford didn't know exactly how far it was from Gearhart's apartment complex, but it had to be at least five miles, perhaps more. And he would have to have driven that distance through some of Atlanta's heaviest traffic.

Could he have committed the crime at six, eluded detection as he made his way out of the Paulson's wilderness tract, and driven back to his apartment through evening rush hour traffic? Possibly. Two hours was enough time, Fulford thought, but just barely. And what had he done with the weapon? A crossbow is a cumbersome thing to conceal. A search of the grounds of the Paulson home had turned up nothing. A crossbow isn't something you could just toss out of your car along the roadside as you might a pistol. And where had he gotten the crossbow in the first place?

If he had done the murder, it was premeditated. He couldn't have, after being released from jail at eleven o'clock, decided on the spur of the moment, to get a crossbow, drive out to Paulson's home, and ambush him as he walked in his arboretum. He'd have to have had prior knowledge about the man's habits and to have made extensive preparations prior to his release from jail. Unlikely as all that seemed, he was still a viable suspect. She had known killers, from previous cases, who had laid plans as meticulously.

Tiring of speculation, she rang Davis on her cell phone and told him what she had learned from the caretaker. He shared her belief that Gearhart could have committed the murder though the time frame would have been close, and agreed they should confront him and demand an explanation.

She picked Davis up and they drove toward Five Points, a confluence of major streets located at the northeast end of Underground Atlanta.

"Would you believe," she said, "in all the years I've lived here, I've never been to Underground Atlanta?"

"It figures," he said. "Locals tend to ignore what's right under their noses. I've never been to the High Museum of Art. I suppose I ought to go just to get acquainted with one of our better known cultural institutions."

"An exhibit is opening there this weekend," Fulford said. "Something I'd love to see. Some jury has pulled together about sixty-five or seventy paintings illustrating how male painters depict women in their works. Should be enlightening. Would you like to go?"

She looked into his startled face with amusement. "Yes, Wade, I'm asking you for a date."

"I'm bright enough to figure that out," he said, looking at her with something resembling wonderment mixed with affection. "I'm just having trouble believing it."

For weeks Fulford had been reserved, distant. She had refused to go out with him on two occasions. She had let him know, in a deliberate way, that she had had dates with Christopher McCalmon, the medical examiner. She seemed intent upon convincing him she had no special affection for him. Now this.

Since their first date when, impulsively, they had slept together, he had been in love with her. His mind, at this new indication of her interest, was suddenly enveloped in a cloud of euphoria.

"Of course, I'd like to go. I think about women in paintings a lot," he said, tongue in cheek. "I'd like to see how some of the great artists handled the subject."

She gave him a half-serious frown of disapproval. "I'm afraid too many of them 'handled the subject', as you so neatly put it, in unflattering ways. Anyway, we'll find out. Sunday afternoon at two okay?"

"Couldn't be better."

Davis parked the car in a multi-tiered parking garage, and the two emerged onto Lower Alabama Street. "The first thing you should know about

Underground Atlanta," Davis said, "is that it's no longer underground. It went underground in 1920 when 'viaducts' were built over the railroad tracks and over slaughter-house-row to avoid congestion. The street was upped one level and underground Atlanta was born."

Fulford listened, fascinated. "You sound like a tour guide, Wade," she said. "Where did you learn all this?"

Davis gestured off to one side. "I've been reading it from that plaque, over there. But I've been here before. We're in Bughouse Square, so named because it was the place where, in the past, medicine show proprietors and confidence men clustered. It's a street market now."

Fulford looked around. The area was filled with restored turn-of-the-century peddler's wagons and pushcarts from which vendors sold every imaginable type of merchandise from hand painted baby clothing to *Gone With the Wind* collectibles.

"I'd love to rummage around among these stalls," she said. "I could spend a whole afternoon searching for treasure, but we'd better not forget what we came for, had we?"

She paused, looking around her, wistfully. Then she said to Davis. "So, Mr. Tour Guide, where do we find Eddie Bauer?"

"We walk a few yards north into Upper Alabama Street," Davis said. "That's were all the specialty shops are."

They moved with the stream of people flowing along Alabama Street and soon found Eddie Bauer. The store was busy. They saw Gearhart helping a customer try on jackets. He had his back to them and when he saw them his face showed anger and dismay.

"What the devil are you doing here? If my boss sees you, it could cost me my job."

"Nothing quite so drastic, I'm sure," Davis said. "Some embarrassment maybe." He glanced at his watch. "I suspect it's soon time for your mid-morning break isn't it? Officer Fulford and I will grab a cup at Gloria Jean's and wait for you there. We have a few questions to ask you."

"Okay, okay. I'll be there in a few minutes." Apparently much relieved at Davis's proposal, he turned back to his customer.

Ten minutes later he showed up, bought a cup of coffee, added precise amounts of cream and sugar to it, and sat down with the detectives. His eyes did not meet theirs. He stared at the cup, which he cradled in his hands, as if it were a source of comfort. As the detectives stared at him saying nothing, he spoke in a petulant manner. "What's this about? I've answered all the questions you asked me. What more do you want?"

"We want the truth," Fulford said. "You told us you were home in your apartment when we asked you where you were on the evening Harry Paulson was murdered."

"I told you I was home. That's the truth." He spoke with great assurance that was visibly shattered when Fulford told him the maintenance man, Mr. Sutter, had seen him leave at three-thirty and had knocked on his door at six to find he was still not home.

Gearhart's face flushed. His hand shook so that he almost dropped the cup he held. "I didn't think my whereabouts was that important and I didn't want you to know how I spent the afternoon."

"Well, how did you spend it?" Davis demanded. "We think you stalked Harry Paulson with a crossbow and killed him."

Gearhart was alarmed. "No! No! I never went near the Paulson place. I didn't want to tell you what I did. I'm not proud of it. And I hate to tell it to a female detective."

Fulford looked at him with a trace of hostility. "You think women should be shielded from disagreeable facts?"

"No, ma'am. It's that I'd just as soon you didn't hear it."

"Well, I'm going to hear it." Fulford said, "So you may as well get on with it."

Gearhart shrugged his shoulders and glanced obliquely at Fulford as he began.

"You must remember I had been in jail for a week in a little cell with nothing but a cot and a toilet that stank. I was treated like scum. I didn't sleep well and I could hardly stand the food. Release was like, I think there is a word for it—an *aphrodisiac,* isn't it? Anyway, I felt an intense sexual excitement. So, at three-thirty I left my apartment and drove to Bethel Street where I picked up a prostitute. I spent the afternoon with her. I returned to my apartment about seven o'clock."

He sat with his head bowed, his eyes averted. He reminded Fulford of a contrite sinner who, having finished his confession, awaited penance.

Davis caught Fulford's attention, indicated his skepticism, and signaled her to carry on the interrogation.

"A touching story, Mr. Gearhart, if it's true," she said. "I assume you can give us the name of the woman who accommodated your acute sexual need."

Gearhart looked up, a trace of irritation in his face. "I never found out her name."

"I see. You were interested only in her body. Everything else about her was irrelevant."

Gearhart got angry. "I didn't ask her name and she didn't volunteer it."

"You see the problem, don't you, Mr. Gearhart?" Fulford continued. "It's impossible for us to confirm your story if we don't have the woman's name."

Gearhart said nothing. Davis intervened.

"You say you spent the whole afternoon with her. You weren't in your car all that time. She must have had an apartment or a room, or some place where you could have a little privacy."

"She drove a van. We parked it on the upper level of a parking garage, in a remote corner, and spent the afternoon there. The van was furnished with a bed."

"What kind of van did she have?"

"An old Dodge, I think. It had side windows that were covered with a dark sunscreen. We could see out but no one could see in."

"I suppose you failed to notice the license plate."

"I didn't look."

"What did you do with your car while you were with her?"

"I parked it on the street."

Davis said, "So you're asking us to believe that after being released from jail, you left your apartment in response to an irresistible sexual urge, that you picked up a prostitute whose name you do not know, that she owned a van, whose license you did not notice, that said van was equipped for sexual liaisons with a bed and darkened windows, and that this woman took you in her portable bedroom to the top tier of a parking garage, where you spent the entire afternoon presumably in an unbroken sexual embrace."

He paused, looking at Gearhart, skeptically. "Doesn't that sound a bit far-fetched to you."

Gearhart responded. "You make it sound that way, but it's the truth."

Davis spoke in disgust. "The truth!" With the air of a man whose patience has been exhausted, he said, "Go on. Get out of here. We'll be talking to you again. Remember you're out on bail. I wouldn't try going anywhere."

Gearhart nodded, got up and walked out.

Davis and Fulford drank another cup of coffee and discussed Gearhart's story.

"It's a total fabrication," Davis asserted.

"Could be. But it's possible isn't it?" Fulford said, remembering Gearhart's embarrassment, and taking it as a sign of possible veracity. "It could have happened that way."

"It could have. Lots of unlikely things could have happened. One of Paulson's daughters could have killed him. Gearhart's so-called alibi doesn't take him off my list of prime suspects."

"Nor mine. But if his alibi does turn out to be true, if, in some way, we can confirm it, who then becomes our prime suspect."

"Lucinda Paulson? Or her lover?"

"You're still assuming the man who was with her at the zoo was her lover?"

"Who else it could he have been? Her psychiatrist?"

Chapter Eleven

"**I** don't see how we're going to find out if Lucinda Paulson has a lover," Fulford said. "We can't just up and ask her." She walked to the window, peered out at the traffic in the street below, where cars moved snail-like through sheets of rain. Turning back, she looked quizzically at Davis.

"No, but we can ask her friends," he said.

"If you're thinking of Adam and Pamela Wharton," Fulford shook her head doubtfully, "I'd forget it. They'll stonewall you. There's an emotional bond between those two families. I could sense it when we were there. The Whartons, in my estimation, will do anything to protect Lucinda."

"You're probably right," Davis said. He thought a moment. "Let's talk to Roger Godwin. I didn't get the impression he was overwhelmingly loyal to his boss. Besides, he was rather shaken when we discovered the infamous blimpie threat came from his own computer. He's afraid we suspect him."

"Do we?" She said, a bit surprised at her use of the pronoun.

"He's a possible. But not because of 'blimpie'. I can't conceive of him being dumb enough to send his boss a threatening letter from his own computer. No, he and Paulson had a serious disagreement over Victor Percy's suit for damages, a disagreement that involved legal strategy for dealing with a suit involving millions of the company's assets."

"Well," Fulford said, "I can't imagine him being dumb enough to kill his partner over that."

He looked at her and smiled. "I said he was a possible, didn't I? He has a flimsy motive, I admit."

He stood up, stretched his lanky frame, and put on his hat. "Get your things together. Let's visit the guy. See what kind of info we can get from him."

They rode in silence most of the way. A few blocks from the Edgeware Pharmaceuticals Building, Fulford asked, "How are you going to handle this? Be blunt? Come right out with it and ask 'Has Lucinda Paulson got a lover?'"

His expression, when he turned his head to look at her, was one of amusement. "That's up to you, Leda. I'm going to let you handle the interrogation."

"Gee, thanks, Wade. This is the second time you've put the monkey on my back. May I ask the reason for your sudden trust?"

"Women are simply better at this kind of questioning than men. They sense nuances of behavior that escape males, and they establish rapport with the suspect a lot easier, especially a male one."

Fulford decided maybe she should be pleased at this delegation of authority, and began to run over in her mind a few gambits to try on Godwin.

As they entered Godwin's suite, they encountered Cheryl, the secretary and gatekeeper. She seemed rattled to see them.

"Mr. Godwin is busy right now. He has someone with him. Could you folks come back later?"

"Not possible," Davis said brusquely. "We'll wait. You might buzz Mr. Godwin and let him know we're here," he said as he and Fulford took seats.

Cheryl flipped a switch on the intercom and said, "I'm sorry to disturb you, sir, but those two detectives are here." They could not hear Godwin's response. Cheryl said, "He'll be glad to see you. He'll be just a moment or two."

Fulford, curious to see how long 'just a moment or two' would be, looked at her watch. She was surprised when, in two and a half minutes, the door to Godwin's office opened and he appeared. What surprised her more was seeing Lucinda Paulson emerge with him.

She didn't know why she found this so unexpected, she told herself. After all, now that her husband was dead, Lucinda would have to confer with his partner. Probably any number of times.

Lucinda greeted the detectives cordially, as if she had expected their appearance. However, a slight almost undetectable flush to her face told Fulford she was a little on edge. She seemed to address the thought that was in their minds.

"Because of Harry's death," she said, "Roger and I have many problems to cope with. I shall be seeing him often."

With that explanation, she clutched her purse as if it were a shield, and strode out the door.

Godwin invited them into his office. He appeared at ease, though he seemed to shuffle papers about on his desk unnecessarily. "Your visit is unexpected. Has some emergency arisen?"

"We happened to be in the neighborhood and thought we would just drop in," Fulford said. "We're compiling background information about Harry Paulson's family and friends."

Even to herself the statement sounded unconvincing. She glanced at Davis, who merely smiled at her. She plunged ahead.

"You've known Lucinda Paulson for many years, haven't you?"

"She and her husband are my best friends. Harry's death has brought Lucinda and me even closer. She's a fine woman."

He spoke those words with evident sincerity. Fulford nodded as if in assent, then said, "She's also a very attractive woman. The kind men look at with more than casual interest. I'm sure she has had many opportunities to enjoy extra-marital pleasures, if I may use such a cliched expression."

Godwin reacted to her remark with an expression of distaste. His reply was resentful, defensive.

"What am I supposed to say to that?"

"Whatever seems appropriate. Whatever suggests itself."

He shook his head in apparent disgust. "I suppose you want to know if she has ever had an 'affair,' which is what you appear to be digging for. I'm sure more than one man has proposed such an arrangement to her. I can tell you with absolute certainty, however, she has never succumbed to such proposals."

He sat silent for a moment. Fulford sat quietly also, looking at him as if she expected him to make an important disclosure. Then he spoke abruptly, a trace of venom in his voice.

"If anyone in that family was guilty of infidelity, it was Harry. I don't like to speak ill of the dead, especially of a man I revered so much, but I must defend Lucinda. Harry was a very attractive man, not only handsome, but a man of power and influence. Those things made him appealing to women. I won't say they threw themselves at him, but they let him know in all kinds of ways they were available."

Fulford, interested in the implications of Godwin's disclosure, asked, "Do you know that Paulson actually had an affair with another woman, or are you merely guessing he did because he was attractive and women frequently came on to him."

"Well, I never surprised him in a hotel bedroom with anyone, if that's what you mean, but it was generally acknowledged that, when he went to our professional conventions, he didn't sleep alone. I don't know if he ever had a permanent liaison or whether he was just took advantage of what the occasion offered."

Fulford was surprised by Godwin's revelations about his partner's sexual activities. He should have been more circumspect out of loyalty. Why had he not been? Was there some hidden motive for his candor?

"Do you think Lucinda knew of his infidelities?"

"She's an intuitive woman. Women can sense when a spouse is cheating."

"So you think she knew?"

"I'm convinced she did."

"Did she ever say anything to you about his cheating?"

"Not openly. I was aware of her unhappiness, however. She couldn't conceal it."

"Do you think she ever had an affair, perhaps just to get even with her husband?"

"No I don't. I think she was a faithful wife. Resentful and angry but faithful."

"Did you ever feel, given Harry's behavior, you might be excused for, uh, consoling her?"

Godwin flushed.

"Why don't you come right out with it, Ms. Fulford?" he said bluntly. "Why not ask me if I ever made a pass at her."

"All right. Did you?"

"No, I didn't." He stared hard at her for a few moments, then said, "I have work to do. I trust you no longer need to impose on my time."

Fulford looked inquiringly at Davis. He indicated he had no questions.

"We appreciate your cooperation," she said to Godwin with just a trace of sarcasm. "I hope we have not unduly inconvenienced you."

As they went through the outer office, Cheryl, the secretary, looked at Fulford in a peculiar way, almost as if she knew the substance of the interrogation of Godwin.

When they got back to the office, Davis brought two cups of coffee from the dispenser, set one before Fulford, and said, "My compliments. You got him to open up in a way I never thought possible."

Fulford stirred a packet of artificial cream into her coffee and followed it with a packet of artificial sweetener. She looked at the cup and smiled. "You never know what's fake and what's real, do you? I don't believe every thing Godwin told us. I don't believe, for instance, Harry Paulson was quite the womanizer he said he was. He gave the impression Harry had a woman on the string all the time."

"That's not too hard to believe. Most men have tendencies in that direction. All they need is opportunity. As CEO of a big company and a power broker of sorts, Paulson could've had plenty of women eager to please him."

"True, but let me give you my fix on Godwin. He was not happy with his partner. That was clear when he told us of their disagreement over the handling of Victor Percy's suit. But he was sour on him for another reason. He coveted his wife. Godwin and Lucinda are kindred spirits, I believe, close to one another socially and close to one another in bed. They've probably been playing house for some time. Remember how protective he was of her when I suggested she might have had an affair after she discovered her husband's alleged unfaithfulness. And remember what Lucinda said of Godwin when we first interviewed her? 'He's a charming man. I'm particularly fond of him.'"

"You're suggesting he revealed Paulson's infidelity to justify Lucinda's having an affair, should that affair ever come out?"

"Exactly. A classic case of the pot calling the kettle black."

Davis mulled over her remarks thoughtfully. "It's an interesting theory, Leda, and I buy your belief that something's going on between Godwin and Lucinda. In fact, I think there's good reason to suppose Godwin was the man we saw her with at the zoo last week. But I also think he was right about Paulson being a habitual womanizer. Don't you remember the impression we got, both from Lucinda and from her daughters, that all was not sweetness and light between the parents. Assuming there really was conflict between the two, what better reason for it than Paulson's infidelity?"

Fulford smiled. "Lucinda's infidelity would be just as good a reason. If Paulson knew about it."

They both chuckled.

"Maybe they were two-timing each other," Davis said, not really believing that possibility was very likely.

"Seriously," Fulford said, "I think we'd better start looking for Paulson's other woman. Maybe she's the one who done him in."

"I'm putting my money on Lucinda," Davis said. "Maybe she and Godwin offed him together."

Fulford added a word of caution. "You realize, don't you, we haven't got a shred of evidence to support any of this."

Chapter Twelve

Davis, idly shuffling through the Sunday paper, found his attention drawn to the story of a Connecticut woman whose husband regularly cheated on her and then bragged about his exploits to her face. After taunting her with details of his latest escapade, he would use her sexually, and complain about how poorly she performed compared to his other women. Driven by his mistreatment, she bought an electric cattle prod, and when, in a drunken stupor, her spouse fell asleep, she tied him to the bed, and goaded him unmercifully in the genital area with the prod. His screaming finally brought the neighbors to his rescue. When arraigned before a magistrate, the wife pled diminished responsibility because of the years of prolonged mental and physical abuse her husband had inflicted on her. Her lack of self-esteem had unhinged her reason, she said, and led her to make what was purely a defensive assault. The sympathetic judge, after dismissing the husband's complaint on the grounds the attack was in self defense, commended her for her restraint in using a cattle prod, saying she would have been justified in "doing a Bobbit."

Davis applauded the judge's decision, and looked at a small box, embedded in the middle of the page, that listed the comments of several psychiatrists as to why men abuse women sexually. For dominance, said one; for sadistic pleasure, said another; for proving his manliness, said a third; while a fourth declared spouse abuse grew from an unconscious hatered the man harbored for his mother which hatred he transferred to the wife.

The newspaper's analysis of sexual motivation, though it focused on deviant impulses, prompted Davis to think about his own sexual behavior toward women. To begin with, he had had sex with very few women in his life. He was in his teens, when he had first gotten laid. His companion had been a prostitute, who took him to her dingy little room. When she took off her clothes, her body, lumpy, slightly obese, and burdened with cellulite around the thighs and buttocks, repelled him. But he was determined to get fucked in order to find out what it was like. He found the act of penetrating her revolting. He ejaculated almost at once, and experienced not pleasure but only relief from the tension of his distended prostate. He felt his friends, who had described the act of sex as something pleasurable beyond description, had badly misled him.

Later, he was to learn the reason for his disenchantment.

When he married, his wife Sylvia taught him that love and respect for each other made sex an exquisite pleasure. His physical union with her was an almost religious rite that culminated in a solemn bond, a bond in which he became an indivisible part of her. After her death, he had been unable to find that level of closeness with another woman.

Then he made love to Leda Fulford. The old rapture of sex returned. But she had disavowed any kindred feeling for him beyond liking and respect, and refused to live with him, even on a temporary basis.

Despite all that, she had, just days ago, invited him to go with her to an exhibit at the High Museum of Art. The invitation rekindled his hope of winning her deeper affection. Against this hope he cautioned himself. He had a habit, in spite of repeated disappointments, of being overly optimistic, of expecting things to turn out well. He tried to think of reasons, other than the hoped for amorous one, that his colleague might have had for inviting him. Perhaps she wanted only a companion so as not to be alone in the crowd, perhaps she felt it wise to keep on good terms with a fellow officer, or, maybe she was a true lover of art who found pleasure in sharing her enthusiasm with someone else.

After a while, he gave up this futile exercise in mind-reading and examined what the paper had to say about the exhibit. Some enterprising jury had collected a number of paintings from famous artists of the early twentieth century, the period that produced the dadaists, the surrealists, the impressionists and their successors. The paintings had been selected to exemplify the way the artists had treated women in their work. He had never been especially interested in painting, but the didactic nature of this particular exhibit appealed to him, and, of course, being able to see it in the company of Fulford made it even more attractive.

His lunch consisted of a tuna fish sandwich, a dish of strawberries in heavy cream, and a cup of decaffeinated coffee. Afterward, he sat in a reclining chair and fell asleep.

The door buzzer awakened him from a frightful dream. He was strapped helplessly to an operating table and a white-gowned, female surgeon spoke soothingly to him. "Castration," she told him, "will not affect your sex life at all. We'll pump you full of testosterone, and you'll be just fine." She was brandishing a scalpel before his eyes as the buzzer sounded.

Disoriented and still trembling from the reality of the dream, he got to his feet, called out, "Just a minute," and shook himself fully awake. The dream faded quickly, his panic subsided, and he opened the door to Leda Fulford.

He was entranced by her image. She wore black slacks of a material that had a faint sheen to it. Over a simple, pure-white blouse, she had on a black jacket of the same fabric as the slacks, tailored to show off the fullness of her breasts and her slender waist. Her black shoes, with two-inch block heels, were made of skillfully woven strips of patent leather. Her hair, pulled back, and tied in a pony tail, focused attention on the remarkable beauty of her face.

"What are you staring at?" she said, pleased at his evident approval.

"I'm not staring," he said, vague memories of his dream roiling in his head. "I'm having a visual orgasm."

The remark amused her. "Is your entire vocabulary tinged with sexual innuendo?" After a pause, she added, "You overdo the erotic stuff, Wade."

She paused, then, looking at his rumpled shirt, his wrinkled trousers, his sweat beaded brow, she said, "Do you sleep in your clothes? You're a mess."

"I fell asleep in the chair," he said apologetically. "Give me a minute to take a shower and put on fresh clothes, will you? Men are always waiting for a date to get ready. It's time you learned how it feels."

She gave him a mock-reproachful look and said severely, "You'd better make it fast, mister, or I'll never ask you out again."

He kissed her cheek swiftly, and made for the bathroom.

When they arrived at the museum, she said, "The building is almost a miniature of the Guggenheim in New York City. Not as imposing, but designed on the same principle."

Davis, who had seen the museum only from the exterior while attending plays at the nearby Alliance Theater, now looked upward into an atrium that rose to the top of the building, where, through a glass skylight, he could see clouds and blue sky.

"I call it 'from-the-top-down' principle," Fulford continued. "The gallery is built in a spiral, ascending from the ground floor upward. Exhibits are arranged starting at the top of the building and curving down to the main floor. So viewers go to the top by elevator and work their way down looking at the pictures as they go."

Fulford paid their admission fee, and they took the elevator to the top of the gallery.

Davis, who was feeling a bit intimidated by Fulford's expertise, asked, "How did you learn all this stuff?"

"I was here once before. They gave me a brochure."

"Ah," said Davis, "I've never been here but I've done a little boning up, too. I read in the paper this morning that the purpose of the exhibit is to show how dada and surrealist painters represented women in their work."

Fulford nodded. She was standing, immobile, her face wearing a look of astonishment and distaste, before a picture of Rene Magritte's entitled, *The Rape.* There was a kind of excitement in her voice, the kind one gets from seeing an automobile accident, or a carnival performer fall from a high wire. The excitement of threat, of disaster.

"You've *got* to see this one, Wade. It's supposed to be a woman, I guess. But a God-awful woman, believe me."

Wade joined her. She stood in a cluster of people gazing with fascination at the painting, whispering awed comments to one another. What he saw was strange indeed. The painting was of a woman's head and neck. She had bushy, unruly hair. In the place of eyes, however, the painter had given her two breasts whose nipples represented pupils. Below the eyes, where a nose should have been, was a navel contrived to look like a petite nose. The creature's mouth and chin were represented by the delta-shaped pubic area that lies between a woman's legs.

"Whew," said Davis. "That's really weird." He studied the picture for several moments as impressions of it filtered through his consciousness. He said to Fulford, "Here's what I think. The picture is telling us a woman is, to use a crude expression, nothing more than tits and ass."

Fulford winced and drew him off to one side away from the cluster of people gathered around the painting. "Don't talk so loud, Wade. People can hear you."

"So," he said, defiantly. "I bet most of them would agree with me."

"You're probably right. Yet, I'm sure there're other points of view. Let's be fair to the artist. Look at the title. It's called, *The Rape.* Maybe Magritte wanted to paint a picture of a woman the way a rapist would see her."

"He might have, but I don't think you can judge a picture by its title. You have to go by what's on the canvas. There's nothing in the picture that suggests anyone's viewpoint except the artist's. Maybe he was a rapist, himself."

"Okay," said Fulford. "Let's agree it's not a very pretty impression of a woman's head."

Davis walked a few paces down the ramp and stopped before another Magritte painting called, *Dangerous Liaisons.* It showed a naked woman standing, her head turned to the left, holding a long rectangular mirror that covered her from her chin to her lower thighs. The reflection in the mirror, oddly enough, was that of another naked woman (or perhaps, the same woman), but the view was from the back showing her torso from the buttocks up to the shoulders. He hair hung luxuriantly down the back.

"Look here," he called to Fulford. "This is a dandy. It looks as if someone took hold of her and wrenched her torso around a hundred and eighty degrees.

That's what's reflected in the mirror."

He paused, watching with interest as his companion looked at the picture with a slight frown. "Tell me," he said, "what does this one mean?"

An elderly lady standing nearby, overheard his question, and gave a firm, and fiercely judgmental, response. "It doesn't mean anything. There isn't a canvas in this whole show that has one iota of meaning. These painters were just competing with one another to see who could insult women in the most outrageous way. Wait till you see Picasso's stuff or de Chirico's." She let out a snort like an angered bull, and strode off toward the elevator.

Fulford smiled. "I told you not to talk so loud."

Davis tried to make a virtue of the incident. "I'd say something good came of it. She probably gave us the best art criticism we're likely to get."

"You'll find better criticism if you read the short quotes underneath the titles." Fulford said, as she gestured to her left. "De Chirico's over here. He's represented by only one painting, *The Two Sisters,* which is probably a good thing, I don't think I could handle another such monstrosity."

The painting, which Davis examined with some incredulity, was of two allegedly female heads. The face in the foreground was a cone-like entity, stood on end, with the point cut off to create a neck. The top of the cone, the wide part, was bedecked with a curly, black wig. The thing had no nose or mouth, and where eyes should have been were two objects that resembled arched windows, or perhaps coffins stood on end, (who could tell, Davis thought). These strange objects gave the face its only features. The second head, to the left and slightly in the background, was nothing but an egg-shaped form, entirely featureless save for two parallel lines that rose from each side and met in the middle where they formed a small oval lying on its side. A bit of sky, and a wooden plank propped at an angle between the two heads, comprised the only background.

"Can there be anything stranger than these two faces," Fulford asked Davis. "If these are sisters, they must have been conceived in a nightmare."

Her face was sober, almost grim. "He should have entitled the thing *'Women As Monstrosities'.*"

They walked a few paces along the descending spiral and saw several paintings that Davis thought of as normal women, paintings like Braque's Bella and a Picasso early work, *Woman in a Chemise.* Then, they came upon Picasso's, *Seated Bather*, the strangest woman of them all. The *Seated Bather* was a jumbled assemblage of what appeared to be rough hewn pieces of wood or some other hard material. One piece resembled a hip and leg joined, but separate from the body, which was nothing but a couple of amorphous slabs. Another slab resembled a sliced-off buttock. An arm, thin and elongated beyond reason was attached to a shoulder that clung to a back bone comprised of an upright two by four. The breasts, on a semicircular arched slab, hung below a neck that rose to a face that looked more like a mechanic's crescent wrench with wide-toothed jaws, coming together in a grotesque grimace.

Davis peered at Fulford, trying to guess her reaction. She stared at the thing, her eyes moving methodically from one part to another as if trying to wrest a whole from the disjointed parts. She shook her head in puzzlement. "I can't see any point to it," she said finally. "If he's making some kind of statement about women, it's beyond me."

"Read the essay underneath the title," Davis said. "One guy calls it a 'subversion of an ideal', another says it's a 'bestial and mechanistic contraption', and yet another says it's like a praying mantis which has 'the capacity to function even when decapitated.'"

"I'm told," Fulford said, "that the female mantis, like some spiders, has a habit of eating her mate once they finish copulating. Is Picasso saying women destroy the artist, after first subverting him through sex?"

He seldom disagreed with her estimate of things, and didn't feel he was doing so now, because there were many ways one could legitimately interpret Picasso's art. "I think he's looking at women, like that guy Magritte, as mechanistic contraptions, a collection of erotic parts, designed for men's pleasure. Picasso was, I read on one of those tablets, a confirmed womanizer. He would use a woman till her novelty wore off and then discard her. He went through a string of women that way."

"I suppose," Fulford said, "it's not fair to tar all these painters with the same brush, yet I get the feeling, from the ones we've looked at, that they thought of women as objects rather than as persons."

Davis had to agree, but offered a reservation. "What we're doing, Leda, is not art criticism. It's sociology, or anthropology, or something. We're trying, from their paintings, to guess their sexual attitudes toward women. Our speculations are not the kind of evidence that would stand up in a court of law."

"But it works in the art gallery, doesn't it? Just listen to the comments people are making around us. Most of them, especially the women, seem to think the artists paint women exactly as they see them—as sexual objects made for male gratification or as mechanistic contraptions to be used like one would use an automobile."

The tone of the conversation began to make Davis feel a little unsure of himself. He had never thought of a woman as an object made solely for erotic pleasure or as a thing to be used as he saw fit. Now, however, he began to wonder if Fulford saw him that way. When they had slept together he had told her how gratifying the act had been, and had urged her to come and live with him so they could continue to enjoy the pleasure that sex had given them. Had he given her cause to believe he was interested only in sex? Sex had been important to him, he had to admit, but it had been only part of a complex emotion he felt toward her. He had not been able to express it very well. Now he felt he was closer to being able to tell her how he felt.

"Have you had enough of dada and surrealism?" he asked. "If so, I've got a proposition to make."

"My mother told me to beware of men making propositions," she said, smiling.

"Nothing to be feared from this one. I've got a refrigerator stocked with chicken breasts, pork chops, flank steaks, and a cabinet full of vegies, pasta, mushrooms, and other goodies to go with meat. I'm proposing we leave this dreary exhibit, go back to my apartment, and see what we can come up with for dinner."

A frown creased her brow. Her sober expression made it clear she was about to turn him down.

"Wade, I'm sorry I can't take you up on that very alluring proposition. I'm having a guest for dinner tonight at my place. Since we were only spending the afternoon together, I didn't think there'd be any conflict."

He put on a show of indifference, but his reply betrayed his disappointment. "Of course. Some other time, maybe... A good friend?"

"Haven't known him all that long, but I like him a lot."

"It's not Chris, is it?" He despised himself for asking the question. It revealed his jealousy and made him feel childish. Christopher McCalmon, the medical examiner, had let it be known, unabashedly, that he was in love with Leda. Davis knew he was in love with her from the way he looked into her eyes. And from the way his voice seemed to caress her when he spoke.

"No, it's not Chris," she said with a sly smile. "It's someone I think a lot more of. I'm not sure I should tell you. Will you promise not to be jealous?"

"Absolutely. Why should I be jealous?" He knew he sounded like a high school kid trying to sound indifferent at being turned down for a prom date.

"I'm fixing dinner for a colleague you should know pretty well. His name is Wade Davis."

Davis covered his astonishment and delight by uttering what he thought was a masterpiece of cleverness. "Congratulations, Leda, you couldn't have picked a better man."

Her apartment was in a complex of condominiums called the Crescent, just off Piedmont. It consisted of a living room, one bedroom, one bath, and a kitchen. When she opened the door for Davis, she waved a hand around and said, "Modest, Wade, but it's all mine—if you don't count the mortgage."

He paused, looking, then spoke with admiration. "Compared to my place this is super. You could be an interior decorator."

"Yeah," she said, "right out of *House Beautiful*. It's furnished, Wade, with garage sale castoffs."

Davis's knowledge of furniture was minimal. Furniture meant kitchen and dining room tables, straight-backed chairs, rocking chairs, upholstered chairs (some of which might be recliners), living room sofas, chests of drawers, and beds—king, queen, full, and twin. If he had to particularize an item in this generic list, he would think of an illustration in a Sears Catalogue.

When Leda told him her table was a Sheraton drop leaf, or that the chest of drawers in the bedroom was a Queen Anne with bow front and claw feet, he nodded appreciatively as if he knew what those definitions meant.

"The corner cupboard is a Shaker," she told him. "It's probably an authentic antique. The other pieces are copies. I was able to buy all of them by keeping my eyes open at garage sales. Got them at ridiculously low prices, even the Shaker."

"How do you know the Shaker's a real antique?"

"Because it doesn't fit exactly into the corner. There's a gap on one side."

"And what does that prove?"

"Old houses were rarely plumb, so when people ordered a corner cupboard, they had the carpenter measure the angle between the two walls. Most of the time it wasn't exactly ninety degrees. This piece isn't ninety degrees. More like eighty-six. If it were modern, it would be ninety degrees on the nose."

"You're really up on this stuff."

"It's a little closer to real life than dada and surrealism."

The remark made Davis realize how far he had allowed himself to stray from some of the really meaningful things of life. After the death of his wife, grim endurance had been his way of coping. He had experienced a gradual loss of feeling that came out of a need to suppress the shocking spectacle of Sylvia's death. Even now, the recollection of the crash from which he emerged with barely a scratch was indelibly etched on his mind. Once again he relived the moment when, as he regained consciousness, his mind still disoriented from shock, he saw his wife's lifeless body, broken and slack, lying on the roadside. For a brief moment, she had seemed to him a puppet whose controlling strings had been cut. Deprived of volition, she lay, a crumpled doll, not ever again to be moved by the engines of love and laughter.

"Wade," Leda's voice broke into his reverie. "Wake up. You're daydreaming." She looked at him, a question in her glance. "What is it? You looked awfully serious."

"I was just thinking how nice it would be if I could get you to join forces with me. We could get a bigger apartment and you could fix it up like you've done this one. We could make some plans for the future. Things like that."

"Don't start again, Wade, please. I know how you feel and I know, that for you, the feeling is urgent. It's still not right for me. I need more time to think things out. Let's just have a good time and let the future take care of itself."

"Heartless woman. You're killing me you know." He put on a wounded face. "I don't have much choice, do I?" He walked to the kitchen door and peered within. "What are we having to eat?"

Busy with pots and pans, she gave him a smile. "Slow-roasted pork loin with apricot chutney, candied yams, fresh shelled peas, and Caesar salad. Sound good?"

"Can hardly wait. How can I help?"

"Open that bottle of zinfandel and pour us a glass."

After they ate, they lingered over dessert, a store-bought lemon meringue pie of exceptional quality. Davis had two pieces. A certain mellowness induced by the wine and the soft background music came over them. They agreed the art exhibit had been beyond understanding, at least beyond *their* understanding, but if one needed support for the hypothesis that men regard women as sex objects, the paintings of Magritte and Picasso, as well as several others, could well be used as supporting evidence.

Davis, warmed by the wine, assured Fulford he did not belong to that class of crude thinkers, that he had never considered her an assemblage of erotic parts but as a marvelous, indivisible entity, that evoked in him chaste, non-visceral admiration.

She seemed amused at his declaration, but thanked him and, with impish solemnity, reminded him of mundane chores.

"We have to clear the table, Wade, and do the dishes. I'll wash and you dry."

He agreed and, to demonstrate his non-visceral admiration for her, he enfolded her in his arms and kissed her lips, her brow, her cheeks. He was aiming to buss her throat and breasts when she wriggled free and handed him a dish towel.

After the dishes were done, Davis opened another bottle of wine and they sat together on the sofa and watched a movie. It was a rerun both had seen earlier, but they thought it worth seeing again.

Davis was aroused as the hero of the movie, with the eager compliance of the nubile creature he had picked up in a hotel bar, had sex, not in ordinary basic ways, but with an unparalleled gymnastic component that led to couplings in such unlikely places as an elevator, a dining room table, and a kitchen sink.

He reached out and took Fulford's hand. She did not withdraw it, but clutched it more firmly as the sexual conjugations on the screen became more fierce and the locales more exotic.

When the movie ended, Wade, momentarily inarticulate, looked into her eyes. She withdrew her hand, breaking the intent gaze between them, and said, "Don't go away, I'll be right back."

In a moment she returned. "I've opened the bed," she said. Her fingers unbuttoned her blouse and in a moment it fell to the floor. She turned her back to him and said. "Unhook this thing, please."

Davis complied, clumsily, his heart beating erratically. When she turned around, he caught his breath. She undid his shirt and pressed her breasts, nipples erect, against his chest. She stepped out of her skirt and deftly removed her panties as he dropped his trousers and boxers. His eyes moved swiftly over her firm, perfectly proportioned body. Then, trembling with desire, he picked her up, and carried her into the bedroom. He lay her on the bed on her side, her round buttocks showing invitingly. He ran his hand gently over the curve of them. Like a cat being stroked, she turned toward him exposing the silky hair between her legs.

It was 5 a. m. Leda was shaking him by the shoulder. Davis roused himself, rubbed his eyes, and still half asleep, looked at the clock. He spoke in indignation.

"Leda. What in the devil are you doing?"

"I'm waking you up, Wade."

"I guessed that. But why?"

"So you can get your clothes on and get out of here before the neighbors wake up."

"Leda, who gives a damn about the neighbors?"

"I do. There's an old lady across the hall who clings to Victorian morals like a leech. I don't relish explaining to her why I had a man in my apartment all night long. She expects more from a police woman. And she's not the only Victorian in this complex. If you're not out of here before daylight, I'll have to spend the rest of the month explaining my lack of morals to the busybodies."

Davis was incredulous. "I can't believe this. Why don't you just tell them I'm your fiancee and we're going to get married soon. That'll shut them up."

"But it's not true."

Davis heard her words and, unable to credit them, said, "Jesus. Leda. What are you saying? Are you telling me that there was no love in all this, that all you and I have in common is sex. Is this just a one night stand?"

"I don't like that term. There's a lot more in my feeling for you than sex. I'm just unwilling to be tied permanently to you because we've slept together. There's nothing wrong about my inviting you here for sex. Men do it all the time.

They wake their girlfriends up the morning-after and shoo them out before they're seen by the neighbors. Why can't a woman do the same thing?"

"She can. That's obvious. You're doing it. You get horney, so you pick a vulnerable guy like me, lure me in for an evening of pleasure, then show me the door."

"Oh, come on, Wade. Self pity doesn't become you. Don't tell me you've never done anything like this. Don't tell me you've never had sex with a woman you had no intention of marrying."

Davis felt the sting of her remark. The truth hurts, and, in this case, the truth hurt like salt on a wound. His mind reeled with confused thoughts. His heart ached at being expelled so summarily. He put his clothes on slowly, tied his shoes, and stood up. He looked at Fulford with resentment, unable to understand her behavior or to forgive it.

"I'll see you tomorrow." He looked at his watch. "Make that nine o'clock today. We have a meeting with Gerry Fillmore."

He walked to the door, opened it, paused on the threshold. His voice was filled with bitterness. "If all you wanted was sex, why didn't you pick up some guy off the street?"

"Don't be insulting, Wade. Quit feeling sorry for yourself and go home."

Chapter Thirteen

Fillmore, with his usual penchant for interference in a smooth running investigation, had assembled everyone, even those who were only remotely associated with Paulson's murder. Davis and Fulford, as principal investigators were to be expected. But why summon Cyrus Orovac, Albert Saffron, and Jeffrey Sailor? Davis wondered what Fillmore expected to learn from them, but being used to the unconventional ways of his boss, he sat back to wait for the answer. He grinned at Fulford and silently mouthed the words, "I love you."

She flushed slightly at his audacity, turned her face away from him, and became totally absorbed in the division head's opening comment.

"I asked you here," Fillmore said, somewhat pompously, "to find out what progress had been made in the Paulson case, one that, as you may know, is generating publicity of the kind the department can do without."

He glanced at the assembled crew with an air of accusation, as if they had been remiss in not shielding him from an impertinent press. Then he spoke directly to Davis. "Wade, are we anywhere near an arrest?"

"Our prime suspect is a guy named Basil Gearhart. He's the guy who clobbered Paulson with a bag of pig's blood at the senate hearing on a bill to restrict deer hunting. He was let out of jail at noon on the day Paulson was killed. He has an alleged alibi we haven't been able to confirm. Says on the day he was released he was with a lady of loose morals enjoying the pleasures of the flesh all afternoon."

"You found this lady yet?"

"No, sir."

"Have you looked for her?"

"Not really."

"Why not?"

"We sort of figured his story was a fabrication."

"Did he give you her name?"

"No. Says he never asked her."

"Where does she live?"

"No address. She entertained him in the back of an old Dodge van which she parked in a parking garage."

"Where'd he pick her up?"

"In Bethel Street."

Fillmore pretended astonishment at Davis's failure to institute a search for the woman. "A lot of whores work out of Bethel Street. Seems like a woman who uses a pleasure palace on wheels would be noticed by a lot of people. Why not send an officer out to question the locals?"

Davis sighed in exasperation. "Because the locals won't talk to a police officer, and we don't have any undercover people to spare for this assignment."

"Why don't you send Albert. Nobody would mistake him for a policeman."

Albert nodded his head in satirical acknowledgment of Fillmore's left-handed compliment.

Davis spoke with ill-concealed irritation. "Albert's an inside man. I can't see him coping with a bevy of prostitutes and their johns."

Albert grinned maliciously. "Give me a chance to prove myself, Wade. Who knows what lies at the core of this corpulent body."

"Suet," said Cy Orovac.

Albert, used to jokes at the expense of his enormous bulk, laughed with the others.

Fulford saw an opportunity to move away from Fillmore's off-the-wall suggestion. "We have another possible suspect, a fellow named Victor Percy, but we have yet to investigate him or to find any direct evidence of his involvement. He suffers from a rare kind of bone cancer and believes a polio vaccine he took years ago was contaminated with SV 40, a monkey virus. Since Edgeware Pharmaceuticals supplied the vaccine, he holds them responsible for his condition and demands monetary restitution."

Fillmore interrupted, speaking in a skeptical tone. "Are you saying he shot Paulson with a crossbow because, years ago, he was inoculated with a contaminated polio vaccine from Paulson's drug company? Sounds far fetched to me."

"We think so, too. But Roger Godwin, Paulson's partner, told us that Percy threatened Paulson with physical violence at an open meeting of the company board. Later Paulson received an anonymous e-mail threat, which we traced back to Godwin's office in the Pharmaceutical Company. Or, rather Jeffrey Sailor did."

Fillmore looked at Sailor curiously. "How'd you do that? Doesn't anonymous mean the sender is not identified?"

Sailor, pleased at the recognition of his expertise, launched into a detailed account of how he backtracked the message through a chain of re-mailers until he found the source. Davis finally quenched the flow of computerese by pointing out that Sailor had identified the computer from which the message had been sent, but not the person who had sent it.

"We think Percy had an opportunity to send that message," Davis said. "He was in the Edgeware building at a board meeting when he threatened Paulson. There were two coffee breaks of fifteen minutes each and a lunch break. Enough time for him to slip into Godwin's office and type out the message."

"A lot of people go into that building at one time or another," Fillmore observed. "You need to ask yourself if there aren't others, besides this guy Percy, who had a beef against Paulson. Maybe a business associate who felt Paulson had injured him with an underhanded deal."

"We're working on that angle," Davis said, although, in reality, the idea hadn't occurred to him.

"Is that it?" Fillmore inquired, looking around as if he had expected a lot more. "Seems you don't have much to go on."

"We're still in the developmental stage," Fulford assured him. "There are other possibilities. We have reason to believe all was not well between the Paulsons, that Harry might have been something of a skirt chaser and Lucinda might have been having an affair with Paulsons partner, Roger Godwin."

"How do you plan to verify your suspicions?"

"We're going to start interviewing friends and acquaintances—and the servants."

Fillmore's demeanor signaled impatience. "You'd better start digging fast. Paulson was a prominent man. The press is going to crucify us if we don't get results soon."

Caleb Burton, a police officer of ten years experience, sat in Davis's office, chair tilted back, feet on desk, when Davis and Fulford returned from their meeting with Fillmore. Burton was not a homicide detective but aspired to be one. As a vice division detective, he had had his fill, he said, of prostitutes, both male and female, crackheads, sexual perverts, and unclassifiable deviates. Occasionally he gravitated to Davis's office, to vicariously experience the atmosphere of the world he much admired and longed to enter. When Davis and Fulford appeared, he rose, greeting them enthusiastically.

"Hello, you two." He cast an appreciative eye on Fulford and gave her a big smile. "I'm here to tell you some big news. One of these days I'll be greeting you as a co-worker. I've got my transfer in and the scuttlebutt says I can expect favorable action soon."

"Congratulations," Davis said. He had known Burton for several years, had come across him first when investigating the murder of a notorious Bethel Street pimp, and admired the fund of knowledge the man had about Atlanta's sexual predators. Burton's background, he reasoned, would be invaluable to the Homicide Division when a murder was connected with sexual deviation, drug addiction, or alcohol abuse.

Fulford, who had met the man several times in the company of Davis, made an effort to be congenial. "You think you'll enjoy nabbing murderers more than yanking crack dealers off the street?"

Burton's glance at her was lingering; his admiration for her evident. "I'm tired of the drug scene," he said. "Too many users and penny-ante pushers get thrown in jail, too few of the big guys." He paused, thinking aloud. "One thing from Vice I'll be glad to leave behind," he added, "is hassling prostitutes. It's a funny thing the way we treat prostitutes in our society. All of our media, movies, advertisements, TV, are aimed to arouse men. Then we get upset when a few enterprising women make a business of meeting the demand."

Fulford looked at him keenly. He was a not-unattractive man. It would be a pleasure to have him on board. "You think we should just ignore prostitution?" she said as a way of establishing a little rapport.

"Why not? It's a victimless crime, in my book. Who's hurt by it? The woman makes a living and the men get sexual relief that probably prevents a few rapes."

"But the women are degraded, aren't they?" Fulford asked.

"Not unless they're forced to be. If the police didn't hassle them all the time, they could lead respectable lives."

"How do you figure that?" Fulford asked.

"Look. The men who patronize them remain respectable citizens, don't they? Why? Because the police never hassle them. They don't even reveal their names. Men get their kicks from the women and then go back to their families and their jobs unscathed. What's right for the men should be right for the women."

"Okay. But it's not than simple," said Davis.

"Sure it is. A few day ago, we arrested a woman, a Thelma Wilcox, who conducted her business with the kind of flair I admire. She had modified a Dodge van into a simple bedroom, and when a john solicited her, she drove him off to some secure place where the two of them left the driver's seat, got in the back, and had a good time. Now, who is hurt by that?"

Both Fulford and Davis looked at him as if he had just discovered the spiral helix.

Davis was the first to speak. "Caleb," he said eagerly, "is that woman still in custody?"

"I'm pleased to say she's back on the street, plying her trade discretely and harming no one. I don't plan, now or in the future, to hassle her."

"I won't ask you to interfere with her business," Davis said. "But you can do homicide a real favor, if you will." He turned to Fulford, "Leda have you got a photo of Basil Gearhart?"

She nodded. Several prints had been made from the mug shots taken at the time Gearhart was jailed. She gave him two, one front, one profile.

Davis handed them to Burton. "Caleb, can you contact this van-driving lady for us? Just show her those photos and ask if she recognizes the guy and if she entertained him during the afternoon of July 30. If she did, find out how long he was with her."

"No problem," Burton said. He appeared pleased at the opportunity to help the people whose world he hoped to enter soon. "I'm pretty sure I can find her tonight. I'll give you a report tomorrow."

When he had gone, Fulford said. "Thelma, bless her, is going to give us a big assist one way or another."

Cheryl Hargert was not in a genial mood. She had agreed, reluctantly, to meet Fulford at the Pullman Diner for lunch. When she arrived, she was coldly formal, insisting on addressing Fulford as Detective Fulford despite Fulford's request to be called Leda.

"I don't think I should be so familiar with a policewoman," she explained. "Especially one who intends to pry into my boss's private affairs."

She sat stiffly in her chair and eyed Fulford warily.

Fulford thought candor might disarm her hostility. "I'll be honest with you, Cheryl. I'm investigating a particularly gruesome murder. You've read about Harry Paulson's death and I hope you're as eager as I am to see his killer go to jail. My job requires me to 'pry', as you put it, into other people's private affairs. I can't be too respectful of their feelings or loyalties."

Cheryl interrupted. "I have been an employee of Roger Godwin's for the past year. During that time he has always treated me with the greatest respect. He has taken me into his confidence on more that one occasion and I do not intend to violate those confidences."

She sat, idly poking at her crab salad with a fork, a severe expression on her face.

"I commend your loyalty," Fulford said. "I'm not asking you to violate confidences. I repeat, this is a murder investigation, and I have to ask certain questions. If a question violates a confidence, you needn't answer. I'll let you be the judge of what to answer and what to refuse. Okay?"

She nodded. Her face reflected conflict, indecision. Fulford thought she could detect an emotional attachment to Roger Godwin that went beyond mere loyalty. Had she ever been Godwin's mistress? The possibility was there. It might explain why she was so fiercely protective.

She thought it best to focus her questions on Lucinda Paulson's relationship with Godwin.

"How often would you say, since Harry Paulson's death, has his wife had appointments with Mr. Godwin?"

"Five or six times. I could check my appointment book if you want me to be more exact."

"Your estimate will be fine. How long did these sessions last?"

"Usually an hour or less."

"Do you know what these meetings were about?"

"Since Mrs. Paulson had to deal with her husband's affairs after his death, I assumed they were about business."

"When she came to these meetings, did Mr. Godwin receive her cordially?"

"Of course."

"Did he ever touch her? Hug her? Put his arm around her shoulder?"

"In a friendly sort of way, yes."

"Did he ever kiss her?"

"No."

"You mean, you never saw him kiss her?"

"I dislike the implication of that question."

"I'm sorry. Did they ever continue a meeting over lunch?"

"Once or twice. They would have sandwiches sent in from the deli."

"This was during your lunch hour. You would be away from your desk while they were lunching in Mr. Godwin's office?"

Her face was sullen. She answered, "Yes."

"Did Mr. Godwin ever call her on the phone?"

"Once or twice he would call and tell her they needed to talk."

"Did he ever ask her to meet him someplace other than his office?"

"I don't know."

Fulford relaxed the rapid pace of questioning. "Thanks for being so cooperative. Let's order dessert, okay? Their blueberry cobbler is supposed to be out of this world."

The cobbler, sweet and baked in a wonderfully flaky crust, occupied their attention for a few minutes. To avoid an awkward silence, Fulford tried to draw out Cheryl on her personal life.

"Are you married?"

"Not now. I've been divorced for a number of years. I'm sure you'll want to know if I have children. The answer is, yes. A son, now nineteen and a student at Georgia Tech. Wants to be an engineer."

She looked at Fulford as if she resented her personal inquiries. Then she said, "What about you? You married?"

Fulford, slightly taken aback at the sudden shift from interrogator to respondent, answered, "Not yet."

"Are you soft on that guy Davis you work with?"

"That's something I'd rather keep to myself."

"Well, good for you. Now you've got an idea of how your questions affect me."

She stabbed her fork into the remains of the cobbler. Fulford, wondering why she found herself so intent on trivialities, found her eyes riveted on her companion's purple tongue. It fascinated her. A ridiculous fixation. Was it an unconscious way of diverting her mind, momentarily, from the disagreeable aspects of her job.

"Point well taken. Hope you don't think I enjoy it."

Cheryl seemed to soften a bit. "Okay. Is there more? I'd like to get this over with."

"Okay. Harry Paulson is rumored to have been unfaithful to his wife. Have you heard such rumors."

"Who hasn't. His escapades seem to have been common knowledge. Mrs. Paulson recently filed for divorce, citing infidelity. I got that from a friend, a paralegal who worked for the lawyer she consulted."

"How long ago did this happen?"

"A month or so before he was killed. According to my friend Mrs. Paulson was enraged when she discovered the identity of the other woman. The woman he was fooling around with."

"Do you know who she was?"

"No. Nancy never found out. I don't think Mrs. Paulson ever disclosed her name. The lawyer convinced the Paulsons to visit a marriage counselor. They were reconciled, sort of. At least, Mrs. P. dropped the suit."

Fulford, reasonably content with the information she had elicited from Cheryl Hargert, called for the check, and thanked the reluctant witness. The two women left the restaurant apart, each going her own way in spite of the fact Fulford offered to drive Cheryl back to her office.

Returning to headquarters, Fulford met Davis, and told him what she had discovered. Davis mulled over the information thoughtfully.

"The cards suggest Lucinda had a powerful motive, don't they? She knew of her husband's unfaithfulness. For some reason, she was outraged when she discovered the identity of his latest lover. Why? She had put up with his infidelities before. What was it about this one that set her off on the divorce trail?"

"Sorry, I haven't the faintest notion. Don't overlook her friend, Roger Godwin. He qualifies as a potential murderer. He had motive. He and Paulson had a serious conflict over how to settle Victor Percy's suit. And he's in love with Paulson's wife. If he got rid of Harry, he would resolve a romantic as well as a business problem."

"Yeah," Davis said. "And he was an expert in the use of a crossbow. Still, as far as both of them are concerned, the case is circumstantial. Not a shred of physical evidence. Nothing that would get us an indictment.

"And there's still Gearhart."

"Have you heard from Caleb?" Fulford asked. "I'm dying to know if Thelma remembered Gearhart."

"I'll give him a ring."

Burton had found Thelma Wilcox. She had recognized Gearhart's picture readily enough, but was uncertain of the date of their afternoon frolic. She corroborated the fact Gearhart had spent the afternoon in her van and that she had parked it in a parking garage. According to her, although she couldn't swear to it, their meeting might well have been on July 30th. But it might have been the day after his release from jail.

"That does it for me," Davis said, as he hung up the phone and shared Burton's information with Fulford. "I'd be ready to move on the guy if we could only tie him to the crossbow. But that weapon poses a real problem. If Gearhart is the perp, did he have the weapon stashed away in his apartment, and if he did, how did he get it to Paulson's place? For that matter how did the murderer, whoever he or she was, get the weapon to the scene and spirit it away without being noticed? A crossbow is a bulky thing. Even if you remove the bow from the stock, you've got an awkward package on you hands. It's not something you can carry unnoticed under your arm."

"Did anyone ever search all of Paulson's little wilderness? Maybe the murderer ditched the weapon somewhere in the woods."

"It was searched, every inch, with metal detectors. Zip. Whoever used that crossbow carried it away."

"So. We're at a dead end." Fulford said. "I think we ought to get in touch with Victor Percy. He probably had nothing to do with Paulson's murder, but I'd like to get him off our list. Then we ought to pay Gearhart a visit. Put the screws on him about Thelma's failure to support his alibi unconditionally. Scare him.

Maybe he'll crack."

"Okay," Davis said. "Then we should get to work on the Lucinda-Godwin angle. I think there's gold in that mine."

Their eyes met. She looked away immediately. Exasperated, Davis put his hand on her shoulder and turned her gently toward him.

"Look at me, Leda. Listen to what I say. Sunday night meant a lot to me. More than I can tell you. I thought you slept with me because you loved me. I believed you were ready to make a commitment. Then, you threw me out."

Her face, when she finally looked at him, carried a hint of reserve, but her smile was tender, compassionate.

"I didn't throw you out, Wade. I asked you to leave to spare myself embarrassment. I like being with you. When we make love, I feel as if I want to be with you forever. But that feeling might not last. I want to wait until we're sure before we commit to one another."

Davis sighed. "I'm sorry you have doubts. I couldn't be more sure of anything myself."

She leaned forward and kissed him. "Let's just go on as we are. I'll have dinner with you, in your apartment, next Saturday. Okay? We'll use up some of that stuff in your refrigerator. If you want to throw me out Sunday morning, you can."

Chapter Fourteen

Because Basil Gearhart had an appearance before Judge Keller on the fourteenth, just two days away, Davis decided to postpone questioning him again until that time. He wanted to attend the arraignment anyway to see how the court-appointed lawyer would plead. After the proceedings were over, he could question Gearhart again, in the presence of his attorney if necessary. He had not found court-appointed counsel very formidable adversaries; in fact, they often showed a woeful lack of diligence in protecting their clients' rights.

He sat in the back of the courtroom waiting patiently as cases were called. The clerk finally intoned, "Calendar 123. The People of Georgia vs. Basil Gearhart. Case number 384."

"Gearhart's lawyer rose and said, "Your Honor, I have been unable to contact Mr. Gearhart. I called him this morning in anticipation of this hearing, but got no reply. I have no idea where he is."

Judge Maxine Keller's annoyance was evident. She frowned. "Did you go to his home to make sure he had not overslept?"

"Yes, ma'am, I did. He was not there."

The Judge spoke to the sergeant at arms in a firm voice. "Mr. Bellamy you are to proceed at once to Mr. Gearhart's address. Make sure he has not returned. Take the arresting officer with you. If Gearhart is there escort him to this court at once. If he is not there search his premises for possible clues to his whereabouts and take steps to apprehend him."

The clerk, after filling in Gearhart's name and address, presented Judge Keller with a search warrant. She signed it and handed it to the sergeant at arms, Mr. Bellamy. Max Bender, the arresting officer, and Bellamy made for the door at quick time. Davis decided to follow them.

Bellamy and Bender questioned the apartment manager, Milford Sutter, who informed them that he had not seen Gearhart for several days. He was certain he was not now in his apartment. Bellamy asked him to bring the key to Gearhart's place and open the door for them.

Davis followed Bellamy and Bender into Gearhart's apartment.

"What do you suppose we should look for?" Bellamy said aloud, not directing the query to anyone in particular.

"I think we should look for correspondence," Davis volunteered. "Letters, memos, credit card bills, bank statements. Anything that might suggest where he might have gone and when."

The search proved fruitless. The only thing of possible consequence that turned up was the summons requiring him to appear in court on the morning of the fourteenth at 9 a. m. A large X, made with a lead pencil, had been drawn over the face of the document.

"Looks as if he never intended to keep his date with the law," Bellamy said. "The Judge should have made his bail higher."

"Five thousand is pretty steep," Bender said.

"Not for the Society of Animal Conservators, Inc." Bellamy said. "They've got hundreds of well-heeled supporters. I think we ought to talk to whoever's the boss of the outfit."

"That would be Madelin Gelbart," Davis said, remembering the woman's fiery speech before the Senate hearing on the bill to restrict bow hunting of deer. "She's the CEO or whatever you want to call her. I think you may not get much out of her, but it's worth a try."

The Society of Animal Conservators, Inc. was housed in a strip mall located off Howell Mill Road near the intersection of Highway 40 and I 75. The niche it occupied, among the fifteen or so stores and offices surrounding it, was distinguished by large plate glass windows and a massive oak door that Davis felt was more suitable to a castle than a cluster establishment. It had a brass plate fixed to a central panel that read: COME IN.

Madelin Gelbart had the regal bearing of one who knows she is a true custodian of righteousness. She received the three police officers with the formality that royalty receives the common herd. Her smile was friendly, but her firm jaw and her steely eyes sent a no-nonsense message.

"Please sit down, gentlemen. To what do I owe this visit. Am I in trouble with the law?"

"It's not like you've broken the law, ma'am. But you're in trouble nevertheless."

Gelbart's smile faded. "Well, out with it man. Don't play cute."

"Yes, ma'am. Basil Gearhart, for whom your organization put up bail in the amount of five thousand dollars, has skipped."

"He failed to show up in court?" She was genuinely astonished.

"This morning, ma'am. There's a warrant out for his arrest, but he can't be found. We wondered if you had any idea where he might be."

"Why should I know where he is? You don't think I would put up five thousand dollars in bail and then encourage him to flee. I put it up because I thought he was being falsely accused. That doesn't make me his baby sitter."

"Unless we find him within forty-eight hours, the court will order you to forfeit the bail," Bellamy said.

Gelbart, appearing upset at the prospect of having to lose a substantial sum of money, shook her head in disbelief. "I can't understand why he chose to run. He had a perfectly good alibi for the time of Paulson's death."

"And what would that be?" Davis asked, recalling the dubious story Gearhart had told him and Fulford.

"Why, he was working here, for me, all afternoon on the day Paulson was killed."

"That's odd," Davis said. "He never mentioned it to us. I assume you are willing to swear in court to his having been here?"

"Of course. Why shouldn't I? You don't think I'm lying do you?"

Davis did not answer her question and managed to keep a straight face.

They rose to leave. Before they were out the door, Davis inquired. "You use computers in your work, don't you Ms. Gelbart?"

"Of course. This operation is not run by amateurs. We have a Hewlett Packard, Vectra V."

"A fine machine," Davis said, although he knew very little about the Vectra V. "I assume you have a laser printer."

"Ink jet," she corrected. "An Epson."

Davis nodded appreciatively. "Quite versatile, I understand. Thanks for your cooperation."

Davis and Fulford were outlining the case against Basil Gearhart to Gerry Filmore, who, anxious to appease an insistent press, was, once again, pressuring them to make an arrest. It seemed to Davis, Fillmore was always on his back, unwilling to allow investigations to proceed at a normal pace.

"Why the foot dragging?" Fillmore complained. "He's run out, hasn't he? That creates a strong presumption of guilt. You've got a fugitive warrant for his arrest already. So, find him. It shouldn't be all that difficult. It isn't as if he's left the country. I'll bet he's no more than a mile away from where we're sitting, right now."

"Probably," said Davis. "But the case against him is weak. Circumstantial, entirely. He doesn't have a compelling motive. We have to assume he killed Paulson out of hatred because Paulson championed a cause he is strongly opposed to. I don't think that's a very good reason."

Fulford, who had never strongly believed in Gearhart's guilt, pointed out that the assault on Paulson with the sack of pig's blood did not justify the assumption that Gearhart was bent on murdering him. "When we questioned him, he denied the act was violent. Said it was symbolic. The logic of that assertion may be a little strained, but I'm convinced the man doesn't have a violent nature."

Fillmore looked at her with disdain and amusement. "Woman's intuition. Is that it?"

"No, sir. Just a woman unwilling to arrest a man on insufficient evidence. . ." She paused, looking at him wryly. ". . .for the purpose of appeasing the press."

Fillmore laughed. "Touche." He turned to confront Davis. "You agree with her, Wade?"

"Not because of her character analysis, though in my opinion it's correct, but because we can't connect him with the weapon. A search of his flat revealed no sign of a crossbow or of anything to suggest he had ever owned one. Whoever murdered Paulson had to carry a crossbow to Paulson's place, use it, and carry it away again once the deed was done. How could Gearhart have done that without leaving some clue?"

"He threw the weapon away after using it."

"Where? Every inch of the Paulson place was searched. The only crossbow that turned up was Paulson's own—inside the house."

"I suppose he has an alibi. They always do."

"Davis smiled. "Yeah. Two of them, in fact. One might eventually be confirmed if Gearhart's lucky. The other, in my opinion, is a clear case of perjury."

Fillmore sighed in frustration. "You know the boat I'm in. The press is nagging me by the minute and the chief, damn him, is a real monkey on my back. Can't you two get something going."

Davis secretly enjoyed his superior's plight. He deserved a little torment, he thought, because of his insistence on unnecessary oral reports. Why couldn't the guy be happy reading the written ones?

Fulford was sympathetic. Fillmore was a convenient buffer, keeping reporters off their backs. He was good at the job especially when he had to resort to artistic invention to hide lack of progress.

"Don't forget we have other potential suspects," she told him. We suspect Mrs. Paulson and her husband's partner are romantically involved. We've also learned that Paulson, himself, was a skirt chaser. Somewhere in those sexual liaisons there may be a clue to Paulson's murderer."

"Well, get on it, will you? The wife strikes me as the most likely perp." Fillmore paused, thinking of the difficulty facing a detective bent on uncovering a wife's illicit sexual activity. "How do you expect to get through the denials and stonewalling of the guilty pair—assuming they are guilty."

Davis and Fulford glanced at one another. They had given those obstacles little thought. They hadn't been ready to move in that direction.

Fulford responded off the top of her head. "We're going to try getting information out of the children."

She hadn't forgotten her failure to break through the reticence of the girls, Kimberly and Gretchen, when the case first broke. But, on the spur of the moment, she thought it a good reply to give Fillmore.

He was skeptical. He acted like a man being offered a counterfeit Rolex watch.

Davis endorsed his partner's suggestion and added that they would question the friends and acquaintenances of the Paulsons, and try to find where the pair's romantic liaisons had taken place.

"We'll give you a full report," he assured Fillmore. "As soon as we've made any progress."

When they left Fillmore's office, Davis expressed reservations about Fulford making another try at the girls. "You've questioned them twice, Leda. What makes you think you can drag anything else out of them?"

"Somehow, I think they hold the key to the murderer's identity. The way they behaved when asked about any trouble between their parents suggests they're hiding something. Maybe I can get them to reveal it unintentionally."

"I admire your persistence, but I think you're going to be disappointed."

Kimberly Paulson was alarmed when Fulford called and said she would come by at three o'clock that afternoon for a 'chat', as she termed it. Would Kimberly be so good as to see that Gretchen was present. Her mother, Ms. Fulford said, had been notified. There was no need to bother her about the visit.

Kimberly told Gretchen of Fulford's call and was surprised at how visibly upset her sister was. She paced the room in agitation, running her fingers through her hair in a distracted manner. "What in the world does she want now?" she complained. "I thought we had seen the last of her. Surely she's not going into Mom and Dad's troubles again."

"If she does, we won't tell her a thing," Kimberly said reassuringly. She knew it was important to keep their parents' quarrels away from the police. If they were to discover the threats their mother had made during her verbal battles with her husband she would become a prime suspect. She had no intention of letting anything of that nature slip.

"I don't know what she's up to," she said to Gretchen. "She's a smart woman. She suspects Mom and Dad were not on good terms. But she's after something else. We have to watch out for what it is."

"What else could she be after?" Gretchen's voice was strained, anxious.

"Maybe she suspects us."

Gretchen was annoyed. "Don't say things like that, Kim. It makes me jittery." She continued in a determined voice. "She's not going to get anything out of me. I hate her."

Kimberly said. "I won't tell her anything, either. Let's just play it cool."

When she saw them, Fulford sensed the wariness. It was almost palpable. Kimberly's jaw was set. Gretchen was behaving with elaborate indifference but Fulford observed her underlying tension. Neither girl showed any sign of warmth as they greeted her. The atmosphere was icy cold. How in the world, she thought, could she disarm these two antagonists? Not by questions aimed directly at the information she wanted. If she hoped to get anywhere at all, she'd have to do it by indirection. She asked a question she hoped the girls would think inoffensive.

"I've just come from a visit with your Daddy's partner, Roger Godwin," she said. "He seems like a nice person. Do you like him?"

Kimberly spoke first, relaxing her reserve a bit at this apparently simple query. "He's nice. He remembers our birthdays and gives us Christmas presents every year."

Gretchen nodded. "When he comes to one of Dad's parties, he always talks to us, like we're adults not kids. When I was sick, he brought me a beautiful bathrobe. I still have it."

She stopped abruptly, concerned, as if she had said something she regretted. Fulford was sure she had not intended to reveal her illness. Gretchen passed off her vexation, however, with an air of one making a casual social remark. "He was always doing things like that."

Fulford's suspicion was aroused at Gretchen's inadvertent reference to her illness. She was obviously upset about having revealed it. Fulford wanted to learn the nature of it, but, she was sure Gretchen would not give that away. "I hope you weren't seriously ill," she said.

"It was nothing. Just a bad case of flu."

Fulford made a mental note to look more deeply into the matter of Gretchen's indisposition.

Kimberly spoke up. "Once in a while, when we visited Daddy's office, Roger would have a little snack made up for us, especially if we were there around lunch time."

"That was nice," Fulford said. "Did you go to your dad's office often?"

"Mom liked to surprise him," Kimberly said. "Sort of drop in on him unexpected. Half of the time, though, he wasn't there. He'd gone out for lunch with somebody."

"Wasn't that dissappointing, not being able to see your dad?"

"We were used to it. It happened all the time," said Gretchen. Her manner implied that her father's absence at lunch time was an ordinary thing. "Roger made up for it," she said. "He would take us all to the company cafeteria. We got to pick anything we liked. It was fun."

She smiled at the recollection. "We even got two desserts, if we liked. Mom didn't mind. She liked Roger. They would sit and talk together after lunch while Kim and I went exploring. I think Roger likes her."

"I'm sure he does," Fulford said. "Your mother is an attractive woman. I suppose Roger's been of great help to her, what with your dad's death and all."

"He comes to the house all the time just to see if he can do anything for her." That from Kim. Gretchen looked exasperated with her sister.

"Didn't Roger have a disagreement with your father about a law suit filed against the company?"

"Oh, that," said Kimberly. "I heard Mom and Dad talking about it. It wasn't any big deal. Daddy wanted the case to go to trial, but Roger wanted to settle. Mom agreed with Roger, but they didn't make any decision. They were still arguing about it when Daddy was killed."

"Did your father and Roger get mad at each other over the suit?"

"Maybe a little. But Mom said they agreed to let things simmer down for a while. Just put a decision aside."

Fulford, pleased with the information the girls had disclosed, decided to move the conversation in a different direction.

"I'm sorry to tell you this," she said, speaking in a confidential manner, "but we haven't made much progress in finding the person responsible for your Dad's death." Her voice indicated regret and frustration. "Perhaps you can help us. In the days before his death did your father seem upset about anything? Was he nervous or anxious?"

Kimberly said thoughtfully, "He was terribly upset about the man who attacked him at the Senate hearing. He said some animal rights people wouldn't hesitate to kill a human being just to save a deer. He felt threatened. He was afraid that the man who threw blood all over him might attack him again. He had heard on the radio he had been released."

Gretchen interrupted. "He's the one who killed Daddy. Why don't you arrest him?" She glared fiercely at Fulford.

"We don't have the proof to convict him," Fulford said. "He's already under indictment for attacking your father at the Senate hearing and he'll be arrested on another charge soon. Unlawful flight. He's run away instead of appearing in court like he was supposed to."

"Why did they let him out? He killed Daddy the minute he was free."

"He might have, but it's not certain. Your dad was killed with a cross bow. As of now we have no evidence Mr. Gearhart ever owned one or that he knew how to use it. We'd have to be able to show that he brought it—the crossbow—to where your dad was killed, used it, and managed to carry it away without being seen."

Gretchen heard this information with obvious dismay. She shook her head in puzzlement. "If he didn't do it, who did?"

"Well, first off, it had to be someone who knew how to use a crossbow and had access to one."

"That's a nasty thing to say," said Kimberly, as she saw the implications of Fulford's statement. "It makes suspects of all of us. Everyone in this house knows how to use a crossbow and could get their hands on one. Roger knows how to use one, too. And so do the Whartons. Both of them."

"Don't let that bother you," Fulford said. "It's not just being able to get hold of the weapon. A suspect has to have a motive. As far as I know none of the people you mentioned had a reason to kill your father."

"Last time you talked to us," Gretchen said, "You tried to make out that my Mom and Dad hated each other. You tried to make out Mom might have killed him."

"I didn't say that at all," Fulford said, feeling a need to be reassuring. "I was looking at possibilities. Being a possibility doesn't mean you're a suspect. As of now our chief suspect is Basil Gearhart."

She thanked the girls and left.

When she had gone, Kim said to her sister, "I didn't like that remark of hers, that the murderer had to be someone who knew how to use a crossbow. She believes one of us murdered Daddy."

The remark seemed to inflame Gretchen. "Why do you keep harping on that, Kim?" Her face was flushed. "When you talked to her earlier, you tried to make out I was in the woods when Daddy was killed. Now you're saying I knew how to use the weapon that killed him. What are you trying to do?"

"Nothing," Kim replied. "I'm not trying to throw suspicion on you. If she thinks one of us was involved, it would surely be me. I was in the woods that day. I found Daddy's body. I know how to use a crossbow."

Gretchen was not appeased. "Well, I wish you'd quit saying things like that. You make me crazy."

Chapter Fifteen

"**H**ow did you make out with Victor Percy?" Fulford asked, as Davis sat slumped in his chair, a mug of hot coffee held gingerly between his palms. He had just returned from a visit to Percy's latest address, the Guardian Angel Hospice, and was not in high spirits.

"I wish I hadn't gone," he said ruefully. "You ever been in a hospice? Cheerful place. Everybody there waiting to die. With dignity. Courageously, with dutiful support of family and friends. Makes you face up to your own inevitable end."

He sighed and shook his head.

"Fortunately," he went on, "Percy is still angry enough to be very much alive. He's at death's door, but refuses to cross the threshold. He gave me a lecture on the wickedness of Harry Paulson and the brimstone furnace he will inhabit in the nether world. Then he lectured me for twenty minutes on the subject of Simian Virus 40 and how it had contaminated the polio vaccine he was injected with when he was a child. And how that virus ultimately caused his bone cancer. He's firmly convinced Edgeware Pharmaceuticals is responsible."

"Do you think he had anything to do with Paulson's death?"

"He's delighted at Paulson's passing, but claims he hasn't the slightest idea what a crossbow is. If he wanted to do Paulson in, he wouldn't have used that kind of weapon. He would have injected him with a slow acting poison so the guy could experience what he is going through with bone cancer."

"So you learned zip."

"Not quite. When I asked him if he felt Roger Godwin was just as responsible for his condition as Harry Paulson, he said he didn't think so. He had talked with Godwin and felt he was more sympathetic toward him than Paulson was. He was willing to settle his suit against the company for a reasonable sum, while Paulson was not. He thought Godwin was more humane.

"He said it amused him that Godwin was getting it on with Paulson's wife.

It was sort of poetic justice. I asked him how he knew Godwin was getting it on with Lucinda. He told me he saw Roger Godwin and Lucinda Paulson kissing in one of the small rooms adjacent to the conference room. He was attending a stockholders meeting. He thought the men's room was inside one of the annex rooms. When he opened the door the two were in each other's arms, kissing passionately, he said. He backed out before they realized he had interrupted them."

"So?"

"After mulling it over, he thought he'd use the information to leverage Paulson. Maybe blackmail him a little. Paulson laughed at him. Said he had known of his wife's affair with Godwin for ages. Didn't give a damn about it."

"If Paulson knew his wife was having an affair with his partner and didn't care about it," Fulford mused, "Lucinda must have known about her husband's dalliances and didn't give a damn about them either?"

"I'm sure she did know. And if she's happy in her relationship with Godwin, what incentive would she have to kill her husband? And why would Godwin want to kill him? To have free reign with Lucinda? Hardly. He probably knew Paulson was aware of their affair and had given tacit approval of it." Disappointment registered on his face. "So there go Lucinda and Roger as potential suspects."

Fulford shook her head, disagreeing. "Not so fast. Don't let Lucinda off the hook yet. Suppose she knew Paulson was fooling around but as long as she didn't know who the woman was, it didn't bother her. But what if she discovered his latest mistress was a friend of hers, or was a known tramp, or was, for some reason, off-limits in her mind? That might have made her angry enough to kill him."

Davis considered this possibility carefully. "I have some trouble imagining who such an off-limits woman might be, but I suppose we ought to see if we can run down Paulson's latest conquest."

"I've got some ideas about how to go about that. But first, let me tell you about my conversation with the girls."

She told him the girls seemed to like Roger Godwin a lot and Roger, in turn, cultivated the girls friendship with presents and random acts of kindness. They admitted he saw a lot of their mother. They believed Basil Gearhart had killed their father and were incensed that he had been released from prison. When they were told that access to a crossbow was a crucial factor in fingering a suspect, they were alarmed because the entire Paulson household became potential suspects. Finally, Gretchen had revealed she had recently been ill enough to be hospitalized but seemed eager to give the impression that her illness was minor. She appeared upset she had let her illness come out.

Davis, reflecting on the information he and Fulford had uncovered, tried to envision the direction the investigation should now take.

"Let's try to find who Paulson's latest girl friend was," he said. "The question is, how do we go about it?"

The call came at 10 a m. Fulford lifted the receiver and heard a familiar voice say, "This is Cheryl Hargert. I need to talk to you right away. Could you meet me for lunch today?"

Fulford was surprised. She had not expected to hear from Cheryl again. When they parted after their initial meeting, she believed her to be irreconcilably alienated. Surprising, too, was the seeming urgency of the request. What was so important as to require a quick meeting?

"Yes, I can. Do you want to meet at the Pullman Diner again?"

Cheryl demurred. "The Diner's always so crowded. We'd have no privacy at all. Do you know where Kellum's Kitchen is? We can get a booth there. And there's fewer people."

"I know it," Fulford said. "I'll meet you there at twelve."

She spent the next two hours doing paper work and wondering what in the world Cheryl Hargert had to tell her. Had she decided to spill the beans on Roger and Lucinda? Somehow she doubted that. Although convinced that Cheryl was in love with her boss, she also believed she had no intention of compromising him.

At a quarter of twelve she gave up trying to guess Cheryl's motives and drove to Kellum's Kitchen. Cheryl was already there, seated in a booth toward the rear of the dining room. She sat down opposite her and looked over the menu the waiter handed her. She felt like demanding to know why Cheryl had summoned her so peremptorily, but said nothing.

"I've not eaten here before," she said, glancing at her companion. "Do you recommend anything?"

Cheryl wrinkled up her nose. "It's not a place I come to for fine food. I picked it because there's less chance of our being overheard." She added almost as an afterthought. "They have a bacon-cheeseburger that's edible. With french fries."

They both ordered bacon-cheeseburgers. As they waited for their food, Fulford studied her companion, and was struck by how Cheryl's behavior had changed from their first encounter. The earlier defiance was gone, replaced by what Fulford thought was a mood of resignation, perhaps even of cooperation.

Fulford also noticed, as she had not done previously, that Cheryl Hargert was an attractive woman. Although probably in her middle or late forties, she had a well-shaped body, the result, Fulford felt, of good health care and exercise.

Her face was an attractive oval, unwrinkled, with soft pliant skin. There was an indefinable aura of charm about her. She would undoubtedly be, Fulford thought, a welcome target for a male colleague seeking an office romance.

"Cheryl, what's this all about?" she asked.

"I've had a change of heart, since I spoke to you last," Cheryl said diffidently. "I know I have been evasive and dishonest. I'm sorry about that. I want to set the record straight."

"Why did you change your mind?"

"My conscience hurt me, I guess. When you asked for help in apprehending Harry Paulson's murderer, I vowed I wouldn't lift a hand to help you. I hated Harry that much." She paused then declared vehemently, "Whoever killed him was a public benefactor."

"What makes you say that?"

"He did something terrible to me. Let's eat our burgers, then I'll tell you about it."

They ate in silence. Cheryl seemed to be arranging her thoughts. She downed her last french fry, and began speaking, softly at first, then with greater intensity.

"When I was first hired at Edgeware Pharmaceuticals, I was an executive assistant to Harry, himself. I thought him an attractive man and I was impressed with his position and the power he wielded in the community. These things often affect a young woman's judgment of a man. They make her overlook his faults and she becomes susceptible to his sexual advances.

"Harry was clever enough. He began by working on my vanity, telling me one of the reasons he hired me was because I was attractive and gave class to the office. Occasionally he would bring a single rose to my desk in one of those florist's flasks. He would put it down, stand back and look critically at me. Then he'd say the rose paled in attractiveness when compared to me.

"When he sensed I was embarrassed, he apologized and said he meant no harm, that I evoked in him admiration he could not hold down, but he would avoid such comments in the future.

"Then he began praising my work. One day I made a suggestion I thought clarified a clause in a contract the company was working on. He told me my suggestion would save the company a great deal of money and my judgment was better than those on the legal staff. He wanted to reward me for my work. He asked me to have dinner with him and I consented, thinking he was being grateful for my help.

"He took me to an expensive restaurant, where we had several drinks before dinner and a couple of shots of brandy afterward. He said he maintained an apartment in the city for important clients and wanted me to see it. I had good taste and I could give him some ideas on decorating and furnishings.

"I wasn't naive. I thought he might want to make love to me, but I told myself I could put him off. We had a couple more drinks after we got there. I think he may have put something in my drink because I didn't remember much after that. Anyhow, I woke up the next morning in bed with him. I should have been ashamed, but I wasn't. He was an attractive man and a good lover. We made love again that morning before we got out of bed."

She broke off her story and looked at Fulford as if expecting condemnation.

"It happens to a lot of women," Fulford said. "Why are you telling me this?"

"Because I think it will help you find his murderer."

"How so?"

"Because I'm sure the person who killed Harry was a woman, a woman he used the way he did me. He really messed up my head. He built up my expectations about my future with him, expectations he knew would never come true. He bought me expensive jewelry so I would think he was serious about me. He took me with him to trade shows and conventions and I shared his room and met his friends. When we made love he would tell me how wonderfully I satisfied him, that I gave him a kind of sexual pleasure he had never known before. His wife was an ordinary, perfunctory lover. He eased my conscience by telling me he and his wife had been estranged for a long time, that each went their own way, having extra-marital lovers by mutual consent. He said it was only a matter of time until they were divorced. I believed what he told me and I had fantasies of one day being the second Mrs. Paulson."

Fulford reached across the table and put her hand over the other woman's. The gesture brought a tear to Cheryl's eyes. She continued in a voice husky with emotion.

"This went on for several years. Then suddenly he dumped me. I mean he really dumped me. No such thing as letting me down easy. He called me into his office one day and told me we could no longer continue as we were, that he had gotten involved with another woman and wanted nothing more to do with me. I was devastated. I really loved him and thought he loved me."

A tear rolled slowly down her cheek and she blew her nose into a handkerchief.

"That same day, the woman who worked for Roger Godwin was sacked and I took her place. I'm sure Roger knew about Harry and me and tried to soften my misery by making me feel he had asked for my transfer. That's why I was so protective of his interests when you tried to link him to Mrs. Paulson.

"I seldom saw Harry Paulson after that. When he came in to talk with Roger, he would ignore me, as if he had never known me."

"Do you realize," Fulford said, "your story makes you a suspect in Harry's murder?"

"Yes, and as I said a few minutes ago, I thought the person who killed him was a woman he had used the way he used me. But I'm not worried. I have an alibi. I worked late on a report the night Harry was killed. I didn't leave the office till after seven."

"Did anyone see you who can verify the time?"

"Roger, himself. He worked late with me. He'll back me up."

"Any idea who the woman was Paulson turned to after he lost interest in you?"

"No I don't, but I know that whoever she was it made his wife furious."

"How do you know that?"

"Because I heard her threaten Harry about this new woman." Embarrassment was written all over her face as she continued. "One day she came into the office looking fit to be tied. She charged into Harry's office and he immediately told me on the intercom to hold all calls. He was not to be disturbed."

Fulford knew Cheryl was embarrassed because she had listened in on the Paulson's conversation. Saying nothing, she waited for Cheryl to continue.

"I always follow Harry's orders explicitly. Unfortunately as I bent down to take a folder from my lower desk drawer, I accidentally hit the intercom switch and before I could shut it off again I heard Mrs. Paulson say, 'If I ever learn you have laid a hand on her again, I will kill you. I mean that, Harry. I will kill you.' I shut the intercom off before I heard anything more."

"Do you realize you are casting a heavy cloud of suspicion on Mrs. Paulson?"

"I didn't mean to. People use threatening expressions of that kind all the time when they're angry. I'm sure Mrs. Paulson was upset and only threatened him to underscore her anger."

"Did she know about you and Paulson?"

"She had to know. We had been lovers for a long time. You can't keep that sort of thing secret indefinitely."

"And she never confronted Paulson with it?"

"I'm sure Harry would have told me had she done so."

Fulford thought a moment about Cheryl's disclosure and then asked, "Why did you think it was so important to tell me all this? So important, you wanted to see me immediately?"

"I had a very simple reason. I wasn't sure about telling you my story. One minute I thought I would, the next minute I decided against it. I was ashamed of how stupid I had been. I despised myself for not having had better sense. It was painful for me to think about and harder to face talking to you about it. Once I decided I would tell you, I knew I had to do it at once or I would change my mind. I hope you understand?"

"I do," Fulford said. She touched Cheryl's hand again in a gesture of appreciation. "And thanks for coming forward. You've helped me a lot."

"They've got Gearhart cornered," Davis said as he hung up the phone. His voice conveyed his excitement. "Get your things together and let's go. I want us to be there when they move in."

"Who's they, Wade?" Fulford wanted to know. "I didn't know anyone from the Division had been assigned to trace him."

"No one has. We didn't need to. His bondsman did the job for us. Put a couple of bounty hunters on Gearhart and they've found him. The bondsman told Fillmore his men were looking for Gearhart, and Fillmore got him to agree that if they found him, they'd call the cops and let them make the arrest."

"Are bondsmen usually that cooperative?"

"More like hostile. They almost never consult the police. But this guy is a friend of Fillmore's. I think maybe he owed him."

"So," Fulford said, "Where did they find Gearhart?"

"In a condo at 710 Palisade Drive. Incidentally, when we talk with these guys call them Bail Enforcement Agents. They're a little sensitive about the bounty hunter label. Seems the movies and TV have portrayed bounty hunters too often in an unflattering light."

Palisade Drive, in spite of its imposing name, was a street of decaying town houses clumped together like a honeycomb, and showing a lack of basic refinements such as paint and intact siding. Condo 710, slightly better kept than most, was at the end of the farthest row. A police car was parked in front of the building and two officers leaned carelessly against it, backs to the building. They were conversing in casual fashion with a man Davis supposed was one of the bounty hunters.

Davis and Fulford joined the group. The cop introduced the bounty hunter as Mike Gillespie. "Fill us in will you, Mike?" Davis said. "You've located Gearhart?"

The bounty hunter said, "He's holed up in the end condo. The up-stairs one." His tone was surly as he added, "He'd have been in custody long ago if we hadn't had to wait for you."

"Sorry about that," Davis said. "It was a special deal. Don't worry, you'll still get your commission." He waited a moment for the tension to lessen, then asked, "How did you find him."

"Easy. Used the phone book. Called his mother, told her he was the recipient of an award for his work in animal welfare, and would she ask him to contact us. When he phoned, we traced him through caller ID."

"Very clever," Davis said.

"Yeah," Gillespie said sarcastically. "Even the police could have thought of it."

Davis was annoyed, but stuffed it. "You sure he's still in there?"

"Has to be. I've been here all the time guarding the front. Haven't been gone a minute. Called you people on my cell phone. My buddy's watching the back."

Davis had arrested dozens of fugitives. Invariably, it was a simple matter. You went up to the person's door, knocked, identified yourself as a police officer, and instructed the fugitive to come out and give himself up. The fugitive invariably come out meekly, allowed himself to be handcuffed and led to a squad car like a lamb.

"Let's go knock on his door," he said. Gillespie and the two officers followed him and Fulford in single file up the concrete stairway to the door of seven hundred and ten. When Davis knocked, they heard Gearhart's voice ask, "Who is it?"

"The police, Mr. Gearhart. We have a warrant for your arrest. Please open the door and come out."

"Okay, okay. Just a minute." They heard the sound of water running in the kitchen.

"What in hell is he doing?" Davis asked.

"Beats me," Gillespie said. "Maybe he's washing the dishes."

Afterward, Davis tried to reconstruct exactly what had happened. First, there was the sound of the key turning in the lock, then the throwing wide of the door. Then the image of Gearhart poised with a steaming bucket of water. Then the involuntary flinging upward of hands and arms to ward off the contents of the bucket—a mixture of hot water, soapsuds, and chlorine bleach. It struck them in the face with the force of hurricane-blown rain.

Eyes smarting, they staggered backward, floundering to recover from their surprise.

Gearhart slammed the door shut in their faces and rushed toward the back door. It opened on a small balcony and a rear staircase that descended to ground level. Unable to check his precipitous flight, he ran squarely into the second bounty hunter who had come up the staircase and was standing just outside the balcony door. The collision knocked the bounty hunter off his feet and against the railing of the balcony. Instinctively, he kicked out with both feet at the hurtling Gearhart catching him squarely in the middle. Gearhart's momentum carried him upward and over the railing. He fell, head-first, into a mass of low growing foundation shrubbery where he lay motionless.

Davis and Fulford, still wiping stinging liquid from their eyes, ran out on the balcony and looked down where Gearhart's body had smashed the shrubbery flat against the hard ground.

The bounty hunter got to his feet, hands and arms shaking with tension. "I couldn't stop him," he said. "The guy was a raging bull."

"Nobody's blaming you," Davis said. "The guy's a nut. I hope to God he hasn't killed himself."

"We'll soon find out," Fulford said. During the excitement, she had presence of mind to phone for an ambulance.

Davis and Fulford made their way down the stairway and bent over the unconscious man.

Fulford felt his wrist. "He's got a pulse. And he's breathing."

"Yeah," Davis agreed. "But he's got a hell of a lump on his head. Probably a concussion."

Mike Gillespie, standing at his side, gave him an ill-concealed look of contempt. "If we had made the arrest there wouldn't have been this kind of fuck up."

Davis, suppressing a caustic remark, said evenly, "You're probably right."

Gearhart lay on the gurney, his face composed and serene as if he were sleeping. The pallor of his skin, however, and the trickle of blood seeping from a lump on his head suggested serious injury. A white-coated doctor bent over him examining his injury as Davis and Fulford watched. The doctor shook his head.

"Not good," he said. "I'll do some X-rays to confirm my guess, but from feeling the wound I think his skull is fractured."

He gave the officers a warning glance. "Don't expect to talk to him any time soon. He'll be unconscious for hours, maybe days."

Aides pushed the gurney into X-Ray and shut the door. As they waited, Davis said to Fulford, "It doesn't make sense, what he did. Why such panic? He was only a suspect."

"Maybe he's guilty after all."

"I don't believe it. There has to be some other explanation for his behavior."

"Such as what?"

"You tell me?"

After several minutes, a radiologist opened the door and held it as aides pushed Gearhart's gurney toward an elevator. When the elevator door closed, the radiologist turned toward the officers. "He has a fracture running clear across the occipital. Swelling of the brain has induced coma. My guess is he'll be unconscious a long time."

Chapter Sixteen

From the window he could see a huge cumulous cloud soaring into the sky blocking out the sun. It grew broad and more menacing, filling the air with black roiling vapor. Suddenly, a jagged spear of lightning leaped from its center and smashed into the ground nearby. Explosive thunder shook the building.

He looked at his colleague. "You afraid of lightning?" She was trembling slightly, picking up the papers she had dropped.

"No. But that one made me jump out of my skin."

"Meteorologists say Georgia gets almost as many lightning strikes as Florida," he said soberly, then smiled at having made such an inane remark. "File that away for playing Trivial Pursuits."

In the distance a curtain of rain, awesome in its black, waterfall-like intensity crept slowly toward them, swallowing up buildings, cars, and trees as it came. Davis watched it with fascination.

As the rain struck and the room darkened, he looked at his colleague with a wry expression. "Snap that light switch, will you Leda? And while you're at it, shed some light on Harry Paulson's killer for me."

Fulford was a little weary of Davis's need to speculate endlessly about possible killers. Dutifully, however, she let her mind assess Basil Gearhart's behavior. Attempted flight is generally the act of a guilty person. Why would an innocent man break and run for it? She had voiced belief in his possible guilt as she watched him being wheeled into intensive care at the hospital. Still, she was not fully convinced. Moreover, she didn't believe he could be convicted if charged. One or the other of his alibis (the presumably phony one of Madelin Gelbart or the uncertain one of Thelma Wilcox) would give a good defense lawyer room to establish reasonable doubt. And then there was the weapon, or rather the lack of it. The fact they couldn't connect Gearhart to a crossbow, would pose a serious obstacle to his prosecution.

"I don't think we can build a good case against Gearhart," she said. "There are too many loopholes for him to jump through. So I ask myself, who else have we got? Not Victor Percy. Even if we did believe in his guilt, he'd be dead before the prosecutor could bring him to trial."

"Cheryl Hargert?" Davis asked.

"Maybe. A woman scorned. Dumped in a brutal way. She has motive enough."

"But Roger Godwin is her alibi."

"That's what she says. What he'll do when the chips are down remains to be seen."

"He'll come through for her. I don't doubt that. She's also an alibi for him, don't forget." He reflected for a moment. "Aren't we being pushed steadily in the direction of Lucinda?" he asked.

"Lucinda had motive and opportunity, that's for sure, and she had access to a crossbow. According to Cheryl she was outraged at Paulson's new liaison and threatened him if he didn't break off with whoever it was. What was to stop her from following him into the arboretum that night, carrying his own crossbow, loosing a bolt into his back, and then returning to the house to put the weapon away in its usual place?"

"Nothing," Davis agreed. "And if Roger Godwin didn't accompany her on her little hunting trip, he could have encouraged and abetted it. Paulson's death would give him the freedom to marry her."

"Sounds possible," Fulford said, "but something's nagging me. Aren't we dismissing the possibility that one of Paulson's jilted mistresses, other than Cheryl Hargert, festered with anger and resentment for a long time and then decided to take revenge?"

"We're not dismissing it. But we're stymied because we don't know who such a former mistress might be."

"Why don't I talk to Roger," Fulford said. "Let him know we suspect Lucinda. He's bound to be protective of her. Maybe that will force him to offer us a sacrificial lamb."

"More than likely Cheryl Hargert. All he has to do is dispute her alibi."

After a few moments of thoughtful silence, he began a tediously long analysis of the probability that any one of the persons they had discussed could be convicted if indicted. Fulford listened patiently but learned nothing beyond what they already knew. She was relieved when the flow of speculation was interrupted by the ringing of the telephone.

Davis lifted the receiver. "Davis here." A momentary pause. "Say again, Burton. Slowly please."

His face became a stolid mask. He turned to Fulford and spoke in a grim voice. "It's Caleb Burton of Vice, Leda. He says a young black man named David Fulford was stopped about an hour ago by traffic officers for running a red light. They had a drug-sniffing dog with them who nosed around the car's trunk and smelled drugs. They opened the trunk and found a package containing marijuana and several grams of another substance not yet identified, but they suspect methamphetamine. He's in the district jail. Caleb wants to know if this David Fulford could be related to you."

"My God, Wade," she said. "David's my brother. And I know for a fact, he's not into drugs. There must be some mistake."

Davis hid from her the disbelief he always felt when a suspected drug user's relatives said they knew for a fact their kin could not be guilty of substance abuse. Too many contrary instances had given him an enduring skepticism.

"Yes, he's Leda's brother, Caleb," he said into the phone. "We'll be over there as fast as we can." He hung up and trailed after Leda who was already out the door.

Leda hugged her brother fiercely. Tall and darkly handsome, David Fulford looked frightened. He held his sister close as she kissed his cheek. They stood in an interrogation room, a stark cubicle without windows, unfurnished except for a dismally plain table and two chairs. The mustard-colored walls reflected a pallid, sickly light from a single incandescent bulb hanging from the ceiling.

Davis and Caleb Burton stood to one side watching the two.

"Lee, I don't belong here," David said to his sister in a plaintive voice. "I don't know how that package got in my car. I swear I didn't put it there."

"I know you'd never use drugs," Leda said, reassuringly. "And I know you'd never be foolish enough to carry drugs in your car. But you have to explain how the drugs got there, David. Tell me how that could have happened."

Davis interrupted. "I'm Wade Davis, your sister's colleague, Mr. Fulford. She's right. If you didn't put the drugs in your car, we need to find out how they got there." He paused to let that fact sink in. "I want to help you if I can. If someone put drugs in your car they had to have access to it. Do you park in a garage?"

"Yes, I do," David said. "I keep my car in a garage that's always locked. And I keep the car locked, too. I know that someone put that package in my trunk but I don't see how they could have done it. You can't forcibly open a trunk without some sign of damage."

"Whoever did it could have used a key," Leda said. "Automobile locks are fairly simple. A few tumbler combinations are used over and over again. Some knowledgeable thieves equip themselves with keys that will open the trunk of almost any car they target."

"Yeah. But thieves break into a car to steal something," Davis said. "Not to put something in. If someone actually put that package in your trunk, Mr. Fulford, what reason would he have had?" His tone of voice revealed the doubt he was feeling.

"I don't know. Maybe he put it in the wrong car. Maybe it was intended for someone else. Someone who has a car just like mine." He looked about him miserably, aware of the weakness of his hypothesis. "I suppose, I'm going to get stuck with this rap even though I'm not guilty."

"Not if I can help it," Leda said. "I'm going to find out who put the stuff in your car if it's the last thing I do. My colleague is going to help me, aren't you, Wade?" She looked him squarely in the eye.

Davis agreed reluctantly. "I'll do what I can." His tone suggested he foresaw serious obstacles to proving David Fulford's innocence.

A turnkey came and told David he had to return to the cell where he would be held overnight, then taken before a judge in the morning. In all probability, he told David, since he was a first offender, he would be released on his own recognizance.

Fulford kissed David and he was led away.

Burton, sensing the tension Leda Fulford was under, took her by the arm and led her, followed by Davis, into his office. He poured coffee for everyone and then said, "Leda, the law in Georgia pertaining to first offenders is lenient."

She gave him a grateful smile. "How lenient, Caleb?"

"Well, section 16-13-2 of the Georgia Statutes says that if a person has not previously been convicted of an offense involving narcotic drugs, marijuana, or stimulant, depressant, or hallucinogenic drugs, the court may skip entering a judgment of guilt, and place the person on probation."

The relief shown on Fulford's face rivaled the brightness of the sunlight that slanted down through the window of Burton's office.

"Are you saying a judge can just put him on probation without an adjudication of guilt?"

"Very likely. He's never been arrested before, he's attending law school, he seems in all respects to be a good citizen."

"Will there be anything that might affect his standing in law school?"

"Not in the court record. He might get some attention from the press. If the unidentified substance turns out to be methamphetamine there's a possibility some reporter might want to do a story on it. Crystal Meth is the rage among Atlanta's drug users these days. In the last year we've seized five labs where the stuff was being manufactured. Cops call it redneck cocaine. There's a possibility law school personnel might read David's name in the paper. But if David keeps his mouth shut, no one in the law school should ever hear of his arrest."

Davis listened with interest. "He won't get off scot-free, will he? Won't the court impose some sort of penalty?"

"He may be required to attend a drug rehab program. Or do some community service or both."

"But he's not an addict," Fulford protested. "He doesn't use drugs and he's actually innocent of the charge of possession."

"Well," Burton said, "that may be so, but we're faced with a question of expediency."

Davis wanted to support Leda but couldn't bring himself to believe David's story. "David will have a tough time proving his innocence," he said. "The stuff was in his car and he can't explain how it got there. Given that fact, he'd be better off to plead guilty and escape a conviction."

Fulford flared angrily. "Wade, I think you believe he's guilty. He's my brother. I know him. He simply wouldn't think of using drugs. Why should he plead guilty?"

"Of course I respect your judgment, Leda. You know that. But what judge is going to believe David's story without some kind of proof? He has to show who set him up and how they managed to plant the stuff in his car. As of now, he can't do that."

"So. You're ready to abandon him, to urge him to admit doing something he didn't do. Well, I'm not. I'm going to find out who set him up." She glared at her colleague. "And I expect you to help me, Wade."

"Okay," Davis said. "Okay, Leda! I'll do what I can. Forgive me, though, if I'm pessimistic."

"This young man, David Fulford, is charged with possession of marijuana and methamphetamine." The clerk read those words from a sheet Caleb Burton had supplied. "Investigation shows he has never been charged with an offense before. He is a law student at Emory University. He seems in the past to have been a law-abiding citizen."

David Fulford stood at attention beside his chair. He seemed chastened by the sobering environment of the court, but there was a firmness to his jaw, and a certain glint of stubbornness in his eye.

The judge, a harassed-looking woman of about forty years, peered at him over her glasses in a perfunctory way. She showed every sign of wishing to dispose of the day's routine appearances as quickly as possible.

"What have you got to say for yourself, young man? Do you regret your transgression and admit you've made a mistake. If you show sincere remorse, I am willing to withhold adjudication and place you on probation."

David Fulford hesitated. He glanced at his sister and the two detectives who sat next to her as if seeking affirmation.

The Judge rattled the paper she held in her hand in a gesture of impatience. "Well, speak up! We don't have all day."

Fulford, looking uncertain but determined, said, "Your honor, I am not guilty of possession. I plead innocent to the charge."

"Mr. Fulford, do I hear you right?" the judge said sarcastically. "Marijuana and methamphetamine are found in the trunk of your car, but you tell me you are not guilty of possession."

"Yes, ma'am. Those drugs do not belong to me. They were placed in my car by someone else."

"And who, may I ask, is the person who put them there?"

"I don't know."

She regarded him with astonishment. "Do you understand the precarious position you are in, Mr. Fulford? If you maintain your innocence I must remand you for trial at some future date? Do you have an attorney?"

"No."

"You had better get one. Bailiff, take the prisoner back to jail."

Davis turned to Fulford. "What, in hell's name, got into him? He had an easy out and he blew it. Now he'll have to make bail and stand trial on a case he can't win."

"I should have known," she said. "He'll never admit to something he hasn't done."

Davis felt impelled to promise something he knew would never happen.

"We'll find the person who did it, Leda. We'll get David out of this mess."

CHAPTER SEVENTEEN

The arrest and incarceration of David Fulford threw his sister, Leda, into an agitated state against which she fought valiantly but with little success. She was impelled to 'investigate' in hope of discovering how some crackhead might have opened the trunk of David's car and left the incriminating substances there. She examined the car, while it was still impounded, for signs of surreptitious entry. She found nothing. She went over the car again after she had posted David's bail, and he and the vehicle had been released. Again, she found nothing.

After that she took a day off from work and went door-to-door in David's neighborhood asking people if they had seen any suspicious characters loitering about. Eight hours of tedious inquiry turned up one lead, the sighting by several of David's neighbors of a suspicious looking fellow who had been cruising the area. Upon further inquiry, he turned out to be a male salesman for Avon products.

After observing her distracted manner and her diminished interest in the Paulson investigation, Davis reproached her. "Leda, David's case is the responsibility of Vice, not ours. Caleb Burton is doing all he can to discover how those drugs got into David's car. Assuming," he added, "someone else actually did put them there."

The remark brought a cold stare and an angry response from Fulford. "You don't believe David, that's your trouble," she charged. "You doubt his story and I'll bet Caleb does, too. You'll never uncover any supporting evidence, if that's the assumption you start out with."

Davis did not lose his temper but changed the subject.

"Tomorrow, I want you to talk to Adam Wharton. He and Paulson were close and he must know of his womanizing. See if you can worm out of him the names of some of Paulson's women. Maybe if you called them 'close women friends' you'd have a better chance of getting somewhere. Okay?"

Her eyes were dark pools of anger, her voice harsh. "I've been sleeping with you every weekend, Wade, and this is the thanks I get. You're ready to throw my brother to the wolves without raising a hand to help him. I told you once I had doubts about our commitment to one another and the way you're acting now raises those doubts to near certainty."

"Leda, that's not fair."

"Don't say fair to me. You don't know what fair is. You can get yourself another woman for your week-end pleasure. I'm staying home."

She stormed out of the room.

Next morning she opened the door to Davis's office and sidled in, a contrite expression on her face. "I didn't mean all those things I said, Wade. It was anger speaking. And frustration over my brother's predicament. Hope you can forget my outburst."

"It's forgotten, Leda. Don't give it another thought."

In spite of her conciliatory words, Davis felt a lingering resentment. Though he tried his best to forget it, her attack still rankled. And he could sense that her bitterness toward him had not fully faded. It would be some time, he guessed, until trust between them would be fully restored, if ever.

"I've made an appointment with Adam Wharton for ten o'clock," she said. "You want to come along?"

"You don't need my help. I'd only be in the way."

"Well, wish me luck. I don't think I'll get much out of him."

"Don't sell yourself short. You have a way of getting to people."

Adam Wharton received her with what she thought was cordial reserve. His greeting was warm enough, and his invitation to enjoy coffee and donuts seemed sincere. But it was evident there was a wall, a barricade, behind which he had retreated when she entered the room.

"Are you making any progress in tracking down Harry's murderer?" he inquired.

"Leads, but nothing very promising. That's why I've come to talk with you."

"I don't see how I can be of help. I haven't the faintest idea of who Harry's assailant might be."

"Often the people we question have information they're not aware of that bears on an investigation."

"So you think I might be a subconscious bearer of vital information?"

"Possibly. I don't want to overplay the subconscious stuff. I plan to be as explicit as possible. I'm going to tell you where our investigation is leading and why we don't like being moved in that direction."

"I take it, from your remark, that you suspect a person you'd rather not believe is a murderer."

"Several persons are suspect, including yourself, on very simple, but logical grounds."

Wharton smiled. He seemed amused but also a trifle miffed. "So you have me on your list. I'm curious why you think I belong there."

"The murder weapon. A crossbow is not an ordinary weapon, not readily available like a knife or a gun. Nor easily disposed of. Few people could get their hands on one and even fewer would think of using it to commit murder. So, in lining up suspects, we have to consider everyone who had access to a crossbow and knew how to use one."

"I see. And since I am a crossbow hunter, I qualify as a suspect."

"As a possible only. In addition to knowing how to use that weapon, the murderer had to have a motive. As of now, we don't know of any reason why you would want to kill Mr. Paulson. You and he seem to have been best friends."

"Then, of what use can I be to you?"

"When a husband is killed, the police are inclined, almost reflexively, to suspect the wife. So we turned our attention to Lucinda Paulson."

Wharton looked at Fulford sharply as if he could scarcely believe what she had said. "Surely you don't suspect her merely because she's Harry's wife?"

"Not without other evidence. But look at it from our perspective. She knows how to use a crossbow and she had access to one. She also had opportunity. She could have followed her husband the night of his murder, shot him in the back, returned to the house, and hung the weapon on the wall in its usual place."

Wharton nodded. The look he gave her was both respectful and disparaging. "But you're stymied because you don't have a motive?"

"That's where you come in," Fulford said. "We think you may be able to supply us with a possible motive."

Wharton shook his head in astonishment. "You think I can place one of my best friends under suspicion of having killed her husband? That's remarkably presumptuous."

"Not really," Fulford replied, "when you look at it dispassionately. We assume you're as eager to apprehend Paulson's murderer as we are. That you want justice done even if someone you like and respect has to be implicated."

"That's mighty high ground you're on, young lady. I'd say unrealistically high."

"Too high for you, Mr. Wharton?" Fulford asked, scornfully. "Would you let loyalty to a friend overwhelm your sense of duty?"

Wharton smiled. "You know how to manipulate people, don't you?"

"I suggest you seriously consider the implications if you refuse to cooperate with us."

"You've made your point. How can I help you?"

"We've been told that Harry was unfaithful to his wife, that, in fact, over the years he had a string of extramarital affairs."

She searched Wharton's face for signs of denial. There were none. She went on. "That fact suggested two possibilities to us. One, that Lucinda lost her patience and did away with her husband, and, two . . ."

Wharton did not let her finish. "That's rubbish. I've known Lucinda for years. She could never do such a thing."

"What makes you so sure?"

"She's not a violent person. She'd never harm another human being. And, besides, I don't think she knew about Harry's indiscretions."

"Surely you don't believe that. Paulson's indiscretions were pretty obvious to other people. Lucinda must have picked up on them, or someone must have told her."

"If she did know, and I truly think she didn't, she would have forgiven him. She is a generous, understanding person."

"Well, let's let that pass. Paulson's womanizing suggested to us the possibility that one of his former mistresses, angry at being discarded, decided to get even by planting a bolt in his back."

Wharton shook his head in disbelief. "I suppose the police have to think of everything, no matter how unlikely."

"We do. And what I've suggested to you is not so unlikely. You were close to him. You must have known the women he had. Or at least some of them. Can you think of one who might have been angry enough at him to want to kill him?"

Wharton picked up a piece of scrimshaw from his desk. He fondled the tusk with evident pleasure, eyeing it from several angles, then looked up at Fulford. "This kind of thing bothers me. It's too much like tale-telling in school. But I suppose I'm obligated to help you in whatever way I can. First, let me say, Harry did not have a string of mistresses as you suppose. He would stick with the same woman for years. He and Cheryl Hargert were together for three or four years at least. Their relationship broke up some time ago, presumably because Harry found a more desirable woman. Or he simply got tired of her. I don't know who his new woman was. I don't think anyone knows. You could ask Cheryl. She might know."

"Do you think Cheryl, herself, could have murdered Harry?"

"I've heard he ended their relationship rather abruptly and without much feeling. Maybe she did something that angered him and he broke it off to pay her back. As for your question 'Could she have done it?' let me quote a line from an old radio mystery show I used to listen to, 'Who knows what evil lurks in the hearts of men' or women."

"Do you know if Hargert knew anything about crossbows, or ever had occasion to use one?"

"She was Harry's executive assistant and he took her with him to business conventions. Ordinarily, he didn't take her on pleasure trips because his wife was along. One time, a year or two ago, she went with him to a crossbow competition he and I had entered. I remember Cheryl competed in the novice class. Apparently, Harry had taught her the rudiments and let her enroll for the fun of it. She wasn't very good, I recall."

"Do you know if she ever owned a crossbow?"

"I'd have no way of knowing. But I doubt it. Unless you're a game hunter or an enthusiast who's into competition, you'd be unlikely to own one."

"Did you work late the night of Paulson's murder?"

"Till about seven o'clock."

"Was Cheryl working with you?"

"I think so. I'd have to check."

Fulford found his answers, if true, an alibi for himself and, perhaps, for Hargert. But she had never considered them suspects, anyway. Having gotten all the information from him she could reasonably expect, she stood up and extended her hand in good-bye. He remained seated, and kept his hands flat on the desk before him. She ignored the rebuff. "You've been a big help, Mr. Wharton. I understand your reluctance to say anything about the Paulson's private lives. I regret I had to pry into their affairs."

Wharton's smile carried a trace of distaste. "I'm glad I don't have your job. Don't think I could stomach it for very long."

While Fulford was questioning Adam Wharton, Davis paid a visit to the hospital. Gearhart's doctor had, early that morning, informed him that Gearhart was sufficiently recovered from his coma to be briefly questioned.

As Davis stood outside Gearhart's room, the doctor warned him that the patient was still in serious condition and should not be subjected to too much stress. Stress might cause a relapse. The doctor wanted to remain in the room so he could terminate the interview if Gearhart showed signs of extreme distress. Davis agreed.

Gearhart turned his head apprehensively toward the door as the two entered. The toll taken by his fall was evident. His pale skin and sunken cheeks were signs of a weakened physique and long confinement. He seemed disturbed by Davis's presence, but he said nothing.

"I'm glad you're recovering," Davis said. "You took a nasty fall."

"Thanks to you," Gearhart said resentfully. Self-pity and a desire to transfer blame colored his voice.

Davis shook his head in negation. "Sorry. I can't take the blame for the fall you took. You acted like an idiot. What got into you anyway?" He paused, his expression quizzical. "The only charge against you was battery on Paulson. There was no murder charge. Yet, instead of appearing in court on this relatively minor count you took a powder, and hid. Did you believe you could hide forever? Your bondsman tracked you down easily."

Tears glistened in Gearhart's eyes. "I knew you guys were going to set me up for Paulson's murder. I knew it. You needed a fall guy. But I didn't kill him. Why should I to go to jail for something I didn't do?"

Davis shook his head. "We weren't trying to railroad you. We *thought* you might have killed Paulson, but we had no evidence to support an indictment and we weren't about to fabricate any. Your running away only strengthened our belief you might have been the killer."

Tears flowed slowly down Gearhart's cheeks.

"I knew you'd find out," he said.

Startled, Davis asked, "Find out what?"

"That I knew how to use a crossbow and could get my hands on one whenever I wanted." As he made that admission, he cowered as if he had just sealed his conviction for murder.

Davis concealed his surprise. "How could you get a crossbow? We searched your place and didn't find one. Did you hide it somewhere else?"

"I didn't have to hide it. It was available whenever I wanted it. I don't own it. It belongs to the Society of Animal Conservators."

"What are the Animal Conservators doing with a crossbow?"

"They've got a number of weapons, not just a crossbow. They've got a longbow, a shotgun, a rifle, a machine pistol, even a grenade thrower. We use these weapons when we give public lectures to demonstrate the cruelty of hunting. We show our audience what ghastly weapons these things are."

"Do you give such lectures?"

"A lot. We get requests from schools, service clubs, and organizations like that for lectures on hunting. We've even given the program before legislative committees. We try to impress people with the brutality of these weapons, especially how devastating it is for an animal to be wounded by one of them as often happens. The wounded animal escapes to die an agonizing death."

"What's with the grenade thrower? Surely you don't contend people hunt with grenade throwers?"

"No. We use it to demonstrate that the pellets from an automatic shotgun, three blasts in quick succession, are just as devastating as if the hunter used a hand grenade. And just as lacking in sportsmanship."

Davis, in spite of his professionally-induced cynicism, thought Gearhart was sincere. But he knew the kind of sincerity exhibited by zealots, could harden a man's will enough to condone murder.

After a moment, he said, "You're right about one thing. We would have found out, given time, that you had access to a crossbow. And I suppose that our knowing about it, would have made us more suspicious of you than ever."

"Of course. So you see why I tried to run away?"

Davis looked at the pathetic, fearful man lying propped up in bed before him, his head wrapped in a huge bandage. In an uncharacteristic display of feeling, he gave him a sympathetic clap on the shoulder, "Hope you feel better."

Gearhart shrank from his touch. "Yeah. I bet you do."

CHAPTER EIGHTEEN

Gerald Fillmore was behaving his worst. He was unreasonable, irascible, and unbending. Stung by the press clamoring for an arrest in the Paulson case, he was demanding that Davis throw someone in jail.

"The press has been chewing my ass for days. They want to know why we haven't made any progress. Are we going to be as slow as the Boulder, Colorado cops were in the killing of that juvenile beauty queen? Will we ever make an arrest? I've been scorched, I don't mind telling you."

He assumed a put-upon look that was supposed to show how hard it was to deal with rapacious reporters.

Davis tried to be sympathetic, an emotion he did not feel. "You know we have to be careful, Gerry. We can't go off half-cocked and arrest someone without evidence to back us up."

"Why haven't you charged Basil Gearhart? You've got the goods on him. His alibis are phony. He had motive. He had opportunity. Now your latest report shows he had access to the weapon, to a crossbow. What more do you want?"

"His phony alibis, as you call them, may very well stand up in court. If Thelma Wilcox gets her mind in gear and testifies he spent the afternoon fucking her, we're done for. We're not sure what she'll say yet, so we can't take the risk. We think Madelin Gelbart's assertion that he was in the headquarters of the Society of Animal Conservators at the time of the murder is probably false. But there's no way in the world we can prove it. Also, we can't prove he took a crossbow from the weapons cache held by Gelbart's society. He could have. But no one saw him take it and no one saw him put it back. We do have a couple of other suspects who had motivation and opportunity to kill Paulson."

He hoped the revelation that there were other suspects would dampen Fillmore's insistence on arresting Gearhart.

"And who are they?" Fillmore made the question sound as if he thought Davis was just being inventive.

"Well, Lucinda Paulson's a good possibility. She had motive. Her husband had been cheating on her for years. And she knew it. Until recently he was getting it on with Cheryl Hargert, his executive assistant. Took her everywhere with him, she said, and she thought they were a permanent duo. Then recently, not more than a few months ago, he suddenly dumped her for another woman. We haven't been able to find out who the new woman is, but the grapevine says Lucinda was enraged when she found out. Cheryl Hargert said she overheard Lucinda threaten Paulson about it."

Fillmore smiled in a deprecating way. "If she knew about his little adventures, and put up with them for years, why did she suddenly decide to kill him for it?"

"We think because his new woman was someone Lucinda couldn't stand. The thought of her husband making love to this new one was more than she could take."

"A lot of guess-work involved here," Fillmore said. "But, in the majority of domestic murders, the spouse is the killer." He paused, then said hopefully, "Are you going to arrest her?"

"Not unless we find more evidence. If you were on a jury would you convict her of her husband's murder on the basis of what we've just outlined?"

"Probably not. Who else have you got?"

Fulford answered. "Cheryl Hargert, herself. I had a long talk with her and she took being cast aside pretty hard. Paulson was brutal about it. He not only dumped her, he demoted her to a lesser job. She says she's reconciled herself to the situation, but I got the impression she's still nursing a bundle of anger and hatred. She also knows how to use a crossbow. Paulson taught her on one of the trips he took to participate in an archery contest. She even competed in an amateur shoot. However, we don't know how she could have got her hands on a crossbow the day of the murder. Biggest obstacle of all, she says her present boss, Roger Godwin, will give her an alibi for the time of Paulson's murder. According to her, they were both working late that night."

"I don't see how you can call her a viable suspect," Fillmore said. "She's got too many ifs on her side."

"Yeah," said Fulford. "It looks as if we're grasping at straws, doesn't it?"

"Well, God damn it," Fillmore exploded. "You've got to arrest somebody. Go do it."

When they returned to his office, Davis said, "I think we'd better confront Lucinda and make some threats. Tell her Cheryl Hargert's story, make her think Adam Wharton gave us some damaging facts, and see if we can't panic her into saying or doing something incriminating."

Fulford concurred, but reluctantly. "Do you really think she killed him?"

"I don't know. She had reason to and I think, in spite of what Wharton told us, she's a hard woman, who if given enough provocation, could and would resort to violence."

"Why don't we just go and arrest her? Hargert's story is enough to establish a presumption, isn't it?"

"Yes, but we don't have a shred of physical evidence to place her at the crime scene. And we don't know who the woman is, who supposedly, made her so furious when she learned Paulson was seeing her. I think we'd have a tough time getting the prosecutor to go along with what we've got. Lets keep digging. One of these days we're bound to hit gold."

Fulford shook her head. "I wish I could share your optimism."

She stood up, went to the window, and looked out at the street below. Car were beginning to jam up in the first of the evening rush hour. She turned to Davis. "You know what's odd about this case? We've got three possible suspects, each one about as likely as the other, and there's nothing to tip the scale toward any one of them. At the moment, I favor Lucinda, but I don't know why. Maybe because Cheryl Hargert has an alibi I trust, and Basil Gearhart's got two alibis, both of which could be bogus."

Davis, who felt their relationship had improved enough to bear a little humor, said, "Good thinking, Leda. Woman's intuition replaces masculine logic."

It was the wrong thing to say. She spoke harshly. "You sound like Gerry Fillmore, Wade. I'm getting sick of it." She turned her back abruptly and stared silently out at the street.

The tense atmosphere was relieved by the appearance of Gerry Fillmore. His face reflected the seriousness of his message. "Here's an item for you guys to chew on. Yesterday Gretchen Paulson tried to commit suicide. Took a bunch of sleeping pills washed down with a heavy dose of vodka. They got her to the hospital in time to empty her stomach and she's going to be okay. Hopefully no brain damage. But it was a near thing."

"How did you find this out?" Davis asked. "Families don't advertise that sort of thing."

"They took her to the same hospital where we're holding Basil Gearhart. The officer on duty saw her brought in and leaned on one of the aides for details."

Fulford, surprised at the news, looked at Davis. "I can't believe it! We've really got a weird family here, Wade. Dad was a philanderer who got himself offed, presumable, by a previous mistress. Mom is playing house with her husband's partner. Oldest daughter aspires to be a Barbie but lacks the equipment, and, consequently, suffers low self-esteem. Youngest daughter, who was Daddy's favorite, has all the right equipment physically to be a Barbie, but is an emotional mess and tries to take her life. Talk about dysfunctional!"

"Yeah," Davis said. "They're a mess. Somewhere in that mess lies the key to Daddy's murder. All we have to do is find it."

"Any ideas on where to start?"

Fillmore spoke up. "I'd start by finding out why Gretchen tried to kill herself. A lot of times, suicides aren't really trying to kill themselves. But just trying to get attention, calling for help."

"Leda," Davis said, "do you feel up to a talk with Lucinda Paulson?"

"If she'll talk to me, which I doubt. She'll know I'm going to quiz her about her daughter's suicide attempt and will probably refuse to see me."

"Well, give it a try."

Lucinda was more cooperative than Fulford had expected. Instead of being hostile, she appeared to welcome the opportunity to discuss her daughter's attempted suicide. She asked Fulford to have lunch in her home and when she arrived, Lucinda seated her at a table set with expensive linen and sterling silver. Lunch was crab salad on a bed of romaine lettuce with warm rolls and butter. The dessert was blackberry sorbet. They talked as they ate.

"Gretchen has always been a precocious child, both physically and mentally. She has the figure of a mature woman, and gets noticed by men wherever she goes. I suppose this has not been good for her. I know it has caused friction between her and her sister. Kimberly is as thin as a rail and plain as an old shoe. She resents Gretchen's looks and, when Harry was alive, she resented the fact he openly favored her sister."

"Are you suggesting Gretchen's relationship with her father may somehow be related to her suicide attempt?"

"Perhaps. I think Gretchen has begun to feel guilty about how she overshadowed Kimberly in her father's esteem. The distance between the girls has widened since Harry's death. Kimberly conceals her hostility, but it's there. Gretchen senses it and deals with it by withdrawal. For several weeks now she has just gone into a shell."

"Have you seen any other changes in Gretchen's behavior, besides withdrawal? That, in itself, could have been a sign of growing depression?"

Lucinda toyed with a bite of crab salad and carefully considered her answer. A dark shadow of some bleak emotion flitted over her face. "Hindsight is always better that foresight, isn't it?" she said. "Your question makes me feel guilty. Yes, there were things that might have aroused my concern if I had read them properly. I've said that she began avoiding Kimberly. That's true. But Greta's avoidance went beyond just Kimberly. She withdrew in other ways, too. She spent a lot of time alone in her room. She'd come home after school, go into her room, and stay there until supper time. Instead of playing music, as she had always done, or reading a romance novel, she would lie in bed with her eyes closed. When I called her for dinner, she was hard to rouse. Then at table she'd eat in an abstracted way and avoid conversation with me and Kimberly."

"Did you ever ask her what was wrong?"

"Yes. She said only that she was thinking about her future and what she would become when she grew up."

"Anything else?"

"She had always been neat and proud of her looks. She'd spend hours fixing her hair and putting on makeup. After her father died, there was a gradual change. She became careless of her physical appearance and tended to be sloppy in the clothes she wore."

"Wasn't she was just grieving at the loss of her father?"

"Yes, but the odd thing is, it didn't happen immediately after his death, as you would expect. It was a week or two later that she began showing behavior changes. Maybe it just took time for the loss to sink in."

"A delayed reaction like that happens sometimes. How is she now?"

"Not good. She's still withdrawn, depressed. I think her mind has been affected by all that has happened in these past weeks. Sometimes she acts as if she doesn't know me or Kimberly. She'll just stare right through us. She has taken to chewing her fingernails and she picks at her cuticles till they bleed. Those things are so unlike her, I could almost believe she has become another person."

She looked into Fulford's eyes for sympathy. She wore an expression of concern, of grief and apprehension, but Fulford had the distinct impression she was exaggerating Gretchen's condition. She chided herself for that thought. Was police work making her cynical? Was she, out of an habitually suspicious bent of mind, unable any longer to credit people with genuine emotion? She tried not to let Lucinda see her skepticism.

"Mrs. Paulson. Do you think your daughter is mentally ill?"

"Something's wrong with her. She's not normal, I know that. She's not the girl she used to be. I don't know what you'd call her condition. She's been acting so strange for a long time now. Her attempt at suicide was just the climax of a terrible emotional upheaval. The doctor thinks she is still suicide prone."

"Are you getting help for her?"

"I'm taking her to a psychiatrist tomorrow."

Fulford nodded approval. "I'm sure he'll be able to help her. If there's anything at all I can do, please let me know." She listened to the words she had just uttered. Trite and insincere, they provided a proper exit line but she didn't leave. She framed a question she had been wary of asking because she believed Lucinda would refuse to answer or would lie about it. She asked it anyway.

"When I last talked to the girls, Gretchen revealed she had recently been hospitalized. I suppose it's none of my business, but I'm wondering if illness might have played a role in her depression."

Lucinda's response was immediate and, Fulford thought, a smooth gloss over Gretchen's ailment.

"Oh, that. It had nothing to do with her emotional state. It was just an intestinal bug that seriously dehydrated her. It took a day or two to get her back on her feet. I don't see how it could have anything to do with her present state."

"Well, I just thought I'd ask."

She had got the answer she expected. After rising from the table and thanking her hostess, she excused herself and left.

When she returned to the division, she saw Davis standing at the coffee machine. He was pounding it in exasperation, trying to make the cup drop into place before the coffee all spilled down the drain. "Damn this machine," he growled. "This is the second cup in a week I've lost. This is supposed to be the age of technological wonders. Ha! A coffee machine should be simple to use. But this one? Half the time all it does is elevate my blood pressure."

"Hey," Fulford said, "calm down. Try this." She handed him a fifty-cent piece.

He dropped it in the slot, the cup fell into place, and, to his satisfaction, was soon filled with steaming coffee.

"Thanks, Leda. Your money seems to work better that mine." He took a sip. "You want a cup. I'll risk another half-buck if you do."

"Thanks. I tanked up at lunch with Mrs. Paulson."

"How'd it go?"

"Surprising. She seemed almost eager to talk about Gretchen. I asked her about Gretchen's hospitalization and she tossed that off as a mere nothing. I got the distinct impression, however, she wanted me to know the girl had emotional problems. She implied she might even be off-balance mentally."

She repeated what Lucinda had told her of the changes in Gretchen's behavior.

"Sounds like she might be on drugs," Davis said. "We'd better get some expert advice on that possibility."

When Caleb Burton called and asked her for a date, she was surprised. She scarcely knew the man. She had met him once in Davis's office and again when her brother David had been arrested for possession. He seemed clean-cut and decent enough, but he hadn't kindled any fire in her. However, she was still somewhat pissed at Davis and saw Caleb's invitation as an opportunity to show her independence and perhaps make Davis a little jealous. And, a thought stirred in the back of her mind; maybe she could get Caleb to help in David's defense.

"Generally, I don't like semi-documentary movies," she said when he named what he wanted to see, "but I've heard a lot of good things about *Midnight in the Garden of Good and Evil.*"

"What say we have dinner first. The movie starts at seven-thirty. I'll pick you up at six. Okay?"

He took her to a restaurant that while, not exactly a fast-food place, was geared to something that couldn't be called leisurely dining. In fact, the waitresses, with management's demand for fast turnover drummed into their heads, were known to snatch an entree plate from under a startled diner's nose a few seconds after the last bite was being chewed and swallowed. Caleb recommended a sirloin steak plate which Fulford reluctantly agreed to order. It consisted of watery mashed potatoes, string beans that were overcooked, and a thin bronze-colored steak that, when chewed, left sinewy fibers lodged in her teeth.

"I hope my transfer to homicide is okayed," Caleb said. "I'm eager to work with you and Wade, and the other people in the division."

"I think you'd fit in nicely," Fulford said politely.

They ate the rest of their meal in silence. Fulford felt an almost irresistible urge to question Caleb about her brother's case, but she held back for strategic reasons.

Caleb glanced at his watch as they ate their dessert, apple pie a la mode. She was pleasantly surprised. It was delicious.

She found the movie fascinating. Such odd and appealing characters. Lady Chablis, the brazen transvestite, was her favorite, but, Jim, the leading man, a charming, devious homosexual antique dealer, accused of killing his young male lover was intriguing. His acquittal, after a trial in which evidence of a dubious nature played a major role, made her think again of her brother's predicament.

When the movie ended, Caleb invited her to have a nightcap in his apartment. She went solely for the purpose of finding possible advantage for her brother. Caleb poured her a glass of wine and said, "Did you like the movie?"

"The characters were. . .well, memorable. The fact they were real people made them even more interesting to me. I don't know if the author had any such thing in mind, but I was struck with the notion of moral ambiguity. Good and evil are sometimes interwoven in the same person and in the things a person does."

She stopped abruptly, struck again by the possible relevance of her observation to her brother David's upcoming trial. An expression of detachment, of inner probing came over her face.

Burton, sensing what was in her mind, said, "You're thinking about your brother, aren't you, wondering if he could actually be guilty?"

She shook her head—negatively. "No. I'm certain he's not."

"Well, I don't know about his guilt," Burton responded. "But this I do know. If he insists on claiming innocence and goes to trial, there's no doubt whatsoever he'll be convicted. He'll get a jail term and a felony record. Isn't there some way you can talk sense into him?"

"I've tried, believe me, and so have his Mom and Dad. He insists he won't confess to something he didn't do. And I really believe he's innocent."

"Well, he might be. Any man willing to risk his freedom and his good name against such odds must be telling the truth."

Fulford, frustration written all over her face, said, "Is there anything at all, Caleb, we can do to help him?"

Caleb eyed Fulford as if to measure how she'd react to what he was about to say. "If something happened to the evidence, if, somehow it got messed up, David's attorney could move for dismissal."

"How could it get messed up? Do you mean contaminated or stolen? You hold evidence in a secure place, don't you?"

"Yes, but evidence has gone missing before. I'm not suggesting stealing it. That would be very risky. I'm thinking it could simply be misplaced so the prosecutor couldn't find it at the time of the trial. That could be done easily, and with little risk. Lacking evidence, the prosecutor couldn't go on with the case."

"Wouldn't the prosecution move for a continuance to try and locate the stuff?"

"Probably. But unless the prosecutor could convince the judge the evidence could be recovered very quickly, she's likely to side with a defense motion to exclude."

Fulford looked Burton squarely in the face. "Why are you telling me this, Caleb?" She tried to read the expression on his face. "Are you suggesting you could misplace the evidence against David?"

Burton spoke in a husky voice, "I would do it..." He hesitated. looking sharply at her. "If I got something in return."

Fulford, astonished as the meaning of his words became clear, said, "Let me get this straight, Caleb. You're willing to risk jeopardizing you career if you got something in return. From me, I assume. Just what do you have in mind?"

"Well, you know...you being nice to me."

She knew what 'being nice' meant. Burton was offering to help her brother in return for sex. So, why didn't she tell Burton to go to hell and stomp out of his apartment in a virtuous rage? Instead, she thought of her brother's peril. The image of him confined for years in a jail cell with nothing but a bunk bed, a wash stand, and a seatless aluminum toilet rose in her mind to torment her. In a wave of emotion, she spoke without forethought, heedless of consequences.

"If you could pull this off, Caleb, I'd be nice to you—really nice."

She spoke out of reckless abandon. Saving her brother was all that mattered. Her judgment was clouded by that overwhelming need.

"I assure you, I can pull it off," Caleb said, as he let his hand rest on her thigh.

"Not so fast." She pushed his hand away. "You're not getting a down payment."

(HAPTEr NINETEEN

The police psychiatrist, a young man fresh out of graduate school imbued with the latest theories on aberrant behavior and anxious to apply them to actual cases, welcomed Davis and Fulford with enthusiasm.

"Hi. I'm Major Smith." He smiled at them. "If either of you want to try making a joke about Major as a name, please do so now, so we can get on with our business." He paused expectantly.

"Okay," said Davis. "Your name is of only minor significance to us."

Smith chuckled with genuine amusement. "That's not the worst I've heard, but it's not the best, either."

"I didn't give it much thought," Davis replied.

"So much for the preliminaries," Smith said. His good humor seemed genuine, a man who liked people, a man happy in his job. "I'm glad to see a couple of detectives in need of help. I haven't been consulted much since I took over this job. Only one case of interest since I came aboard. Maybe you remember the serial arsonist who got referred to our division because two people died in his last torch job."

"I remember him," Davis said. "You drew an interesting profile of the guy. Unfortunately, he hasn't yet been caught."

"So I've heard. If investigators depend very heavily on my profiles to lead them to a perp, they're bound to be disappointed. The trouble with such profiles is that, while they may fit a criminal, they can fit a lot of ordinary people as well."

"I'm not sure we're looking for a profile," Davis said. "More like an opinion about the behavior of a young, sixteen year-old girl, called Gretchen, who tried to commit suicide after her father's death. The odd thing is this girl has a sister, Kimberly, who seems to be coping perfectly well. Kimberly suffered the same loss as Gretchen, but never, as far as we can tell, thought of suicide or teetered on the brink of mental collapse. So we wonder why one daughter adjusts well and the other tries to kill herself. Why one copes and the other suffers severe personality changes."

Davis told Smith of the changes Lucinda Paulson had observed in Gretchen's behavior following the suicide attempt.

Smith was especially interested in Gretchen's untidy personal habits and her penchant for biting her fingers and mutilating her cuticles.

"You tell me this girl is attractive physically and in the past was proud of her appearance. Now she's become slovenly, neglects her hair, and uses no make up. Moreover she picks at herself as if she were carrion. What does that suggest to you?"

Fulford responded. "Loss of self-esteem."

"Exactly. And a person can lose self-esteem because he or she has done something they know to be wrong. So what has Gretchen done wrong? You tell me her father was murdered. Does she think she was, in some way, responsible for his death? It's not uncommon for children to feel that way after a parent dies."

"We don't know if she blames herself, but if she does would that be enough to drive her to suicide?" Davis asked.

"If she felt that some action of her's endangered him. Often children imagine they have somehow contributed to a parent's death. Such feelings are irrational, but they seem very real to the subject."

"Okay," Davis said. "Let's assume for the moment she *doesn't* imagine she was responsible for her Dad's death. What else could make her show such behavior changes?"

"She might be experiencing guilt over something she has done, some kind of behavior she knows is wrong."

"Like what?"

"The ripeness of her development suggests she might have been a target for sexual abuse possibly by a member of the family or by a close friend of the family. That would make her despise her own body, cause her to pick her nails and cuticles, and neglect her appearance. It would also explain her withdrawal, her loss of interest in family and friends."

Fulford ventured an opinion. "Her father was the only male in the household, and we know for a fact, he had sexual partners outside the home. Are you suggesting he might have molested his own daughter?"

"We can never be sure about such things, Miss Fulford. There are many clinical cases of fathers having an incestuous relationship with one of their daughters. But it's also possible Gretchen had an affair at school or with a neighbor boy. Maybe she engaged in oral or anal sex, acts she, herself, thinks of as wrong. As a result she could have become obsessed with shame, seeing herself, now, as dirty, unworthy. That, rather than a sense of responsibility for her father's death, could have been the cause of her changed behavior."

Davis nodded. "Are you of the opinion, Dr. Smith, that, all things considered, Gretchen's problem is rooted in some kind of sexual behavior?"

"Not necessarily. But it seems highly probable."

As they rose to leave, Fulford could not resist saying. "You've had a major impact on our thinking."

Smith chuckled. "It never fails!"

"You don't believe Harry Paulson was screwing his own daughter, do you?" Davis inquired.

He and Fulford were drinking coffee and reflecting on the opinions expressed by Major Smith.

"I wouldn't put it past him," Fulford said. "Men like him are always on the lookout for new sexual kicks. Biggest obstacle to that scenario, however, is how he could keep it from his wife and Kimberly."

Davis gave that a thought. "Maybe it wouldn't be so hard. He and Lucinda slept in separate rooms. So did Gretchen and Kimberly. What was to prevent him from slipping out to Gretchen's room after the rest of the household was asleep. After he'd had his little fling with Gretchen, he could slip back into his own room easily enough. In the morning no one would be the wiser."

"But what about Gretchen? Wouldn't she have had a tough time facing her mom and sister after one of those nocturnal visitations?"

"Why not call Major Smith and ask?"

Fulford rang him and posed the question of Gretchen's probable response if she had been abused by her father. She put the phone on speaker as he responded. "A child who has been repeatedly sexually abused by a respected adult has to learn to accept the situation in order to survive. Children develop coping mechanisms, one of the most common one is to make the behavior seem acceptable. Was Gretchen close to her father?"

"She was his favorite and she adored him."

"That would help her adapt. She could make herself believe she was in love with her father and that he was in love with her. Everything would then have been all right in her mind. She may even have treasured the affair, thought of herself as having a special relationship with her dad."

"So it wouldn't have been hard for her to confront the rest of the family."

"Might even have made her feel superior."

"Then why," Davis inquired, "her sudden plunge into depression?"

"Maybe she thought her relationship with him had something to do with his death." He paused expectantly. "If so, she would be plagued with overwhelming guilt."

"Enough to drive her to suicide?"

"Could very well be."

The two looked at one another, their expressions quizzical.

"Thanks," Fulford said. "You've been a big help." She hung up the phone. "Well, that opinion opens up a new avenue of speculation, doesn't it?"

"More than speculation," Davis said, "I'd call it a major breakthrough. No pun intended. I think it comes close to putting a noose around Lucinda Paulson's neck. We said that Lucinda might have been motivated to kill her husband because she found out he was having an affair with another woman, a woman she couldn't stomach. We were assuming the other woman would be an adult. What a jolt to Lucinda if she discovered she was her own daughter!"

"If that's what happened," Fulford cautioned. "We're placing a lot of credence in Major Smith's opinions. He cautioned us not to do that."

"I know. We can't condemn Lucinda on guesswork. So where do we go from here?"

"I'm not sure. I've had a nagging feeling, however, that Gretchen's illness has something to do with the case. I think we should find out why she went to the hospital a few weeks before her father died."

"That won't be easy. Legally, medical records are sacrosanct."

David Fulford's trial on the charge of possession was just two days away. Fulford's mind was filled with alarm over what she and Caleb Burton had conspired to do. The full import of it suddenly seemed to hit her.

Filled with dread, she rang up Burton. When he answered she said, "Caleb, I'm getting cold feet. I don't want you to touch that evidence."

"What do you mean?" Burton said hastily. "I don't know what you're talking about. I'm glad you called, however. I'll be in your neighborhood this morning on business. Why don't we meet for coffee someplace?"

Fulford realized her mistake. Since David's arrest, she seemed to have lost all sense of reason. Burton's terse response told her that she should not have called on his office line. Her words might have been be overheard by unintended ears, placing both of them in peril. "Okay," she said. "Meet me at the Burger King at ten."

"I'll be there."

At ten o'clock she sat in a booth waiting. When Burton arrived, he was still upset. Scowling, he carried a cup of coffee to the booth and sat down opposite her.

"Why in the devil did you call me at the office? We're playing a dangerous game, Leda. If I get caught, it means jail time. Probably the same thing for you."

Fulford winced at the prospect. To have endangered him and herself by a stupid act was unconscionable. Where had her mind been? Suddenly she saw the whole idea of tampering with evidence for what it was. A despicable folly!

"I want to abort the whole thing," she said. "It's not only illegal, it's morally wrong. Don't do it, Caleb."

"It's too late, Leda," he said ruefully. "It's already done."

"You destroyed the drugs that were in David's car?"

"Nothing so drastic. I simply misplaced them. I changed the name on the bags from Fulford to Buford and filed them under B. It would take days before anyone could untangle the mess. And no one would know what happened. It would appear to be a simple mistake."

Fulford winced in anxiety. "My God, Caleb. What a risk that was." She shook her head at their ill-starred plot. "David's trial is not until Monday." She said decisively. "I want you to go back and put those evidence bags where they belong. You understand? We've got to call this whole thing off."

"Okay," Burton said in quick agreement. "But putting the stuff back doubles the risk of getting caught." He looked at the floor, then picked an imaginary piece of lint from his sleeve, dropped it on the table. "I'll do it as soon as I can."

He paused. "And everything else is off, too, I guess."

Fulford could hardly believe his effrontery. "Jesus, Caleb! What do you think."

Monday morning, Fulford sat in courtroom 126 awaiting her brother's appearance. The lawyer she had hired, Orville Samson, a man who had represented dozens of drug offenders, had repeatedly sought to persuade David to change his plea to guilty and escape conviction on a felony charge. David continued to maintain the drugs had been planted in his car. He refused to enter a guilty plea. Leda's entreaties, added to those of his attorney, continued to be of no avail.

After conferring with Leda, David's attorney opted for a bench trial, believing no jury in the world would believe David's uncorroborated story. A judge on the other hand, while doubting David's story, might be compassionate enough to give him a break. Judge Owen Shelfer, who was to hear the case, was, unfortunately, not renowned for legal generosity.

"Our best hope," Samson told David and Leda as they sat awaiting the appearance of Judge Shelfer, "is to get the evidence quashed. From what you've told me, David, I may be able to show the arresting officers lacked probable cause to search your car. But first I want to determine if the evidence has been properly handled. You'd be surprised how often the police contaminate evidence by careless handling."

The opportunity for further discussion ended when Judge Shelfer appeared and the clerk admonished, "All rise." The clerk then spoke the formal legal words, "Calendar 19—case 201. The State of Georgia vs David William Fulford."

The prosecutor, Vernon Kline, presented his case in short and simple fashion. "On September twenty-fifth, defendant was stopped for a traffic violation, namely running a red light. A specially trained K9 Corps dog, smelled the odor of marijuana coming from the trunk of Mr. Fulford's car. Mr. Fulford gave the officers his key, they opened the trunk and discovered an ounce and a half of marijuana and ten grams of methamphetamine in a package bound with masking tape. Mr. Fulford denies having placed the drugs in his car trunk and contends they were put there by some one else. He has been unable to name the person or persons who put the drugs in his car and has been unable to suggest how they managed to do so. The trunk of the car shows no evidence of having been forced or otherwise being tampered with.

"Given these facts, there can be no doubt Mr. Fulford is guilty of possessing two controlled substances and should be punished accordingly."

He offered two brown paper bags containing drugs as people's exhibit number one and sat down with a satisfied expression, as if he were assured of a favorable verdict.

Judge Shelfer examined paper work relating to the case and then peered over his glasses at David's lawyer. "Your client has pleaded not guilty, Mr. Samson. What do you have to say in his behalf?"

Samson arose and spoke, a grave expression on his face. "I should like to examine people's exhibit number one," he said, as he walked over to the clerk's desk and picked up the two brown packages. He examined them minutely, and with a face expressing puzzlement, said. "Your Honor, the name 'Fulford' on these exhibits appears to be smudged as if erased and rewritten. If a name has been erased, I am entitled to know why the erasure took place and what name was deleted. I think the matter calls into question whether these bags contain the actual contraband allegedly taken from Mr. Fulford's car."

"You are indeed entitled to be concerned," the judge replied. He then turned to the prosecutor. "Mr. Kline, can you explain why these exhibits show an apparent erasure?"

"Yes, your Honor. A very simple mistake was made when the evidence was catalogued. Someone misread Fulford as Buford. Upon discovering the mistake, instead of affixing an entirely new label with the proper name, he or she—we do not know who actually made the mistake—simply erased the mistaken name and wrote the proper one, Fulford."

Leda Fulford looked across the room at Caleb Burton. Burton met her glance momentarily, then dropped his eyes.

Samson shook his head as if he could scarcely believe what he had heard. "Your Honor, given the careless handling of people's exhibit number one, handling which makes doubtful whether the contraband in these two bags is actually what was taken from David Fulford's car, I move the evidence be suppressed and Mr. Fulford found not guilty."

"Not so fast, Mr. Samson. I'm not sure if serious doubt exists about this being the contraband taken from Fulford's car. Mr. Kline, was the evidence lost or contaminated in any way?"

"No, your Honor. All that happened was the bags were mislabeled at first and the packages filed away alphabetically. When the error was discovered, the wrong name was erased, the right name substituted, and the drugs were properly stored."

Judge Shelfer rubbed his chin, adjusted his glasses and after a moment's reflection, said, "For the time being, the motion to suppress is denied."

Samson shrugged his shoulders. "Your Honor, I wish the record to show that because there was a mistake in labeling the evidence, we cannot be certain that these drugs are actually those removed from Mr. Fulford's car. How do we know that when the evidence was mistakenly labeled 'Buford' it was not mixed up with evidence from another case?"

"Let the record show Mr. Samson's objection."

Although momentarily defeated, Samson showed no sign of being ready to throw in the towel. "I call Officer Jeff Walton."

Walton was sworn in and took the stand.

Samson asked. "You were one of the officers who arrested Mr. Fulford, were you not.?"

"Yes, sir."

"And you are the handler of the dog that supposedly sniffed the odor of marijuana coming from the trunk of Mr. Fulford's car?"

"I am."

"Does this dog have a name or an identification number?"

"Officially she is K9 Corps number twenty-seven. I call her Maggie."

"Okay, is Maggie certified as a trained drug-sniffing dog?"

"She is."

"And when was she certified?"

"I don't remember the exact date, about a year and a half ago."

"Isn't there a requirement that such dogs be recertified on a regular basis?"

"Yes. They're supposed to be recertified every year."

"Has Maggie been recertified?"

"I don't think so. I could find out."

"So as far as you know, however, Maggie has not been recertified?"

"No, sir."

"How many drug sniff searches has Maggie performed since she has been in service?"

"We keep a record. I could refer to that for the exact number."

"I don't think that's necessary. As her handler you must have a pretty good notion how often she has been used. How often would you say?"

"About two hundred and forty times."

"Over a year and a half. Isn't it possible because she was not recertified, she could have gotten a little rusty?"

"It's possible."

"Among those two hundred and forty times she has been used to sniff marijuana, how often has she been mistaken?'

"About ten or fifteen percent of the time."

"So there's a ten or fifteen percent chance she was wrong when she indicated there were drugs in the trunk of Mr. Fulford's car."

"Since we found drugs in his car, I'd say that's proof she wasn't wrong."

"When you said Maggie had a ten or fifteen percent error rate, you based that figure on the times when she indicated a car or a piece of luggage held marijuana and a subsequent search showed the sniffed object did not contain marijuana. Right?"

"Yes."

"Did you keep a record of the times the dog alerted you and no drugs were found?"

"No. We did not."

"So the ten or fifteen percent figure was just a guess on your part?"

"An opinion based on experience."

Samson shook his head as if weary of half truths. "Your Honor, I move the evidence in this case should be excluded. Let me cite a precedent. In 1994, in the case of the *U. S. v. Florez,* DNew Mexico, the court held 'Where records are not kept to establish a drug-sniffing dog's reliability, an alert by such a dog is much like hearsay from an anonymous informant, and corroboration is necessary to support the unproved reliability of the alerting dog and establish probable cause.' I submit Maggie's reliability is in doubt because she has not been recertified in timely fashion and a proper record of her reliability has not been kept. Therefore David Fulford's car trunk was searched without probable cause."

Judge Shelfer looked at Samson with something akin to hostility. "Just hold on a minute." He turned to the prosecutor. "What have you got to say about this, Mr. Kline?"

"I can't cite a specific case off the top of my head, but I refer you to the 'good faith' doctrine. In several instances, courts have held evidence is admissible if officers acted in good faith, that is, believing they had probable cause for a search even if their warrant was defective. I think you should keep that in mind when making your decision."

Samson responded immediately. "The good faith excuse has only been applied in cases where police searched a home with a warrant that later proved to be faulty. To my knowledge it has never been applied in a stop and search situation."

Judge Shelfer played with his left ear lobe and scowled. "Well, I intend to research this question before I make a decision. I will announce my finding two weeks from today. Next case."

Leda embraced her brother in the hallway as they emerged from the courtroom. "Things look good, David. I'm sure the Judge will suppress the evidence. You owe Mr. Samson a great deal."

David grimaced, not wholly satisfied. "You were very good, Mr. Samson, and I appreciate what you've done, but I would rather have been found not guilty than get off on a technicality."

Samson smiled indulgently. "I'm sure a not guilty verdict would have been satisfying, but it was an unrealistic hope. Incidentally, the exclusionary rule is not a technicality. It protects the public from police abuse. It protected you, David. They never should have searched your car trunk."

"David," Leda said reproachfully. "You should be more grateful. Mr. Samson has gotten you out of a mess."

Samson spoke a word of caution. "Let's not be too confident. We haven't won yet. Maybe the judge will rule against us. Most law enforcement personnel, including judges, dislike the exclusionary rule and do their best to weaken it. He may find in favor of the prosecution. Kline made a strong appeal to the doctrine of good faith."

"Which way do you think he'll go?" David asked.

"Case law is inconsistent," Samson replied. "Judges, as I said a moment ago, are constantly trying to restrict the exclusionary rule. A lot depends on whether Judge Shelfer reads the right cases and is willing to be influenced by them. I'd say we have a better than average chance of a favorable verdict."

David forced a smile, but concern lurked behind his effort to be cheerful.

Chapter Twenty

Leda, her mind freed from the worst anxiety about her brother, returned to consideration of the Paulson case with something like enthusiasm.

"I have a feeling," she said to Davis, "we're getting close to identifying the killer, and I'm convinced, after my talk with Lucinda, that Gretchen holds the key to the puzzle."

"How do you mean, 'She holds the key?'"

"I think her suicide attempt and the changes in her behavior after her father's death are signs she knows or suspects who killed Paulson. Holding it in is driving her crazy."

She paused for a moment, thinking of what she had learned in her interview with Gretchen's mother. "I want to know more about Gretchen's illness. Her mother passed it off too quickly, too glibly, when I asked about it. That illness is somehow related to Paulson's murder. I'm convinced of it."

"Then find out what it was."

"Easier said than done. Asking the Paulson's doctor would get us nowhere, I'm sure. He'd invoke the confidentiality of medical records and I'd be unable to budge him."

"Why not try talking to Kimberly. See if she backs up her mother's story. There's always a chance her story won't jibe with her mother's and that will give you a wedge to break her down."

"If I pull zilch with Kimberly, then what can I do?"

Davis thought about that before responding. His hesitation sprang from knowing that what he was about to propose had only a small chance of success. "I think I'd tackle Wharton. He's an MD isn't he? A gynecologist. And a good friend of the Paulsons. He probably knows what happened to Gretchen, but I'm sure he didn't treat her. Doctors who are friends of a family rarely treat one of them. If he didn't treat Gretchen, he wouldn't be bound by medical confidentiality. Maybe you can get him to talk."

"If he wasn't Gretchen's doctor, how would he know about her?"

"I'm guessing the Paulsons took him into their confidence. After all, Lucinda and Pamela Wharton are great friends. It would be a natural thing for Lucinda to lean on Pamela for advice."

Fulford fell silent. She was thinking of her verbal assault on Davis when her brother was arrested for possession. Her emotions at that moment had been raw with anxiety. The attack had been unbelievably harsh. Although she had apologized for her behavior, and Davis had graciously accepted the apology, the atmosphere between them was still tense. She wondered if she should suggest resuming their weekend dates and the intimacy those dates involved.

She was about to make a tentative move in that direction, when Davis abruptly said, "I had a call from Caleb Burton a while ago. A strange conversation. He's withdrawing his transfer from Vice. I couldn't get him to give me any reason for his doing so. Just said he had thought it over and felt it was wiser for him to stay where he is."

The revelation hit Fulford hard. She guessed that Burton had decided to stay in Vice because of the evidence tampering business he had agreed to do with her approval. She was overwhelmed with guilt. She had tried to use Burton's weakness for her own selfish ends. Moreover, she had connived with him in a corrupt deal that dishonored both of them.

Davis looked at her closely. "What's wrong, Leda? Burton's decision is nothing to you, is it?"

"Nothing at all." She resolved that the Caleb misadventure, as she now chose to think of it, would remain buried forever in the deepest recesses of her mind. Maybe the guilt would eventually go away.

"You still mad at me?" Davis said.

"Wade, I was never really mad at you. I transferred my anger at my brother's arrest to you. That wasn't a nice thing for me to do. I'll make amends. What do you say to our having a weekend together sometime soon?"

"Just say when."

"After the judge has ruled on my brother's case. Okay?"

Kimberly looked haggard. Her face was drawn in painful lines. She sleeps poorly, Fulford thought, and that has sapped her vigor—and her spirit. She sat opposite Fulford, her posture slumped, her manner dejected. Fulford disliked the necessity that drove her to begin an inquisition of this unhappy child, the purpose of which would be to worm information from her by hook or crook. She had done more agreeable things.

"Your Mom said it would be all right for me to talk with you. Do you feel like talking?"

"I guess so."

"You look tired, Kimberly. Aren't you sleeping well?"

"Could you sleep if your father had just been killed and your baby sister has tried to kill herself?"

"No. I suppose not. I'm sorry to tell you we seem to be no closer to knowing who killed your father than we were the last time we talked."

"I'm not surprised. If whoever killed him keeps her mouth shut you'll never find her."

"You said 'her', Kimberly. Do you think a woman killed him?"

"I don't know. I just said 'her' without thinking. It probably was a man. Momma thinks it's that Basil Gearhart. I think so, too," she added, but Fulford got the distinct impression the pronoun 'she' was no accident.

"We've got Gearhart in custody in the hospital. He hurt himself trying to escape. If we think he's guilty he'll be charged and held without bail."

"Do you think he might not be guilty."

"Well, he has an alibi for the time of the murder. And we have other suspects."

At the mention of other suspects, Kimberly came sharply to attention. "Can you tell me who these other suspects are?"

"No, Kimberly, I'm sorry. I'm not permitted to disclose their names."

"Are they men or women." She seemed extraordinarily eager to hear the answer to that question. She searched Fulford's face expectantly.

Fulford toyed with the idea of telling her that a major suspect was female, but thought better of it. "Sorry. That's another area where division policy keeps me from answering."

Kimberly pouted momentarily. "I should think members of the family would be exceptions to your rule."

"Perhaps they should be. I'll raise the question with the administration."

She changed the subject. "How is Gretchen doing now? Your Mom tells me she's depressed and withdrawn."

"She won't talk to me much. Stays in her room. Cries a lot."

"Do you have any idea what's bugging her?"

"This whole business of Dad's death has made her sick."

"But you've gone through the same ordeal, and you haven't gone to pieces the way Gretchen has. What's the difference, Kimberly?"

"She was much closer to Daddy than I was. He used to visit her at night before she went to bed. Told her stories and soothed her till she fell asleep."

"Kimberly, there's something I've been curious about for a long time. When I last talked with you and Gretchen, she let it slip that she had been ill, physically ill I mean, and was hospitalized for several days. She passed it off as nothing.

When I asked your Mom about it, she said it was an intestinal bug that had dehydrated her. Do you know what it really was?"

Kimberly looked at Fulford with an almost crafty expression. "What it really was? Are you saying Mom lied to you? That it was actually something else?"

Fulford thought quickly. "Some people don't like to talk about certain diseases. Cancer is a good example. Or certain kinds of surgery like a colostomy."

At the mention of the word surgery, Fulford thought she detected a slight, odd, flicker of tension in Kimberly's expression.

"I was never told exactly what the illness was. If Momma says it was something like colitis, then that's what it must have been."

"Didn't Gretchen ever confide in you?"

"She didn't know what was the matter with her. She just knew she felt bad."

"So she told you how she felt, what her symptoms were?"

"She had pains in her belly, that was all she ever said."

"She never complained of problems with her menstrual cycle, like PMS?"

"We both had bouts of PMS at times, but that had nothing to do with her going to the hospital."

"How can you be sure?"

"Because she went to the hospital weeks after her menstrual cycle."

Fulford was tempted to ask exactly how many weeks after her cycle, but decided not to."

"Did Gretchen have lots of dates with boys?"

"She only dated once in a while. Daddy was very protective of her. Insisted on her staying home most weekends."

"Didn't that upset her?"

"No. When she stayed home, he paid a lot of attention to her. Visited with her a lot. Took her places."

"Did he do the same for you?"

Kimberly's voice was bitter. "He didn't think that much of me."

When she left the Paulson house, Fulford carried with her the distinct impression that Kimberly knew more about Gretchen's hospital visit than she was willing to say. She was certain the hospitalization was for something more serious than an intestinal infection. Exactly what it was, she did not know. But she had guesses that promised an answer to the question, "Who killed Harry Paulson?" with a name that was growing more and more probable in her mind.

She got into the office at eight, earlier than usual. Davis was there waiting for her.

"I phoned you," he said, "and got no answer. So I figured you were on the way. Judge Shelfer is going to make his ruling on David's case at nine. We'd better be on the way."

"Buck me up, Wade," she said as they got in the car. "I'm about to have a panic attack. If he rules against David, I don't think I can stand it."

"Yes, you can," Davis said. "You can cope with anything. But if it eases your mind any, Shelfer, unlike a lot of judges, usually researches case law carefully. I think that's in David's favor. But we'll just have to wait and see."

They had not been seated in the courtroom for any length of time when David and his lawyer, Orville Samson, came in and took seats at the defendant's table. The prosecutor was already seated. Judge Shelfer appeared shortly.

After the clerk identified the case, Shelfer donned his glasses, glanced over the room, and began to read from a prepared text. "The exclusionary rule was adopted to prevent police from making unreasonable searches and seizures. The question before us is whether the evidence discovered in David Fulford's car should be suppressed because of police misconduct. Mr. Samson moved to suppress because the police mislabeled the evidence attributing it to another case, that of a person named Buford. Had that mislabeling cast serious doubt that the drugs brought to court were the actual drugs taken from Fulford's car, the court would have agreed to suppress. But the prosecutor and the personnel of the evidence repository swear under oath the drugs were never misplaced. They were merely mislabeled. Given those facts the court believes the drugs presented were indeed those taken from Mr. Fulford's car. The motion to suppress, on that ground, is therefore denied.

Fulford's face reflected her alarm. Davis leaned over and whispered, "Don't give up, Leda. There's still the question of the dog." She grasped his hand.

Judge Shelfer resumed reading his opinion. "The question now to be addressed is Mr. Samson's move to suppress on the grounds the police lacked probable cause when they searched the trunk of Mr. Fulford's car. The Supreme Court of the United States has ruled that the police may make warrantless searches of an individual's car if they have stopped the motorist for a law violation. However, they must either have the individual's consent to the search, or they must have some evidence that a law has been broken unrelated to the original cause for stopping the motorist. Visual evidence, such as drugs lying on a car seat or on the floor is sufficient to justify a search. The smell of marijuana coming from the car has also been held to be sufficient cause for a search.

"In the case of David Fulford, the police were not given permission to search the trunk of his car. In fact, Fulford protested the search. The police relying on the alert given by a trained K9 drug-sniffing dog believed they had probable cause and opened Fulford's trunk. Case law has established that an alert from a drug-sniffing dog is admissible if the dog is regularly recertified and records are kept of the dog's success rate in alerts. In the case of the dog used in the Fulford case, neither of these criteria were met. A presumptive case for the suppression of the evidence is thus established."

Fulford grinned happily at her brother. Samson's solemn face, however, dampened her spirit.

Shelfer continued. "The prosecutor urged the court to invoke the good faith doctrine. The good faith doctrine is based on case law having to do with defective warrants used by police to conduct a search. When, after a search is completed, it is discovered the warrant was defective, the courts have sometimes held that, because the search was carried out by officers who acted in good faith, believing the warrant to be valid, the evidence obtained in the search should be allowed. According to the specific circumstances of the case, judges have sometimes allowed the evidence to be used or have suppressed it. Decisions seem to be based on whether the officer knew or should have known that the warrant was defective.

"In this case, the question is, did the officers have probable cause to search the trunk of Fulford's car? The dog used to alert them to the presence of the drug played the role of a search warrant, and it is the contention of the prosecution that the officers acted in good faith after being alerted by the dog.

"The key question in this instance is: Did the officers know or should they have known that they had, in a sense, a defective warrant? The officer who handled the dog knew the animal had not been recertified for over a year and he also knew that no record had been kept of the percentage of times the dog was mistaken when she made an alert. Given those facts, it is my opinion the officers lacked probable cause to search Fulford's car and they did not act in good faith. The evidence derived from the search is suppressed."

He turned to David and said, "Young man, you have escaped the consequences of your act because of police error. I urge you to seek help in breaking your narcotics habit. Let this be a lesson to you. You are released from the custody of this court."

David stood, anger and frustration in his face. He appeared about to speak when Samson pulled him back into his seat, stood up, and addressed the judge. "Thank you, Your Honor. My client is grateful."

He seized David by the arm and propelled him from the room. Fulford and Davis followed. In the hall, Leda put her arms around her brother and calmed him.

"David, for heaven's sake, let it go. So you weren't vindicated. But you're free."

Davis shook his hand and said. "Sometimes, David, the law dispenses justice by accident."

Samson, overhearing the remark, said, "Don't forget, the accident was arranged by your lawyer."

David finally smiled and embraced Samson. "Thanks for everything counselor. I'm a law student and this experience has been good for me. For one thing, I've found a great role model."

Chapter Twenty One

I t was afternoon. Davis and Fulford had shared a victory lunch with David, his lawyer, and David's parents. The atmosphere had been jovial and spirits had been good. Now, back in Davis's office, they again faced the question, Who killed Paulson?

"What's your take on Gretchen's hospitalization?" Davis asked. "How do you think it ties in with her father's murder?"

"I don't know. I hate to say I'm guessing, but I am. Here's one possibility. Gretchen is a lush, little number. She's bound to have had dozens of admirers. She fucks around with a boy at school and gets herself pregnant. Momma is enraged. Blames Daddy for being too indulgent with the girl. Blames him for being a corrupt role model. Daddy arranges for an abortion but Momma has had it up to here with him and opts for a final solution. How does that sound?"

"All right, except there's a more powerful motivation for Lucinda to want to kill Harry. I'm sure you've thought of it."

"If you're talking about sexual abuse, I have. Suppose Harry Paulson, who everyone agrees was close to Gretchen, got too close and got her pregnant. Lucinda would not only have to tolerate her daughter's pregnancy, but would have to swallow the fact that her husband was the father of the child. That drove her over the edge. She followed Harry on one of his evening rambles in his little wilderness. She let him have a bolt in the back, returned to the house, put the crossbow away, and pretended nothing had happened.

"When Kimberly found her father's body, she was in shock. Grief stricken at his loss, she at first blamed Basil Gearhart. Soon, however, she became certain that either her mother or Gretchen had killed him. She learned of Gretchen's pregnancy and realized it gave Gretchen and her mother an urgent motive for murder."

Davis nodded agreement. "I'm convinced that's what happened. It's critical we get Gretchen's medical history to back up our theory."

"Shall we try Adam Wharton? We thought he might cooperate because, if he knew her condition, he has no legal or moral obligation to keep it confidential."

"True. But loyalty to the Paulson family may cause him to button his lip."

"It's worth a try. If we have to subpoena the records, it'll be a hassle."

"I'm willing to give it a go this afternoon. How about it?"

"I'll tag along, but you do the talking. You've got more charm than I have."

She laughed. "More brains, too, Wade."

Adam Wharton's last patient left at four-thirty. Davis and Fulford were ushered into his office by an officious secretary, who had been keeping an eye on them since they arrived. She, clearly, had not been told of their mission nor of their position as law enforcement officers, and apparently regarded them as carriers of some loathsome disease. Her relief at getting rid of them was apparent as she ushered them to seats in the doctor's office, and assured them the doctor would be with them shortly. She backed, watchfully, out the door.

Wharton appeared almost at once. He was nervous and tense as if anticipating a disagreeable session. "Are you here in connection with Harry Paulson's murder?" he inquired.

"Indirectly," Fulford said, following Davis's instruction to do the talking. "We're concerned about Gretchen Paulson's mental health and thought you might have some insight into why she tried to kill herself."

Wharton assumed a puzzled expression. "How could that possibly be related to Harry's murder?"

"We're theorizing she might know who the murderer is but is unwilling to tell what she knows. By keeping such information bottled up she may have driven herself into an emotional breakdown."

"Why do you think I know anything about the girl's state of mind? Since Harry's murder I've had little contact with the family and almost none with the children."

"I see. Well, there's another matter you might be able to help us with. Some weeks ago, Gretchen spent two days in the hospital. We think her hospitalization is related to her emotional problem and, in some fashion to Paulson's death."

"I don't see how it could possibly be connected."

Fulford eyed him carefully watching for the slightest cue as she said, "We think there was something seriously wrong with Gretchen. But her mother told us she had nothing more than an intestinal bug. Paulson was killed just a few days after her release from the hospital. We think those events were related."

Wharton was impassive. He simply sat staring at the detectives as if to say, "What do you want of me?"

"We figure as a close member of the family, you might be able to tell us what her ailment was."

"But her mother has already told you."

"Frankly, we don't believe she's being truthful."

He spoke scornfully. "So you want me to impugn the veracity of a dear friend."

"Sometimes murder investigators have to seek the truth without regard for people's sensibilities. We think you might have been consulted about the daughter's problem."

"Had I been, I wouldn't tell you. Medical records are confidential."

"But you, as a friend rather than the doctor in charge, have no obligation to respect the rule of confidentiality."

Wharton gave her a look that at once was an acknowledgment of her astuteness and a condemnation of her probing. "I hate to dash your expectations, but I don't know what was wrong with Gretchen and I wouldn't tell you if I did. So you must take your inquiries elsewhere."

Fulford smiled. "Detectives have no choice, Mr. Wharton. We find it very frustrating when good citizens, for reasons of misplaced loyalty, refuse to help us. I had hoped you would understand and cooperate."

Wharton was affected by what she said. "That's pretty harsh," he said. He paused seemingly torn between two impulses. "Perhaps, I deserve it. I don't want to be completely uncooperative, Miss Fulford. The doctor who cared for Gretchen was Gerald Barker. His office is in this building. Perhaps you can get something out of him."

"Thanks," Fulford said. "We'll try. What's his specialty?"

"Gynecology."

"We're on a roll," Davis said, satisfaction in his voice. "I see the net closing around Lucinda. If this guy, Barker, refuses to cooperate, we'll subpoena his records."

Fulford was just as elated as her companion. Their big break was about to happen. She had no doubt of it.

In what seemed almost a reprise of their visit with Wharton, they sat in Barker's office awaiting his appearance. When he came in, they abandoned the idea that he'd be a pushover. A granite jaw in a stolid face suggested an iron will. He greeted them and did not wait for questions.

"Adam Wharton has told me you want information on Gretchen Paulson's hospitalization. You, of all people, should know that medical records are confidential. Nothing could destroy doctor-patient trust more swiftly than a doctor willing to abrogate that responsibility."

He paused. Davis thought to himself that they'd have to tighten the screws on him pretty hard if they expected to get anywhere. Aloud, he said. "We are investigating a murder case, Dr. Barker. The illness you treated Gretchen for and the reason you hospitalized her, may be of great importance to us. If necessary, we can get a court order to examine her records. If we are forced to do that, I promise you we'll bust into your office during your busiest hours and make a scene you and your patients won't soon forget."

Barker's face blanched. "You wouldn't. You're using that as a threat to get me to talk."

Fulford spoke up. "Don't be mistaken, Dr. Barker. I know this man. He means what he says. And," she added, "he can be as ugly as they come."

Barker nervously shuffled papers on his desk, his face a mantle of indecision. "I'd rather you'd subpoena the records," he said. "That's the proper way to do it. But I don't want you bursting into my office making a scene. You wouldn't really do that, would you?" he asked, looking hopefully at Davis.

"Just try me," Davis replied harshly.

"Well, I want to avoid that kind of scene, so I'll tell you about Gretchen. But you *will* subpoena the records afterward, won't you? Just to cover me?"

"Of course," Fulford said. "That's a promise. Now, why was Gretchen Paulson hospitalized?"

"Because I had to perform a surgical abortion. When her mother first brought her to see me, I tried a medical abortion, but it failed."

Fulford was curious. "A medical abortion, Doctor?"

"We try to induce abortion by giving a woman two drugs that adversely affect the uterus. First, I use methotrexate which is injected intramuscularly. A few days later the woman returns and I insert two suppositories of misoprostal into her vagina. An abortion occurs at home usually within a couple of days."

"And this didn't work with Gretchen?"

"The method is not foolproof. Five to ten percent of medical abortions fail. I was forced to put Gretchen in the hospital for a surgical abortion."

Davis showed as much interest in the topic as Fulford. He was aware of abortion procedure generally, but he wanted to hear how an abortion was done from a doctor's mouth. "Tell us about a surgical abortion," he demanded.

"The woman's cervix is dilated and a suction tube is inserted into the uterus. The fetus is removed by suction. Sometimes, as happened in Gretchen's case, it is necessary to insert a curette and gently scrape the walls of the uterus to make sure everything has been removed."

"Does this procedure take very long?"

"Ordinarily no more than a few minutes."

"But Gretchen was in the hospital for two days. Why?"

"She was hemorrhaging and her mother thought it best to keep her in the hospital till the bleeding had stopped. I agreed."

Barker's face was troubled as if he regretted having made the disclosure. Davis and Fulford weighed the impact of the information on their case. Davis inquired, hopefully. "I don't suppose you were told who the father was?"

"It was none of my business," Barker said. "I simply did the work and asked no questions."

Chapter Twenty Two

They appeared at her home to arrest Lucinda Paulson at 8 a.m. instead of coming at six o'clock, the time they preferred when a suspect was thought likely to flee or to resist arrest. Lucinda surrendered meekly enough, asking only that she be given time to put on a decent dress and apply her makeup. They informed her of her Miranda rights, cuffed her, and took her to the station where they escorted her into an interrogation room. Davis told her she could call a lawyer if she wished. She declined.

She sat down, bent forward, and covered her face with her hands. She remained in that position for most of the interrogation.

Davis sat down across the table from her and asked the questions. He spoke quietly. He felt a lot of sympathy for Lucinda Paulson. She had been driven to murder by circumstances few women could be expected to tolerate and he wanted to treat her as gently as possible.

"As officer Fulford told you, the charge is murder in the first degree. We believe you were driven to kill your husband because of his unfaithfulness. He cheated on you, over the years, with numerous women. You knew about these infidelities, and we believe you swallowed your pride and put up with them for the sake of your children."

Lucinda looked up at Davis momentarily, her eyes red rimmed, tears seeping out onto her cheeks. "I put up with his affairs until I learned he was carrying on with Cheryl Hargert. He was so brazen about her, I could stand it no longer. I thought all our friends knew about her and were secretly feeling sorry for me. I had some pride left. So I filed for divorce. Harry wouldn't hear of it. Too much negative publicity for the family and the business. He promised he'd break off with her and give up future entanglements. I dropped the divorce on condition he sever his relationship with Hargert at once."

Davis glanced at Fulford. Both now understood why Cheryl Hargert had been so abruptly and callously dumped by Paulson. Davis continued, telling Mrs.

Paulson his version of events leading to Paulson's murder.

"Mrs. Paulson, this is the worst part of what I must say. Please understand I regret the necessity."

He paused, his eyes on Lucinda. As he spoke there was sympathy in his voice.

"When Gretchen matured into a very attractive girl, your husband began to pay attention to her. She became his favorite, and they grew very close. You watched this development with apprehension and suspected something was wrong, but you couldn't bring yourself to believe he was abusing Gretchen sexually."

He stopped a moment as the grieving prisoner began to cry. She lifted her hands from her eyes and looked at Davis. She merely nodded in assent and then dropped her head into her hands again. Davis looked at Fulford as if to say: "I hate doing this. I wish I didn't have to." But he went on.

"Then Gretchen became pregnant. Your worst fears were confirmed. Although Gretchen swore the father of her child was a boy from school, you knew better. You challenged your husband and he admitted the affair. You forced him to arrange for Gretchen's abortion. When the abortion was over, you determined that he would never again abuse your family sexually. You stalked him one evening as he took one of his customary walks and shot him in the back with a crossbow. You must have been startled out of your wits when you heard Kimberly call out, 'Who's there?' Fortunately she did not see you and thought the person might have been Gretchen."

He paused. "Mrs. Paulson would you like to rest a bit. Maybe have a cup of coffee?"

Lucinda shook her head without looking up. "Please. Let's get this over with."

"Okay. Are you willing to sign a statement that events happened as I have just described and that you are the person who shot Harry Paulson in the back with a bolt from a crossbow?"

"I am."

"Let the record show Mrs. Paulson waived the right to have a lawyer as she gave this testimony." He then spoke directly to Lucinda. "You were not coerced into making this statement, were you.?"

"No."

"You assent to this statement of your own free will and do not harbor any mental reservations nor do you intend to deny what you have admitted at some future date?"

"I have no mental reservations and I do not intend to repudiate what I have said at some future time. Now, can I go some place and lie down?"

Fulford said, "Just a couple of quick questions. Early in our investigation, you claimed someone left a teddy bear pierced with an arrow on your front porch. Was that your own doing?"

"Yes. It was silly wasn't it? I did it to throw suspicion on animal rightists."

"And what about the death threat that allegedly came from *blimpie*. Did you send it?"

"I typed it one day when I was in Harry's office and no one else was around."

Fulford tried to recollect the content of that message. "The message said something to the effect, you have invaded my body and corrupted it for your own ends. What did you mean by that?"

She did not reply immediately, and seemed unsure what to say. "I got genital warts once, transmitted to me by Harry, from one of his sexual partners."

"I see," Fulford said, almost apologetically. "I have no further questions."

Davis's memory was jogged by Fulford's inquiries. "Did you prepare and plant the note that was left in your mailbox? The note with the drawing of the deer having an arrow in its body?"

"No. I'm sure that was sent by someone opposed to hunting, especially hunting with bow and arrow." She had quit crying but sat, bent and shriveled, like an old woman. Her face was drawn and her body wracked with fatigue. Davis instructed a matron to take her to a holding room and bed her down.

Gerry Fillmore had watched through the glass the entire session. He smiled exultantly at Davis and Fulford. He was so manifestly happy at the outcome, he could scarcely sit still.

"Congratulations! I always thought you two were one of my best teams. Now I'm sure of it. What a neat package! We'll get a first degree murder indictment with no trouble. And a conviction."

Davis smiled at the praise but expressed doubt that a conviction would come easy.

Fulford had doubts, too. "I'm not so sure of a first degree conviction, Gerry. Her act was premeditated, true enough, but she suffered extreme provocation. A jury is likely to be lenient with a mother who murdered to avenge the sexual molestation of her daughter."

Fillmore nodded assent. "Okay. A jury may go easy on her, but the case itself is a model of good detective work."

No one disagreed with that.

The morning papers were filled with stories of the arrest of the woman who killed her husband because he sexually abused one of her daughters. Some writers didn't know what to call her act. It wasn't patricide. She killed a husband not a father. But they hated simply to call it murder. Maybe it was spousicide. Whatever, they had a field day denouncing the father who had sexually abused his daughter and they portrayed the mother as having performed an act of simple justice. Thus began the outpouring of sympathy for Lucinda Paulson. "Avenging angel," "Lioness protecting her young," "Courageous defender of family values," and similar metaphors were spread over the pages.

Fulford and Davis found little satisfaction in all this. The press, as usual, was conducting a trial before the courts had even held an arraignment.

"I feel sorry for Lucinda," Fulford said. "But I feel even sorrier for the girls. I don't think Gretchen will ever get over the lurid press accounts of how her father abused her. It will be a kind of death for her...a death of innocence."

"And think of Kimberly," Davis said. "She has a mother who killed her father, and a sister who made illicit love to him. How will she cope with that? She'll need help."

It was as if Kimberly had heard his words, for just then the phone rang and when Fulford answered, she heard Kimberly's distraught voice.

"Ms. Fulford, I need to talk to you right away. Can you come to our house now."

"Yes, of course. I'll be there as quick as I can. Fifteen minutes at the most."

"Should I go with you?" Davis asked.

"I don't think so, Wade. This is going to be a woman thing."

Kimberly was in a state of great agitation. She had been crying. Her eyes were red, bloodshot, her cheeks tear-stained. A muscle in her upper lip twitched uncontrollably and she twisted a handkerchief into a sodden rope. She took Fulford by the hand and drew her down on the couch beside her.

"You've got to help me, Ms. Fulford. I've no one else to turn to."

"I'll help you any way I can, Kimberly. Tell me what's wrong."

"It's Momma. I can't let her go to jail for Daddy's murder. It's too horrible to think about."

"But your mother admitted she killed him."

"I know she did. But she was protecting Gretchen."

Fulford found the remark profoundly disturbing. "Kimberly, let me get this straight," she said. "Are you aware of what you're saying? Do you mean to tell me that Gretchen killed your father?"

"Yes."

"How do you know?"

"She told me."

"Gretchen told you she killed your father? When?"

"I think it was about a week after Daddy was killed. I went by her room and heard her crying out in her sleep. She had been doing that a lot. I opened the door and listened. I thought I heard her say, 'Oh, Daddy. I didn't mean to kill you! I didn't mean to kill you! Daddy, I just meant to hurt you so you'd leave me alone.' I woke her up and told her what I'd heard. She admitted she followed him into the arboretum and fired the bolt into his back. But killing him was an accident, she said. She meant only to hit him in the bottom or the leg. But the bolt went too high and struck him in the back. She was frantic, afraid I had seen her. Now, by talking in her sleep, she had given herself away. I knew her secret, but I couldn't tell anyone. If I didn't keep silent she would go to jail, she said. Maybe she would even be put to death. She wanted me to promise to keep quiet."

"And you agreed to keep her secret?"

"I didn't want her to go to jail, and the thought of her being executed terrified me. I had a terrible time holding it in, especially when we had to talk to you and Mr. Davis."

"Kim, a court will not believe your story. Legally what you've told me is hearsay. Hearsay is what you learned from someone else. No court will accept it. Greta's confession has to come from her, not you."

"Then ask Greta. She'll tell you."

"I can't ask Greta. That's the problem. She's in the hospital under a doctor's care. She's mentally incompetent and deeply depressed. The doctor won't allow anyone to question her."

"Why won't people believe me." Kimberly complained. "I'm grown up. I'm not a child."

"You're only seventeen, Kim."

"Do you believe me?"

"I don't know. It seems possible Greta could have done it. She had a powerful motive, she had the means, and the opportunity. But your mother has confessed to the killing. Without additional evidence I don't know who to believe."

"Why don't you ask Mom? She knows Greta did it."

"That's exactly what I plan to do." She paused a moment, uncertain. "Kim, is anyone staying with you now?"

"Aunt Celia, Mom's sister, is spending nights here."

"I'm going to talk with her, then I'm going to the station. In the meantime, you keep all of this under wraps. Okay?"

Fulford's mind was in a turmoil at Kim's disclosure. Had Lucinda, in an effort to protect her daughter, really confessed to something she had not done? If confronted with Kimberly's story would she continue to say she had committed the murder? Or would she admit her confession was false, given to protect her abused child?

She hurried back to headquarters and put the question of whom to believe to Davis. He had little hesitation in deciding what to do. "We'll have to confront Lucinda with Kim's story and see what she says."

"Do you really think she would confess to save her daughter?" Leda asked.

"I doubt it. But I have a devious and cynical mind. I think Lucinda's a very crafty woman. I think she may have set up this whole thing to create doubt about her confession. She knew Gretchen was in a terrible state after her father's death. The girl was ashamed of the sexual acts going on between her and her father. Her mother exploited that shame. She added guilt to the shame by suggesting to Gretchen that she was responsible for her father's sexual advances. She told her he never would have molested her had she not seduced him. Gretchen was deeply depressed and highly suggestible. She began to feel, with her mother's prompting, that she had actually done the killing. Lucinda harped on Greta's guilt till the girl became mentally unbalanced, started hallucinating and, eventually, attempted suicide. Kimberly has unwittingly helped Lucinda's plan by telling you of Greta's confession, a confession spoken out of delirium."

"Wade, you don't really believe all that, do you?"

"Well, it could have happened, couldn't it? Let's put it to the test. Let's see what Lucinda has to say for herself."

Davis invited Major Smith, the psychiatrist, and Gerald Fillmore to attend the questioning of Lucinda Paulson. He wanted Smith to judge the truthfulness of Lucinda's responses when she was confronted with Kim's story. He asked Fillmore to view the proceedings with an eye to the effect Lucinda's remarks could have on the legal case.

Before the interrogation, Davis inquired of the jailer, "Has she had any visitors?"

"She saw a man, a Roger Godwin, briefly. They got into a fierce argument shortly after he arrived. She ended the interview with him in less than five minutes. She told us she didn't want to see him again."

"Anyone else?"

"Adam and Pamela Wharton tried to visit. She refused to see them."

Davis looked questioningly at his companions. "Looks as if she's cutting herself off completely, doesn't it? I wonder if that has any significance?"

When the jailer brought Lucinda into the room, Davis was surprised at the change in her. She wore a prison gown, a god-awful looking garment she had made no effort to spruce up. Her skin was sallow, prison pallor, he supposed, and her face was without makeup. Her eyes were darkly shadowed as if she had slept little or not at all. Her hair, always so meticulously coifed, was now uncombed, dull, almost matted. She sat utterly uncaring of her appearance, a woman seemingly beaten down by outrageous fortune.

Fulford, who remembered how Lucinda had always striven for a youthful appearance, felt like saying something supportive to her, but seeing Davis's stern, cold manner, she restrained the impulse.

"Mrs. Paulson," Davis said. "I would like for you to tell us once more how you killed your husband."

She spoke from great weariness, and with a resignation that spelled total capitulation to the demands of her interrogators. "I have done this so often, I can't understand why you want to hear it again. It was very simple. When he took a walk that night, I followed him into the arboretum and shot him in the back with a bolt from a crossbow."

"Had you planned this or did you act on a sudden impulse?"

"That afternoon I sat in the study thinking, obsessively I'm afraid, about what his uncontrolled sexual appetite had done to me and the children. I was especially angered by what he had done to Gretchen. That poor child not only endured his advances for God knows how long, but she had to endure the most heartbreaking act a woman can experience—an abortion. I suddenly felt a kind of rage I had never felt before. I went into the game room, got his crossbow and a bolt, and followed him into the woods. When I got close enough to be sure I couldn't miss, I shot him in the back. Kimberly almost saw me and called out. But she thought it was Greta."

"What did you do then?"

"I went back to the house, staying out of Kimberly's way, and put the crossbow back in it's place. I waited, knowing Kim would find the body."

Her precise narrative sounded rehearsed to Fulford. She thought that Lucinda, prompted by maternal instinct, might have subordinated her own self-interest and confessed to the murder to shield her daughter. But her story did not ring entirely true. The look on Davis's face, however, told her he was convinced Lucinda was the actual killer, not a mother sacrificing herself for her daughter's sake.

Davis continued. "Mrs. Paulson, are you making this confession in order to save your daughter, Greta, from being punished for murder."

She lifted her head to face him, anger and dismay in her expression.

"For God's sake, Greta didn't kill her father!"

"We've been told, by a reliable source, that Greta *did* kill him."

"That's not true! Who would say such a thing?"

"Kimberly. She says that Greta told her she committed the crime a day or two after her father was killed."

"That's nonsense." She seemed off balance, however, as if uncertain how to respond. After a long pause, she said, "Kimberly has always been jealous of Greta. Harry's attention to Greta was obvious and Kim resented it. When she learned her father was having sex with Greta, it was almost more than she could bear. She was hurt and angered. Now she's getting even."

Davis shook his head, as if her explanation was beyond belief. "That's a pretty harsh thing to say about Kimberly."

"Well, it's true. You don't understand what children can be like."

Davis paused, uncertain what direction he should take. At last he said, "Mrs. Paulson, are you willing to take a polygraph test?"

"Of course. How can I make you people believe me? My daughter, Greta, could not have committed this crime. She loved her father dearly. She would not have hurt him in any way, let alone kill him."

"Are you sure you don't want a lawyer's advice before taking this step."

"When the time comes, I'll want a lawyer to plead me guilty. I have no other use for legal advice." She sat, face in hands, without moving. Her rigid posture seemed to say, "I've had enough. Let's end this torture."

Davis motioned the jailer to take her back to her cell.

Major Smith thought her responses were convincing.

"She's forthright and open. I don't sense any effort at deception. I think she's telling the truth." He paused a moment, thinking. "A polygraph test might confirm my opinion, but there would still be doubt. Polygraph tests can't be used in court. Too great a margin for error. A professor at Baylor university says the tests are wrong thirty percent of the time. That may be a bit high. But spokespersons for the American Polygraph Association admit there is probably a ten percent error rate even with a trained examiner. If the examiner is not well trained or has had little experience, the error rate would be higher."

Davis listened, thoughtfully, then said. "Assuming you're right, we'd still gain if she takes the test. We'd have a seventy percent chance the result is reliable."

"Yes, but most errors have found allegedly innocent people guilty. In Mrs. Paulson's case, we'd be trying to confirm that an admittedly guilty person is actually not guilty. I'm not sure how an operator could phrase questions that would test for innocence rather than guilt."

Fillmore, who had been listening silently, said, "Hadn't we better talk to Gretchen? If she confesses to the crime, her mother must be lying."

Smith shook his head. "Maybe and maybe not. We couldn't be sure Gretchen is telling the truth. Or that she even knows the truth. She could be remembering what her mother planted in her mind. Regardless, there is no prospect, at least for a long time, of our questioning her. The girl is in the psychiatric division of the hospital, diagnosed as suffering from stress induced depression—what we used to call a nervous breakdown. She's incompetent. Any statement she makes while in that condition would be worthless. She's unable to distinguish fact from fancy, and is expected to remain in that state for the foreseeable future."

"Well," Fillmore said, scratching his chin and adopting his oracle look, "the lawyer who represents Mrs. Paulson is facing a hell of a problem. When he pleads her guilty, he'll be morally bound to tell the judge about Kimberly's testimony. The judge will have to decide if her testimony is reliable. The only way he could do that is to question Gretchen. But he can't question her. So, if he wants to send Lucinda to jail, he has to disbelieve Kimberly. If he believes Kimberly, he has to brand Lucinda's confession false. And then what? Prosecute Gretchen for murder? Even if she were competent to stand trial, which she isn't, he probably couldn't prosecute Gretchen as an adult."

Davis shrugged his shoulders in frustration, smiled at Fulford, and said, "Well, Leda, you and I have topped our usual superior work. We've ended up with not one but two confessed murderers. I don't see how we could have done better."

"Yeah," Fillmore said. "A clean, clear-cut resolution. All loose ends tied up neatly. Baloney! We still don't know who killed Harry Paulson and probably we never will."

"You're convinced Lucinda killed him, aren't you, Wade?"

They were sitting in Davis's office, drinking coffee and rehashing the case. Both were thinking of the odd resolution or, more accurately, the odd lack of resolution, of their investigation into Harry Paulson's murder. "I'll back off that Machiavellian plot, I spun earlier," Davis said, "that she played on Greta's frazzled emotional state to make her believe she killed her father. I don't think Lucinda planned to hide the murder. She was going to kill her husband and take the consequences if she were discovered. I think she could no longer put up with Harry's philandering and the emotional devastation it had brought her and the girls. You remember we once said Lucinda probably went after Harry because he was screwing some woman she couldn't abide. Well, at the time, we couldn't have guessed that he was screwing Gretchen, her daughter. That was the last straw for Lucinda."

Leda considered his version of events carefully. There was good reason to accept it, but she had a different scenario. "You build a good case, Wade, but I still believe Greta did it. Think of the state that poor girl must have been in after she had aborted her child, her father's child. Her mind must have been in a turmoil, and her emotions were tearing her to pieces. She had to find relief, and punishing her father was the only way she knew how to get it. If Lucinda killed him, why didn't she do it the moment she discovered Harry had made Greta pregnant? Why would she wait and suffer that indignity for weeks before taking action?"

"You've got a point. There are arguments on both sides."

"A couple of other things bother me, Wade. Lucinda said she faked the teddy bear incident to throw suspicion on the animal rights people. That sounds phony to me. It's much more reasonable to assume the bear was Gretchen's work. Forensics told us the bear was given away with a cosmetics purchase. God knows Gretchen used plenty of cosmetics and could easily have acquired the bear that way. Remember the mascara incident? The arrow came from a child's archery set, something Gretchen probably had tucked away in her toy closet for ages. She took the rubber suction cup off the arrow sharpened the tip, and with a little help from a screw driver, thrust it through the bear's chest. Doesn't that sound more like a child's work than the work of an adult woman trying to cast suspicion on animal rights people? Anti-hunting people would have rigged up something a little more sophisticated. Gretchen was telling her mother, through the bear, that she had killed her father. The bear was her way of saying, 'Can't you guess who fired that arrow?'

"Then there was that *blimpie* note. The exact words were *you have invaded my body and corrupted it for your own ends.* That doesn't sound to me like a wife damning her husband for giving her genital warts. It sounds like a daughter damning a father for getting her pregnant."

"You make a lot of sense, Leda, but you can't establish Greta's guilt with certainty. As good a case can be made for Lucinda as the killer. I think Gerry was right. We'll never know for sure which of them did it. You and I can argue till doomsday and not reach agreement."

"Okay. Let's drop it."

She paused, wondering how he would respond to the proposal she was about to make, a proposal that held for her a promise of agreeable things to come. "Why don't we spend the afternoon at my place? Sort of celebrate the end of a frustrating case, or should I say, our unresolved case? Whatever! I've got a couple of bottles of champagne in my refrigerator just waiting to be drunk."

"Can't think of a better way to spend an afternoon," Davis responded. He put his hand over hers and looked at her eagerly. "With two bottles of champagne, I can see all sorts of possibilities."

However, they were not to know the pleasures that might have followed the consumption of Fulford's champagne because Fillmore suddenly appeared, radiating the kind of excitement he showed when he bore news of an especially fascinating homicide.

"I want you two to get over to 221 Milledge Street, apartment 401 right away," he ordered. "Some poor bastard was striped naked by a couple of goons, bound and gagged with duct tape, and tortured with a cattle prod till he died of a heart attack. Just the sort of case you two like."

"Yeah," Davis said dryly. "Grisly murders. Right up our alley. We were planning to take the afternoon off, Gerry."

"And you deserve it. You do. It pains me to ruin your plan." He put on his *I-hate-to-do-it-but-duty-calls* expression and said with exaggerated solemnity, "But you know as well as I do, death never takes a holiday."

Davis winked at his colleague, a wink conveying his amusement at Fillmore's pomposity. "You've got a way with words, Gerry."

Resignedly, he turned to Fulford. "Come on, Leda. I guess we'd better head for Milledge Street."

Wayne Minnick is the author of *The Art of Persuasion, Public Speaking* (Houghton Mifflin), and *Butcher Bird* (Creative Arts). He holds a Ph.D. in Speech Communication from Northwestern University, is a professor emeritus at Florida State University, and was an associate professor at Northwestern University. He began writing short stories and mystery novels upon retirement.